A DELICATE QUESTION

So what the devil was Butler up to? Roskill felt a cold tingle of caution crawl up his back. Butler was a good fellow, solid and sensible, but an establishment man to the core, prepared to put his hand to any awkward job loyally. And notoriously he was given such awkward jobs...

But it would be useless to ask outright for the truth. Butler would be ready to fend off such a question. Better simply to play it straight, with caution.

"And why would anyone want to blow up Llewelyn?"

"Perhaps Dr. Audley could tell us that."

Audley slowly put down the empty glass he'd been nursing and stared at Butler...

THE ALAMUT AMBUSH

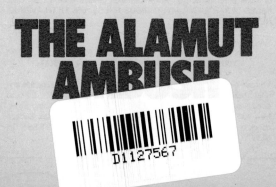

Also by Anthony Price

Sion Crossing
The Labyrinth Makers
Colonel Butler's Wolf*
Here Be Monsters

Published by

MYSTERIOUS PRESS   *forthcoming

THE ALAMUT AMBUSH

BY

ANTHONY PRICE

THE MYSTERIOUS PRESS • New York

To
Katherine, James
and Simon

MYSTERIOUS PRESS EDITION

This Mysterious Press Edition is published by arrangement with the author.

Mysterious Press books are published in association with
Warner Books, Inc.
666 Fifth Avenue
New York, N.Y. 10103
A Warner Communications Company

Printed in the United States of America

First Mysterious Press Printing: November, 1986

10 9 8 7 6 5 4 3 2 1

Prologue

JENKINS WALKED SLOWLY round the Princess, fumbling with the buttons of his overalls.

It was late—he had heard the chimes of midnight on his way in from Blackheath—and he was dog-tired. And it was also an imposition to be called out during what were at least technically the last hours of his leave, which he had purposed to spend getting some order into his new flat.

Yet he knew that it was neither the hour nor the imposition which were sapping his concentration, but the suppressed excitement of the day's events. For a year now he'd felt ambition stirring, and for the last three months he'd sensed the faint scent of promotion trailing him like after-shave. Tonight it was strong in his nostrils: he had the feeling that life hadn't let him down after all.

The trick was to do things right, and there he had Hugh Roskill to help him. Hugh could be trusted to advise him without trying to steal any of the credit—although it wasn't like the old days, Hugh was still almost family.

He ran his finger idly along the thin buff-gold line that ran the whole length of the Princess, just below the meeting place of the black and the grey, the line that was the last lingering memory of the great days when there was coach-work to car bodies.

He'd never quite been able to make his mind up about Hugh. Up on the Eighth Floor they all had some sort of façade, and Hugh's was the familiar, nonchalant RAF one that he'd long grown accustomed to during his childhood, when Hugh and poor old Harry had been inseparable. Yet Harry had been no great brain, and it was certain that non-chalance alone never got anyone to the Eighth—which was where he himself intended to go. So there had to be a lot more to Hugh somewhere, as Aunt Mary had always main-tained there was...

He shrugged, running the finger down from the line into the mud splashes.

The mud was the most obviously interesting thing about the Princess. No rain for ten days, and the gale tonight blow-ing miniature dust devils in the dry gutters, but nevertheless the lower half of the car was thickly coated with mud, and undeniably recent mud.

It might be this that had alerted someone, even though it was the oldest and crudest cover-up trick in the book. But the Special Branch man who'd delivered the Princess had been uncommunicative. It was far more likely that the un-known but influential owner of the car had delusions of gran-deur...

Jenkins yawned, rubbed his eyes and looked down at the red rexine-covered handbook, with its gold lettering—an-other subtle touch of class there. It reminded him that he'd never had a Princess through his hands before—a few months ago that would have been a challenge in itself, to prove that no matter what came along, he was the best. But now it was just another car to be cleared, just routine, and he was mildly niggled that Maitland had found himself some other pressing engagement while McClure and Bennett were still snarled up in Northern Ireland.

Abstractedly, his mind still half on Roskill, he plugged in the tape recorder and began to unwind the flex ... It was true that Hugh did seem more serious these days, almost preoccupied, on the occasions they had met. But that wouldn't make any difference now; it was serious advice he wanted.

He shook his head. Best to get the matter in hand over quickly, to salvage some hours from the night. For tomorrow he'd need to be on top form...

He picked up the little microphone.

"Vanden Plas Princess 4-litre-R, black and grey, registration number..."

1

THE RATTLE OF the chain was much louder than the bell itself: after one dull clunk the bell had jammed, but the chain went on rasping and clattering against the stonework.

It was, thought Roskill, almost the last bit of Audley's old house that hadn't yet been transformed by his new wife. The carpets were new and the curtains were new, and the new central heating roared away in the distance. The splendid old furniture was still in place, but now it shone with polish in the candlelight. The house even smelt different, with the mustiness of age overlaid by an amalgam of odours suggesting female efficiency. And there didn't seem to be any back-teasing draughts any more—the place was almost cosy.

But the bell was a genuine piece of Audley before the Age of Faith, as eloquent as a 'Do not disturb' sign.

The only other unchanged object was—surprisingly—Audley himself, for the evening had so far revealed exactly the same confusing mixture of arrogant humility and courtly rudeness which had first fascinated Roskill years before in the famous Mirage briefing, when the big man had casually forecast Israeli intentions with such uncanny accuracy.

Roskill had marked him then as an acquired taste worth cultivating for the future and possibly one day the man who'd take Sir Frederick's job. It was only when he had come to know him better that the doubts had been born: the ruthlessness was there, and the brains, but the singleminded drive was lacking. At heart Audley was an amateur.

Yet out of this insight had come a curious, almost masochistic affection. He didn't really trust Audley, but he *liked* him—

"That frightful bell!" Faith grinned at Roskill as she rose from the table. "I must get it fixed so that David can't just sit there ignoring it. You know, Hugh, I sometimes think he's got—what do you call it?—xenophobia, is that it?"

Audley regarded his young wife tolerantly.

"Xenophobia? Perhaps I have. But then it's an ancient and very sensible disease, love. The xenophobes survive long after the xenophiles have been knocked on the head during the night by the strangers they've let into their homes."

Roskill gestured to the table in front of him. "And the law of hospitality? Isn't that ancient too?"

"A simple extension of the laws of self-preservation, Hugh. And a fiction more often than not: 'The raven is hoarse that croaks the fatal entrance of Duncan under my battlements'. That's the true face of hospitality. And the other face shows the guests quietly opening the back door for their friends outside after lights out."

The bell chain rattled again and the clapper briefly unjammed itself.

"And I suppose I should say 'the bell invites me' now!" Faith started for the dining room door. "I wish I could tell you that he doesn't believe what he's saying, Hugh, but I'm afraid he does believe it. Only I'm miscast as Lady Macbeth, hopelessly."

Audley watched her out of the room. "And I'll tell you something else. Bells that ring after ten at night are alarm bells."

Roskill frowned across the candlelight towards the grandfather clock which ticked away heavily in the shadows. The front door banged and there was a murmur of voices.

"So now it's only a question of whether the trouble is yours or mine. Probably mine, but I can still hope it's yours. In fact it puts me in mind of the old tale of the Rake and the Hounds—do you know it?"

Roskill shook his head. He had heard and disbelieved that there was an irrational side to Audley, and now here it was. Perhaps the flicker of the candles brought it out.

"It's a Hebridean tale. The rake was coming home over the hills early one morning after a night's debauch when he saw a man running in the valley below, looking over his shoulder all the while. And although there was nothing else to be seen the rake knew at once that the man was being pursued by the hounds of Hell.

"Then the man looked up the hillside and saw the rake, and he turned and ran straight towards him. And when he reached the brow of the hill he stopped to catch his breath, looked at the rake, and then staggered on past. And the rake knew very well what he had been thinking: 'He's a black sinner too—maybe the hounds will stop and take him instead of me'."

The door opened behind Roskill.

"It's Major Butler, David," said Faith. "He wants an urgent word with Hugh."

Roskill swung round. Butler loomed solidly in the doorway, silhouetted against the brighter hall behind him. There was a glitter of raindrops on his head—the weather had broken at last.

"For Hugh?" Audley didn't look at Roskill. "Well, Butler—we've just reached the brandy stage—allow us to finish that before you take him away. And join us in the meantime— sit down. Your ill tidings can wait a few minutes."

"No need to take him away, Dr. Audley." Butler dabbed at the damp red stubble on his head as he sat down. "A brandy would be acceptable though. As to the ill tidings—your leave's up tomorrow anyway, Hugh. What other sort of tidings can there be?"

Roskill knew then with certainty that he was about to be

double-crossed—knew it and was filled with gladness. All that remained was to act out a convincing role: should he struggle in the snare or submit with cold dignity? Which would be more in character?

"Jack, you know darned well when my leave ends." Struggle, then—even a rabbit struggled. "At 8 a.m. tomorrow I shall shave off this beard. At 10 I'll pick up my mail at the office, and by 3 I'll be at RAF Snettisham. There's not one thing you can do about it—it was all settled months ago. I belong to the RAF for the next ten weeks. Not to Sir Frederick, and certainly not to you."

He looked round the table for moral support. Faith radiated honest sympathy, but Audley's sympathy was tinged with relief: the hounds had passed him by...

"Ten weeks' refresher, Jack—that's the agreement. Ten weeks to keep me up to the mark so I'll still have a career when Sir Frederick puts me out to grass. They wouldn't be thinking of breaking that, would they, Jack?"

Go on—break it, Jack.

"The beard." The suggestion of a perverse smile passed across Butler's mouth. Butler had been due for some leave when Roskill returned, but then the best press gangs were always made up of pressed men. "That's one reason why I'm here. They'd like you to keep it, even if it does make you look like a pirate."

"I'm not going to Snettisham with a beard."

"You're not going to Snettisham at all, Hugh. Not for the time being, anyway."

"The beard's coming off and I'm going to Snettisham." Struggle harder and feel the wire tighten.

Butler looked pained. "Don't be childish, man. If you put your pretty uniform on again tomorrow you'll stay in it. And not at a nice lively place like Snettisham. More likely somewhere like Benbecula—or wherever they send the awkward ones nowadays. On the ground, certainly. There'd be no more flying."

They had to want him very badly to spell it out as crudely

as that, with what they took to be the ultimate threat. Or so they thought. That might well be the only thing they didn't know about him—that one big, secret ace in the hole. And as long as they didn't know it, it was his strength, not his weakness.

One final protest should be enough for the record.

"They might as well ground me anyway. If they won't let me keep up with my flying they're as good as doing that already. Is this Sir Frederick's idea of a gentleman's agreement?"

Faith pushed her chair back from the table and stood up. "I think I'll go and make a lot of strong coffee—before I'm sent packing."

Butler turned towards her hastily. "Don't go, Mrs. Audley. The brandy's fine—please don't leave us."

Audley grunted angrily. "I don't think she likes watching Hugh blackmailed any more than I do. It's too much like old times for both of us."

"At least hear me out," Butler looked at Roskill. "I think you may not want to go back to the RAF quite so quickly then—I mean that, Hugh. And it really is perfectly in order for you to listen, Mrs. Audley. You may even have something to contribute."

Faith sat down again willingly enough, and Roskill felt a pang of disquiet. It was like her to be curious, and it wasn't like Butler—solid, security-conscious Butler, who mistrusted women and hated amateurs.

And of all women, Faith. For Butler had deplored Audley's original involvement with her—"that over-bred, under-sexed schoolteacher with foam-rubber tits." It was an uncharacteristically facile assessment, except possibly as regards the foam rubber, but what mattered was that it didn't fit this sudden partiality: Faith wouldn't hold her tongue, and Butler would know it.

"Get on with it, then, Jack. I can't wait to hear why I have to keep my beard."

Butler took a slow breath, almost a sigh. "On Tuesday

night somebody stole a car belonging to a Foreign Office man named Llewelyn."

Audley sat up. "Llewelyn? David Llewelyn would that be?"

"You know him?"

"I used . . . to know him." Audley began guardedly and ended casually. "I played rugger against him as a matter of fact."

"So someone pinched Llewelyn's car," said Roskill after a moment's silence. Butler had evidently hoped that Audley was going to elaborate on his acquaintance, but Audley's mouth was tightly closed again. "That's a normal occupational hazard in London these days."

"It was taken in Oxford."

"Still close enough for the city gangs."

Butler ignored him. "He parked the car at 6:30 p.m. in Radcliffe Square, just next to All Souls—he was having dinner in All Souls that evening. By midnight it had gone. They picked it up at Bicester at 7 p.m. next evening."

Roskill looked at the map in his mind. Bicester was just north, or maybe north-east, of Oxford. And hardly more than a dozen miles away. There was an RAF maintenance unit there, not far from the American base the F IIIs were moving into soon. And an Army camp—a fair-sized ordnance depot.

"So some jokers missed the last bus home and picked their own transport. It happens."

Butler nodded. "It happens—aye. In fact it's what the police suggested. They found the car in an Army depot area, beside a public road."

Audley began to say something, and then stopped abruptly, and looked down into his brandy glass. And if Butler was normally resistant to Faith's charm, Audley equally could never resist hypothesizing. So now they were both acting out of character.

Roskill started to stroke his chin and rather to his surprise encountered his beard: the very idea of preserving it was ridiculous, and also out of character . . .

Butler was a colleague, a friend even, so he must now be doing simply what he had been told to do. But Audley ranked as a friend too, and there was something which had scared him off—even though the hounds of Hell had passed him by. So there was something very wrong with the idea of some RAOC private lifting the Foreign Office man's car—

"What sort of car was it?"

"Vanden Plas Princess—the 4-litre one."

The poor man's Rolls-Royce, the company director's tax dodging limousine.

"All right, Jack. If you want me to play 'spot the deliberate mistake' I'll play it, though you could just as soon have told me. For starters—the wrong sort of car lifted from the wrong place. How's that?"

"Why was it wrong?" asked Faith.

"Too obvious. It's not a popular make. If I wanted to get back to barracks I'd pick something easier to get into and easier to drive. And something less conspicuous. *And* I wouldn't lift it from somewhere in the centre of Oxford like Radcliffe Square, if my memory of the place is right. I'd pick up a Mini from a dark sidestreet. Right, Jack?"

"But it did turn up at the depot, Hugh," Faith persisted. "Why make a mystery out of nothing?"

"The mystery's all Jack's, not mine, Faith. But as it happens it also turned up too late. If it was a substitute for the last bus it'd have been ditched within an hour. Once there was a call out for it they'd have spotted it before midday."

"They still could have missed it. A parked car is just a parked car if it's not in a 'no parking' zone."

"No, Mrs. Audley," said Butler. "They didn't miss it, we do know that. It was parked near enough to one of the depot entrances to be in the way. When it was noticed the engine wasn't even cold."

"All of which you could have told us in two minutes flat, Jack." Roskill masked his unease; again, it wasn't like the man to go the long way round. "You're being rather a bore now. Why don't you just come to the point?"

"The point?"

"I don't know what Llewelyn does, but if David doesn't want to say, it's probably veiled in bullshit. So some bright boy in security will have smelt the same rats I have, and after that the procedure's straightforward: they checked it out and they found it was bugged. The point is—where do I come in?"

"Aye, it smelt," said Butler heavily. "It smelt of fish and chips and it had the previous evening's Oxford paper in it, and it was muddy. Which suggested to the local police that it was a casual job. But they had a look for prints and they couldn't find one, not one. Which made them think again, because it was a bit too careful."

"I thought everyone knew enough to wipe off their fingerprints these days?" said Faith.

"Just so, Mrs. Audley. But only the professionals do the job really thoroughly. When the police delivered it back to London they suggested a closer look might be in order. Young Jenkins was given the job of looking—you met him last year, Mrs Audley."

"I did indeed!" Faith smiled reminiscently. "Lots too much hair, but very good-looking. He's nice."

"He's damn good, too," Roskill said. Jenkins was the star up-and-coming performer of the electronic backroom boys, which excused his hair and the irreverence that went with it. "If there was anything in the Princess, Alan Jenkins would have found it. And I take it there was something?"

"There was, Hugh."

"Well, for Christ's sake, man, don't be so mysterious. What sort of bug was it?"

"We don't know." Butler looked obstinately at Roskill, as though he wanted to look away, but couldn't. "Jenkins is dead. It blew him apart, whatever it was. He's dead."

"He's what?"

It wasn't a question: Roskill knew he'd heard perfectly well—he could hear the distant thump of the boiler and the whisper of the hot water in the pipes. It blew him apart, whatever it was ... *Not Jenkins, of all people.*

"He was told to remove any bugs he found," said Butler flatly. "Llewelyn wanted his car back on the double. Jenkins was working alone, taping his report as he went along. He'd checked out the interior of the car, and the engine and the boot. He was working in the pit underneath when he spotted this bug, just about under the driver's seat. He started to remove it, and then he said, 'That's interesting'. Just that— and then there was an explosion."

Faith put her hands to her cheeks.

"They haven't reconstructed things accurately yet—it happened just after midnight, this morning. But from what he said just before it sounds as though someone took a lot of trouble. All we know is that it was one of the latest plastic explosives almost certainly, with maybe one of those new proximity activators. But it must have been attached to the bug as well—it can't have been just bad luck, otherwise he wouldn't have spotted something interesting."

Not Jenkins. Roskill groaned to himself inwardly. Lots of hair but very good-looking. But not good-looking any more.

He'd never thought of Jenkins as good-looking. Just intelligent and eager—that had been how he had looked that first time, at the Battle of Britain Open Day at Snettisham. Harry's younger brother who was a genius with electronic gadgets and bored with his trainee managership. It had seemed such good sense to find a useful square hole for so square a peg ...

"It was quick, Hugh," said Butler. "He never knew what hit him. He wasn't expecting it—damn it, no one was expecting it."

No one had expected it—and bloody Llewelyn had wanted his precious car on the double. But that was half-baked, unfair thinking; of course no one expected it. Chicago in the twenties, maybe Berlin in the worst days of the Cold War. And Northern Ireland today. But this wouldn't be an IRA job: if the police had driven it all the way from Oxfordshire it was a real professional piece of work.

"But why, Major Butler—why?" said Faith. "Why should anyone want to blow Jenkins up?"

"Not Jenkins, Mrs. Audley. Jenkins was an accident, an innocent bystander. Killing Jenkins was like poisoning a food taster—no sense to it. It was Llewelyn they wanted, and it looks as though whoever rigged the device was plain bloody-minded. But then the whole thing was a botched up affair, half clever and half stupid: if they wanted to kill Llewelyn they could have done it with much less fuss. And if they wanted to put the fear of God into him they needn't have taken so much trouble."

Butler was right. It was like a futile accident—as futile as a sudden skid on a patch of oil. Better to think of Jenkins skidding into a lorry: nothing anyone could do about it, and at least it was quick.

Except that this patch of oil had been deliberately spread by someone, and it would be a sweet thing to see that same someone's face rubbed in it.

Roskill savoured the prospect for a moment: Butler had been right about that, too—for him Alan Jenkins overshadowed Snettisham. So for the first time a desire for a tangible revenge—a new sensation that—would coincide with a job.

Then he stopped short in mid-thought, suddenly at a loss. That wasn't how things worked at all. Rather, they worked the opposite way round: any sort of personal involvement, however innocent, was anathema. In this instance he ought to be the last person conscripted, not the first.

And doubly the last. Whatever Llewelyn did it had nothing to do with aviation or avionics, or he would have encountered him already. A bungled assassination was first and last a Special Branch matter, not a fit assignment for an avionics man. One might just as well despatch a chopper to intercept a bomber.

So what the devil was Butler up to? Roskill felt a cold tingle of caution crawl up his back. Butler was a good fellow, solid and sensible, but an establishment man to the core, prepared to put his hand to any awkward job loyally. And notoriously he was given such awkward jobs...

But it would be useless to ask outright for the truth. Butler would be ready to fend off such a question. Better simply to play it straight, with caution.

"And why would anyone want to blow up Llewelyn?"

"Perhaps Dr Audley could tell us that."

Audley slowly put down the empty glass he'd been nursing and stared at Butler.

"The last time I set eyes on the man was maybe ten years ago. It was a pub in Richmond—he apologised for treading on my hand in the game we'd played that afternoon. He'd trodden on it deliberately, of course; it was just part of *his* game. And that was the last time I met him. Ten, maybe eleven, years ago."

"But you know *of* him, then," Butler prodded.

Audley looked at Butler reflectively.

"Too late, I did. He was a bastard." Audley turned towards Roskill. "But he knows what he wants—just as Butler here knows what he wants. Unfortunately for him, he's not going to get it."

"David, what on earth are you talking about?" Faith's face, turned towards her husband for the first time, seemed thinner and whiter in the candlelight.

"That's your cue, love," said Audley. "In a moment you're going to start disapproving of me. So will Hugh. Or on second thoughts maybe Hugh won't. Hugh's a downier bird than they think—not just an overgrown ex-fighter pilot with a crafty streak. I think Hugh's smelt a rat too."

A rat, certainly. But what sort of rat?

"Hugh's not talking, very sensibly, love. And Major Butler's not talking either now! Perhaps I'm being rather unfair to Butler, though. He's only doing his job."

"Unfair?" The irritation was plain in Faith's voice. "Aggravating and pompous. And under the circumstances callous too, I think."

"There—you've started to disapprove." Audley's sudden enjoyment of the situation *was* aggravating: this was the old Audley, one maddening step ahead of the play and relishing the fact. Again, it was all very well for Audley to enjoy himself; Butler hadn't come for him.

Or had he?

It flashed across Roskill's mind that Audley was now behaving exactly as he himself had done when Butler calmly cancelled Snettisham: wriggling in the snare. But Audley was an altogether more formidable creature. When it came to traps he would be a wolverine, almost untrappable . . .

"You never did finish your story about the hounds of Hell, David, did you?" Roskill murmured. "I take it that the rake was lucky: the hounds passed him by and he turned into a prodigal? The question is, which of us are the hounds going to take?"

Audley smiled appreciatively. "You were just a touch slow there, Hugh, but you got there in the end. I think they were after me all the time, don't you?"

Faith looked from one to the other of them. "What hounds?"

Roskill watched Butler. "What David means, Faith, is that Jack there could just as easily have waited for me at home if he wanted to preserve my beard. More easily, in fact. But instead he had to come here and tell you all about it, and make a great performance of it, when strictly speaking he shouldn't have done so at all.

"And normally he wouldn't have done. But he did—didn't you, honest Jack? Because it wasn't me you wanted at all. It was David!"

Butler lifted his chin. "Audley can help. It's as simple as that."

"Well, why the bloody hell—pardon, Faith—can't you ask him straight out?"

"Simple again. He might have refused."

"No one gives orders to him any more? Are you an over-mighty subject now, David?"

"No 'might' about it. I have refused. In this matter I *am*

an over-mighty subject, as it happens. Llewelyn can stew in his own juice...".

"David!" Faith was outraged. "You can't say that, not when someone wants to murder him—not when they've already murdered Alan Jenkins. Don't you want to catch the people who did *that*?"

Audley shook his head at her. "Faith, love—can't you see that's what you're supposed to say to me? Can't you understand that nobody's ever going to catch whoever booby-trapped Llewelyn's car? He'll be away and long gone. And even if he wasn't and we caught him, then we'd only have some stupid devil who thought he was doing his patriotic duty.

"And that wouldn't stop them blowing up Llewelyn if they're set on it, any more than it would bring young Jenkins back to life. And they don't want me to avenge Jenkins, anyway—no one's ever going to do that—"

No one would do that, no matter what, thought Roskill bitterly. No one could avenge an accidental death.

"But if they find out why it was done they can still save Llewelyn," said Butler. "You can help there."

"You can't refuse, David," said Faith.

"I'm not supposed to have any choice, and that's a fact. Your tender social conscience and Hugh's special relationship with Jenkins are designed to weight the scales—just what was so special about Jenkins, Hugh?"

Coming from almost any other man it would have been offensive in its implication. But Audley was curiously naïve about such things, and prudish too. He meant exactly what he had said, and if he had suspected anything else he wouldn't have spoken at all; Roskill simply wouldn't have been sitting at dinner with him.

But none of his business nevertheless, and it was on the tip of Roskill's tongue to say so when he glimpsed Faith's face, stricken with ludicrous embarrassment; she was all of fifteen years younger than her husband, but a million years older in this—the embarrassment was for his naïveté, not for any homosexual tendencies Roskill might possess.

Ludicrous, though——and how Alan would have laughed at it, with his obsessive pursuit of dolly girls who needed no pursuing!

He had to take pity on her.

"Nothing like that, Faith. Jenkins was a friend of mine. I got him into the service."

That would have to do. It was as much as the service knew, anyway. The private guilt and grief was all his own—his own and Isobel's . . .

"Hugh—I'm sorry. But it wasn't your fault."

Not his fault. An accident. Nothing they could do about it and he never knew what hit him. Epitaph for both the Jenkins brothers. One way or another he'd done for them both now.

But this was mere self-pity. The important thing now was somehow to succeed where Butler had failed: to do what the bastards wanted him to do—to involve Audley. And that could never be done by moral blackmail, or not so crudely anyway. Nor could it be done while both of them were still in the dark.

"I know it isn't my fault. It isn't David's either, so you might as well let him off the hook. Just tell us this, Jack: am I still in on things, or was I just the sprat to catch the mackerel?"

"They want both of you."

It might be true. Or it might be that Butler was still trying to catch the mackerel.

"They'll just have to make do with me then." He couldn't risk winking at Butler, with Audley sitting directly ahead of him. More likely neither of them would see it in the candlelight, anyway. "Just tell me what Llewelyn is up to that might make a target of him."

Butler shook his head slowly. "That's the rub, Hugh. Apparently Llewelyn isn't up to anything."

"Nonsense!" Audley exploded. "Llewelyn isn't the sort of man who is ever up to nothing. He isn't capable of doing nothing."

Faith said: "But you said you didn't know anything about him."

"I said I hadn't met him for years. Until last year I'd forgotten about him, and when I came up with him again it was too late to take precautions. He'd got me kicked out of the Middle Eastern group."

Roskill looked at him incredulously. Audley had been the brains of that group and virtually a law unto himself. And under Sir Frederick's special protection.

"Nobody told you that, did they, Hugh? Come to think of it, why does everyone think I transferred to the European section? What do people say about it?"

Roskill strove to rearrange his thoughts. The rumor was that Audley had been miffed at having his warnings ignored, and that after the Aden withdrawal he had schemed diligently to manoeuvre himself out of an area in which there was no longer either credit or honour to be gained.

"They say you were—prudent," he replied cautiously.

"I abandoned a sinking ship, did I?" Audley smiled bitterly. "It was thoughtful of Fred to put that around—better for my image! But actually I was sacked—kicked upstairs and promoted out of Llewelyn's way. I asked too many awkward questions and gave too many inconvenient answers."

So Llewelyn was definitely Middle East; it had been on the cards from the moment Audley had been involved.

"I can't think how I didn't meet up with him much earlier. He must have kept very quiet until he was sure the power was in his hands. Then—wham! I think he damn near convinced the JIC that I was an Israeli agent."

Rumor had said that too: Audley had worked far too closely with the Israelis.

"I did a little quiet research on *him* after it was all over." Audley sighed. "Just for my peace of mind, of course.

"Outwardly he's all empiricism and pragmatism, outsmarting the Russians and the Chinese. But inwardly he's a raving idealist. I think he dreams of becoming a political Lawrence of Arabia—or at least getting back to the UN partition lines of '47 if he can't undo 1920. An admirer of all things Arab, anyway—providing they fit in with his dream of the new Middle East."

"Would you say there's any substance in his dreams?" Butler asked.

"There's something in it, certainly. He wants to underwrite the new nationalisms, and that would seem to be backing a winning streak. But he thinks that deep down the Arabs would rather deal with us than with anyone else because we're the only ones who have had any sort of love affair with Arabia.

"The trouble is that the real Lawrence types always seem to turn up on the wrong side—like those bright characters in the Yemen. And he tried to stop them."

Audley gave Butler a sidelong glance, as though it had suddenly dawned on him that he was being drawn. "Anyway, that was why I was —promoted: my advice didn't always fit his scheme of things. And admittedly I'm not exactly anti-Israeli."

There was a lot left unsaid there, thought Roskill. If Llewelyn was a schemer, so was Audley. In fact Audley could probably be as bloody-minded and obstinate as anyone when it came to the crunch, for all his air of donnish reasonableness.

But for the rest, it made sense. The great powers might be chary of blowing up each other's civil servants, but some of the smaller powers were much less inhibited, particularly the Middle Eastern ones. There were harassed bureaucrats in Washington and Moscow who sweated without great success to curb such tendencies. The Israelis went their own remorseless way, apparently regardless—and some of the Arab guerrilla groups were both uncontrollable and unpredictable...

"But if he doesn't approve of you, darling, why does he want your help now?" Faith asked. "And why doesn't he ask you straight out?"

"It would stick in his throat. But I suppose he thinks I've got some useful private contacts." Audley shook his head. "He's wrong of course."

"He doesn't think so," said Butler. "The truth is, Mrs. Audley, your husband was the sharpest man in the group, and they know it. And he had his own grapevine."

"'Had' is right. I haven't got it now. I've been out nearly a year, and that's a lifetime—I'm out of touch completely. They should know that I can't pick up the threads just like that. It won't do—it simply won't do—and I'm surprised Llewelyn ever thought it would."

"He's seen the driver's seat in his car, Dr. Audley," said Butler harshly. "He's frightened."

"Frightened? You're damn right he's frightened. So am I—and so should you be. But he'll put himself on ice and expect me to go poking around. And I'm not going to! I'm not equipped to deal with maniacs."

"You don't have to. Just get a line on the who and the why—that's all.

Audley gestured abruptly. "No! It's not on. Besides, I've got Faith to think of now. So even if I could, I wouldn't. You can tell them I'm just not interested."

Not interested—that would be the heart of the matter for a man like Audley in anything that involved choice. Only because of that would he allow other, weightier reasons to become decisive.

Butler pushed back his chair and stood up.

"I'll tell them just that. But on your head be it then, Dr. Audley."

"Not on my head, Major Butler. That's a hat I don't choose to wear. It doesn't fit."

Butler's eyes shifted momentarily to Roskill, and then back towards Audley, calculation naked in them now.

"If it's not yours then it's Hugh's, whether it fits or not—spare me a moment outside, Hugh—so I'll see myself out, Mrs Audley. And I'm sorry to have troubled you."

Roskill followed Butler to the square of cobbles in the angle of the old house, in the pool of light from the porch lantern. It didn't help to be dragged out like this—Audley would know very well what he would be up to—but if there was anything to be salvaged now he had to know more.

"Don't ask me to go straight back and convince him, Jack. It won't do any good now. You've botched it—you've bloody well botched it. It'll be damned difficult now."

Butler faced him, relaxed and without a hint of apology.

"I warned them. I told them he'd tumble to it. But Stocker reckoned he might quit if they tried to force him—he's got just enough money of his own to do it—and Fred would play merry hell if that happened. So they seemed to think they'd got nothing to lose."

He snorted. "They're running scared, that's the trouble."

"I don't wonder at it. But what the hell has Llewelyn been doing? They must have some idea."

"Stocker said they hadn't the faintest idea, but things must be bad for them to come crawling to Audley like this when they both hate his guts. But Audley's got a big reputation for puzzle-solving, especially after the business with that Russian last year. *And* he's got some juicy Middle Eastern contacts of his own, remember."

"He swears he hasn't now."

"So he says. All I know is they want him and they want him badly. And now it's up to you to get him—you and Nellie No-tits in there. She's probably giving him hell now. I hope she is; it'll make it easier for you."

Roskill knew he had to make allowances for Butler's blind spot, but there was a point at which allowances became pusillanimity.

"You really are a bugger sometimes, aren't you? And not even a very clever one this time, as it happens. You want to watch it, Jack. It might become a habit—making mistakes about women."

Butler's heavy shoulders slumped and then stiffened again, and Roskill was aware too late that he had hit harder than he intended. The man had children—three little snub-nosed, red-haired, miniature Butlers, all female—but he had never once mentioned a wife. Roskill had never thought to ask about that, and now he never could.

"Aye, that could happen." Butler stared into the darkness before meeting Roskill's gaze. "But this is strictly business. They say she has a well-developed social conscience and they aim to catch at him through it. And through you too, Hugh—through you."

Now there was regret in his voice, and a curious echo of that lost Lancashire accent. If there was anything more to be got out of Butler, now was the time.

"And that was the only reason why I'm involved?"

A shake of the head. "I don't know. They know you got Jenkins into the service, that you know his family. And Audley likes you, they know that too. But I think there was something else behind that . . . You went to Israel before your leave, didn't you?"

"That was nothing. I only met a few of their pilots—I saw their tame Sukhoi 7 and some Mig 21 modifications, and we talked about the SAMs. It was pure routine."

Butler nodded. "I don't know, then. But they want you sure enough. There's a briefing tomorrow at 11:30—not at the office, either. Officially you're at Snettisham. The meeting's set up at the Queensway Hotel, just off Bloomsbury Square. Room 104. You and Audley, if you can swing it. You and your beard, anyway."

Butler eased himself into the driver's seat of his Rover. He reached for the ignition.

"And Hugh—I'm sorry about young Jenkins. It was bloody bad luck, pure bloody bad luck."

Alan Jenkins was already a little unreal, thought Roskill sadly. Already one of the absent friends, fixed forevermore in the past tense, merely to be remembered and regretted. Not even a ghost, but just another of the shades, like Harry. It was appalling how quickly death could be accepted. But then he'd never really known Alan as he had known Harry: the age gap had been small enough, yet impassable.

Yet it was civil of Butler to regret him, a decent gesture after their recent passage of words. It called for a civil answer.

"If it hadn't been him it would have been some other poor devil."

"But it was doubly bad luck for him, though. It should have been Maitland. He was the one on call."

"Why wasn't it Maitland, then?"

Butler switched on the engine. "Act of God, the insurance companies would call it. That gale last night brought half a tree across Maitland's telephone wires—he lives out of London, down East Grinstead way. They couldn't get through to him. The other two chaps were out of town and Jenkins had just come back. He was the second stand-by. Pure bad luck."

He looked up at Roskill as he reached for the transmission selector. "But if you want to get your own back on bad luck, Hugh—get Audley. It's as simple as that."

Roskill watched the Rover's tail-lights down the drive until the beech hedge cut them off. So Jenkins' death had been doubly accidental—a useless, cruelly coincidental death. He turned despondently towards the porch. It would take more than coincidence to make Audley change his mind.

He stopped with his hand on the iron latch, staring at the weathered oak. Were those the original adze marks on it? Pure bad luck ... yet perhaps Audley would be more interested in bad luck, at that—he had once said that he was not a great believer in luck, either good or bad: he maintained it was very often something a man received according to his deserts ...

There was a germ of an idea there: a trick and a deception, certainly, but also an idea. Yet it would have to be good to catch a suspicious-minded Audley; it must do better than fit the facts, but must carry its own inner conviction. It must intrigue him. It must—

Roskill caught his breath, still gripping the latch. *It did fit the facts*. It fitted them so perfectly that it ceased to be a deception even as he tested it in his own mind.

God! It was like carrying a supposedly forged masterpiece

to an art dealer, only to realise at the last moment that the forgery bore the irrefutable marks of authenticity on it!

He started as the latch moved under his hand and the door opened suddenly in his face. A gust of warm air hit him.

"Hugh! What are you doing standing out in the cold? You look as if you'd seen a ghost."

Roskill stared at her. "I think I have, Faith—I think I have."

Faith put her hand on his arm. "It's Alan Jenkins, isn't it? I'm so sorry—I can't quite believe it even now."

"I'm going to ask David to help me. Do you mind?"

"Mind? Of course I don't! I think it's his duty to help you."

"Even after Jack Butler tried to use the way you felt as a lever?"

Faith shook her head ruefully. "I'm used to that sort of thing now. It's the way they think—always the indirect way. It's the way David himself thinks half the time. He can't help it. You're the only normal one among them I believe, Hugh. And don't you dare change."

Roskill looked at the floor in confusion, thinking guiltily of what he was planning, and worse still why it would appeal to her dear David. Really, she deserved better than this...

"But it's no use, Hugh. He won't help you. It isn't that he doesn't care about people, because I know he does. But they hurt his pride terribly when they took him off the Middle East—he won't admit it, and he laughs it off like he did this evening. But it mattered to him much more than he pretends because he really cared about the Jews and the Arabs. He had real friends among them, on both sides—that was why he was so good at his job. And I think he really hates that man Llewelyn. So it won't be any use—I haven't even tried to convince him, so I know you won't be able to."

A pity Butler was on his way back to town; it was a speech he ought to have heard. And if true a valuable insight equally into Audley's mind: beneath that air of calculation the man might even be committed to some sort of humanitarian ideal.

He might have a dream like Llewelyn's in fact. Perhaps that was what really fed his dislike of the man.

So much the better now, Roskill thought.

"I must try nevertheless, Faith," he said gently. "Because there's something I believe we've all overlooked up to now."

Audley was sitting back, waiting for him, his final refusal cut and dried and ready for use.

"It's 'no' to you, too, Hugh. I'm sorry, but I'm like that American statesman who said that if he was nominated for the presidency he wouldn't stand, and if he was chosen he wouldn't sit. So have another drink and don't bother to ask me."

Roskill smiled. It seemed so clear now: it was like saying that the earth was round. But they had all been so busy thinking of themselves that no one had noticed it—except Faith, who had spoken the truth because she hadn't understood at all.

"Hugh, what's the matter?" Audley was looking at him, perplexed. "Have I said something amusing?"

The matter was that it was amusing: Llewelyn scared enough to pocket his pride and try to manoeuvre a man he disliked—and who hated him—into rescuing him. And all for nothing.

That was what Audley would surrender to: not the tragedy of it, but the savage joke.

"The bomb in the Princess, David—it wasn't for Llewelyn at all. It was for Jenkins. Just for Jenkins."

II

ROSKILL LAY ON a groundsheet in the soaking bracken, watching Mrs Maitland shepherd her children into her Volkswagen half a mile below him.

The 8 o'clock sun was low enough behind him for the forward slope of the ridge to be a textbook observation position, which made him feel slightly foolish. If she had walked right by him she still wouldn't have known him from Adam: she was a perfectly innocent housewife running her kids to school. But Audley had been insistent on every precaution being taken; nothing must be allowed to alert anyone about what they were actually doing.

He watched the little car bump down the rutted track to the metalled road, and then along the curve of the road for a mile until it disappeared from view. Then he backtracked to the exact point where the Maitland's telephone wires left the main cable, their more slender poles striding across the open field to the cottage and the farm beyond.

He adjusted the binoculars fractionally, scanned the area for the umpteenth time and saw nothing fresh. In all probability there *was* nothing, or if there had been it had by now been hopelessly obliterated by the repair men whose tramplings were evident even at this distance. At best it was a long shot, but everything had to start somewhere, and this was that inescapable starting place.

He replaced the binoculars in their leather case and folded the groundsheet. Mrs. Maitland would not return for at least forty minutes; Maitland himself had been gone half an hour and would be on his train by now. It was time to move.

He searched the landscape once more, wondering as he did so if he was duplicating the actions of an earlier observer. Then he turned and retraced his way to where the Triumph was parked among the pines. He unlocked the boot and replaced the binoculars and the sheet. Shutting it he glimpsed his reflection in the shining cellulose, distorted and wholly unrecognizable. In leather jerkin, flat cap and gumboots—and with the ludicrous beard—he wasn't quite sure what he resembled. An itinerant Basque revolutionary, perhaps, but hardly a pirate and certainly not a stray GPO linesman. Equally, however, not his elegant self.

He stumped off heavily down the hillside. The break in the weather hadn't lasted, thank God; the ground was still wet, but was drying fast, which was just as well if there was going to be much crawling about like this. It was no use telling himself that he was a country boy, born and bred, for over recent years he had become half-naturalised into a townsman. Not that this little bit of heath, field and woodland was true countryside; anything as close to London as this was little better than the enclosures at Regent's Park Zoo, open space preserved to give the human animals the illusion of a natural setting.

He shook his head. If there was nothing left to show that the wires had been deliberately brought down, should he invent evidence to keep Audley happy? It had been what he had originally intended, after all, before the possible truth of it had dawned on him. Yet Audley had taken little convincing; it was almost as though he'd welcomed the idea, despite his previous intransigence. Perhaps deep down he knew that he wasn't quite big enough to turn Llewelyn away.

Or perhaps it was simply that the logic of Roskill's solution made such crude proof unnecessary. It was there in the events themselves: every step of the car theft and booby-trapping had been marked by the same contradictory cleverness and stupidity. But the cleverness and the stupidity had both been carefully calculated to lead directly to the removal of the fatal bug by an expert—and by one expert in particular.

The Jenkins Gambit, Audley had called it: *the best way to kill a food taster is by poisoning his master's dish—it looks like an occupational hazard!*

And it had so very nearly worked, too. With someone as important as Llewelyn menaced, Jenkins was almost certain to be overlooked. The assassins could not reasonably have expected anyone like Roskill, with a personal commitment to sharpen his perception, to appear on the scene—and even he had only stumbled on the more likely truth by accident.

The only real flaw in their planning was the telephone wire: the coincidence that had alerted Roskill. They should have waited until Jenkins came on duty by normal routine—unless for some reason they were unable to wait, in which case it was not a flaw, but a calculated risk...

At least finding the place had been easy enough. Although the repair men had worked on the other side of the hedge their vehicles had chewed up the roadside verge, deeply rutting the debris of the previous summer. He had had no difficulty spotting it on his early morning reconnaissance drive along the road, in the half-light.

The tree itself, contrary to Butler's report, had not come down—it merely leaned drunkenly away from the road, ten degrees out of true. The damage had been done by a huge dead limb which appeared to have snapped off two-thirds of the way up. Falling in the field it had brought down Maitland's wires and conveniently left the main cable intact.

Roskill squelched his way over the ruined verge. The elm had grown up on the far side of a deep roadside ditch; with its one-sided root system—he could see the stumps of roots which had been severed when the ditch had last been cleaned out—it was hardly surprising that it had started to fall away from the road. Elms, he remembered, were notoriously unstable at the best of times.

He peered up at the new scar high up on the trunk where the limb had been ripped away. There were no signs of saw marks, nor any tell-tale sawdust scattering at the base either. It looked depressingly like a natural break, the result of the extra pressure when the tree canted over.

Not for the first time he felt a touch of doubt chilling his beautiful theory. It would be damned embarrassing if he was forced to double-cross Audley into making a fool of Llewelyn. Worse, if Jenkins wasn't the target it was Audley who would be made to look the fool, and Audley would be a nasty enemy to make in the department.

He launched himself clumsily across the ditch, throwing his weight forward and embracing the elm as the soft earth crumbled under him.

The grass on the other side of the hedge was also torn and trampled and sprinkled with legitimate sawdust, where the fallen limb had been cut up into manageable sections and stacked. It was good burning wood, too, dead but not rotten.

Dead, but not rotten: there was something maybe not quite right about that. He ran his eye up the trunk again: it was odd how the great branch hadn't fallen in a line with the tree itself—yet if it had done so it would almost certainly have missed Maitland's wires. As it was it had peeled off towards the left, almost as though it had been . . . pulled.

Pulled! He kicked himself mentally for missing the simplest method of all: hitch a cable to the dead branch and pull obliquely. It was not only the obvious way but virtually the only way, and he'd been a monumental idiot not to see it at once.

And yet it would take immense strength to do it—not only bringing down the branch, but also very nearly the tree itself. It would take more than manpower to do that.

He looked up at the elm again, then down to the torn turf, trying to gauge the likely direction from which the pulling had been done. It had to be out in the field to the left of the wires.

He moved carefully away from the hedge, searching the ground intently. It had been dry on that night, and for some days before, but this land was low lying. Further out in the field there were tussocks of coarse marsh grass. It would never be less than damp here.

And there they were!

Hardly more than twenty yards from the elm, and somewhat closer to the hedge than he had expected, were four symmetrical bruises in the grass where the wheels had spun for a moment before winning their tug-of-war with the branch.

Roskill's pulse beat with excitement: *four* tyre marks made the evidence conclusive. The act of dragging a heavy object on the ground would have produced deeper rear wheel marks and shallower front ones, even if the vehicle was four-wheel drive. But the downward pull had equalised the forces at work—another few yards, indeed, and it would have been the front tyres which would have dug deeper into the ground. These marks were exactly those which a Land-Rover would make in the act of sabotaging the line, unremarkable in themselves but irrefutable evidence in context.

He experienced a curious mixture of gratification and anger. His logic—and Audley's confidence—was vindicated by this tattered piece of low-grade pasture. Here Maitland had been deliberately cut off, so that Jenkins should keep the appointment.

Somebody knew too bloody much about the technical section, that was certain. And somebody knew too much about Llewelyn's movements.

Roskill felt for the camera in his webbing haversack. And somebody, he thought grimly, had come unstuck, nevertheless.

III

AUDLEY WAS STANDING on the pavement in Grosvenor Gardens, ten yards from its junction with Buckingham Palace Road, which was precisely where he said he would be, to the yard.

In fact, thought Roskill, he looked rather like a solitary, oversized waxwork which had been stolen from Madame Tussaud's and then abandoned to become a pedestrian obstacle: he stood unmoving, engrossed in a dull-looking, stiff-covered magazine, oblivious of the passers-by who eddied round him and of the traffic which accelerated past his nose.

Even when Roskill slid the Triumph alongside the kerb beside him he did not move at once. And nor, when he did move, did he bother to verify that it was Roskill. He methodically closed the magazine, turning down the page—so much Roskill could see from the driver's seat—and simply got straight into the car, without a word.

Roskill engaged the gears. "Well, we were right," he said.

Audley grunted and nodded. "You mean *you* were right. I was reasonably sure you would be, whether you found anything or not. But I'm glad to hear it; it's always nicer to be certain."

He subsided into silence and it occurred to Roskill that he

wasn't going to ask for details. That might indeed be proof of a touching confidence, but now seemed far more likely to indicate that Audley was trying to forget how very nearly he had missed the chance of making a laughing-stock of his enemy.

But he wasn't going to get off as easily as that.

"They pulled it down with a Land-Rover," said Roskill. "Not the whole tree—just one big branch. The tyre-marks are perfectly plain when you know what you're looking for."

He reached under the dashboard for the envelope.

"Photographs, diagram and report—all in there."

Audley slid the material half out of the envelope, riffled through the photos briefly and then pushed it all back.

"You didn't talk to anyone?"

"I didn't talk to anyone. Nobody saw me. And I developed the pictures myself." Roskill kept his tone neutral. "It's our own little Top Secret."

"We'll keep it that way, then." Audley slipped the envelope between the pages of his magazine. "I don't want anyone around while we're checking up on Jenkins. I don't even want them to know that we're checking on him, in fact. The chances are that they'll find out sooner or later, but I want to put that off as long as possible. But I don't want to tell any lies, so I think our lines should be what Kipling called 'suppressio veri, suggestio falsi'—do you understand, Hugh?"

Roskill understood very well, and bitterly too: once Llewelyn found out that they were investigating Jenkins he would soon put two and two together. And the moment he realized he was in no danger the joke was over. Indeed, to get a full and perfect revenge Audley needed to complete his assignment first, for only then would it become a matter of record and unsuppressible.

But it was a sad thing that the only way Jenkins could be avenged was by enabling Audley to indulge his own private feud . . .

"I understand that perfectly well," he said evenly. "We're going to make him sweat."

"Make him sweat—yes." Audley turned in his seat and looked hard at Roskill for a moment. "But I don't think you do fully understand, all the same. At a guess I'd say you're thinking that there's not much to choose between Llewelyn and me—a couple of right bastards. But I just happen to be the bastard who suits you at the moment—is that right?"

It was a question that didn't admit equivocation.

"I think," said Roskill reluctantly, "that you can do the right thing for a paltry reason. In this case your reason doesn't—dignify—what we're doing."

Audley nodded thoughtfully. "A petty vendetta? Yes, I can see your line of thought. I ought to have seen it before. And there's something in it, too. But you knew that when you came back to tempt me last night, and it didn't stop you."

"I'm not complaining. You asked me a question and I gave you an honest answer. And as you said, it suits me well enough."

"Then perhaps I ought to question your motives too, my dear Hugh—I ought to wonder why they were so sure of you."

"I told you last night—I recruited Jenkins in the first place."

"Not good enough."

"I know his family too."

"Still not good enough. You also admitted last night that you weren't to blame. There isn't enough there for a guilt complex."

Audley paused, waiting in vain for an answer.

"Very well, then! Let's get back to my base motives for a moment. I admit that the chance of making a fool of Dai Llewelyn did attract me—it still does. But it wasn't enough to make me change my mind. It was the fact that it was Jenkins and not Llewelyn who was the target—I find that *very* interesting. The poor boy said it was interesting the moment before he died, and by God he was right!"

Roskill frowned. He had been so busy with practical problems that he hadn't really faced up to the ultimate one. It had simply hidden itself at the back of his mind, nagging at him: why the hell would anyone blow up Alan?

"You see, Hugh," Audley continued, "Llewelyn isn't such a bad candidate for assassination, because in his own way he's a pretty important person. I know Butler said he wasn't up to anything. But when you wield the sort of influence Llewelyn does there'll always be sufficient motive for somebody to have a go, if that's the way they're inclined.

"But Jenkins wasn't important. At least, he shouldn't have been. Yet he suddenly became supremely important to somebody..."

"Somebody who knew too bloody much about the way the Department works, too," said Roskill. "They must have known exactly what would happen if Maitland couldn't be contacted."

"They also knew where Llewelyn was. They knew how everyone's minds worked." There was a note of puzzlement in Audley's voice. "Yet if it was accidental death they wanted to stimulate they set about it in the most extraordinary manner. A simple road accident would have been so much neater. Nobody would have thought twice about it. Unless of course they didn't know where Jenkins lived. Did he live in some inaccessible place?"

"I really don't know." Roskill thought hard. "He was always changing his digs, certainly. I think he did it to get his old girlfriends off his back—he'd never leave a forwarding address."

"Well, that might account for it." Audley's head bobbed. "They had to catch up with him quickly and they didn't know where to find him. But they knew what his job was—that really might explain it!"

It was a cold thought: failing to find him, they had created a situation in which Jenkins and his death had converged on each other, with death riding in a Vanden Plas Princess.

There were both silent for a time. Then Audley spoke.

"The point is, Hugh, I don't think other people will see things quite the way we do. When they realize that the heat's off Llewelyn I think there'll be a great big sigh of relief higher up. Then the reaction will set in; they won't want too much fuss and bother. They won't want any awkwardness. And that will mean that they won't want *us* poking around, because we're liable to become awkward. They know me too well already—and you've got this mysterious personal stake of yours..."

Audley tailed off, waiting once more for an explanation. But that was in line with what everyone said about the man: the facts and figures were never enough for him—he nagged endlessly at the whys behind them. So now he'd never give up, he'd never leave such a loose end as Roskill's motive for vengeance untied behind him.

"Let me put it another way, Hugh. There's got to be some mutual trust between us. I've trusted you. Don't you think you can trust me?"

Roskill looked at him in surprise. "You've trusted me?"

"I have indeed! Last night I chose to believe that you thought out the Jenkins angle on your own, without any prompting from Butler. I've given you the benefit of the doubt, in fact."

"What doubt?"

"My dear fellow—hasn't it occurred to you that Llewelyn might have calculated that I couldn't resist making a fool of him? I wouldn't put it past him, you know!"

"But the facts—when you look at the facts, David. Llewelyn didn't bring down that tree, damn it!"

"Facts can be arranged. But, as I say—I chose to believe you. That's why I've let you convince me—which is what they'd planned in the beginning. If Butler failed, there was Faith. If Faith failed, there was you—I simply want to know why in the end it was you!"

Roskill sighed. It would have been better if he had revealed rather more the previous night, when Audley wasn't concentrating on him. Now, in simple self-defence, he'd have to give him Harry.

Harry ...

"I didn't know Alan Jenkins very well really, David. He was in electronic counter-measures, the bugging business. It was his brother I knew—his elder brother."

He paused, searching for the right words. But how could one explain a man like Harry to a man like Audley? He would know all the theory of it, from David and Jonathan onwards, but his understanding would be as two-dimensional as the pages he'd gathered it from.

To talk about comradeship and friendship was inadequate; to mention affection debased it with physical undertones— though by God if it had been the army of Alexander the Great instead of Queen Elizabeth's air force, there probably would have been that too!

Harry...

"Harry Jenkins—he was a good friend of mine in the squadron. My wing-man. He was a first-rate chap."

Friendship is Love without his wings—was that Byron? But they had had their wings too.

"I spent several leaves at Harry's family place at East Firle, down in Sussex."

East Firle...

Up in the morning at cock-crow and over the hills, past the old burial mounds and down into Alfriston. On over the Cuckmere, up the hillside again, down under the Long Man, beer and pickles at Jevington. Then onwards more slowly until Pevensey Levels spread out below, along the last magnificent roll of the Downs towards Beachy Head, where the car would be waiting for them with Mrs. Jenkins at the wheel. It was a golden memory.

"We used to walk a lot. I got to know the family pretty well—nice people. Harry's father had a fighter wing in '45. He's dead now."

Dead too, thank God. All the Jenkins males were dead now, but at least the old man hadn't been the last, chafing in a house full of women, even women as delightful as Aunt Mary.

"Oddly enough it was Alan I knew least—he was always

away at school. I didn't actually meet him until just after I'd left the squadron. He'd just started with Alpha Electronics and he didn't much like 'em. And you know how Sir Frederick is always on about keeping our eyes open for talent."

"What happened to Harry?" Audley drew him gently back to the point.

"Harry had my flight—my job—on my recommendation. He took over from me when I came into the department."

For Roskill, read Jenkins.

"He flew into a hillside in Wales a week later."

Carnedd Dafydd—he'd seen it from the pass beyond Capel Curig on the way to Holyhead a few months afterwards, the clouds driving like smoke across it.

"And you feel it should have been you, not him?"

"No, hardly that." Roskill shook his head sadly.

Poor Harry! The better man by far, but never the better pilot. "It was Harry's mountainside."

"But your guilt nevertheless?"

"You might call it that—I don't know what else you could call it. I suppose I might feel better if I'd left the squadron for pure patriotic reasons . . ."

Instinctively Roskill felt that a shadow of the truth would satisfy Audley now.

"The fact is, David, that I was rather bored with flying. Fred dangled this job in front of me—this job and a step in rank. So Harry and Alan are dead because I was bored. I know I didn't kill them—I just recommended them. And now I'd feel a lot better if I could wipe someone's eyes. Silly, isn't it?"

Audley nodded slowly. "Yes, it's silly. But I know the feeling, Hugh. It's like slashing a bed of stinging nettles when you've been stung—silly, but very satisfying."

Roskill relaxed carefully. More by good luck than calculation he had struck the right note for Audley.

"Tell me, Hugh," said Audley conversationally, "how would they accept you down at—where was it—East Firle now? Do they blame you in any way?"

"Good Lord, no! They don't know I had a hand in anything. They probably wouldn't blame me if they did know, either—they aren't that sort of people."

With his mind on a parking space thirty yards ahead Roskill's guard was momentarily down and it wasn't until he was actually swinging into the space that the significance of the question hit him.

"You don't mean—Christ, David! You're not going to ask me to go down to East Firle?"

"Someone's got to go."

Roskill grabbed blindly for the handbrake, grappling with the implications of what appeared so obvious to Audley. That anything could have happened at East Firle, snuggled so peacefully under the Beacon, seemed not only unlikely, but unthinkable. Yet—

"Don't play dumb, Hugh, just because you don't want to go. It has to be you, because you can go down there as a friend of the family. You've got a perfectly innocent motive for being there. If I was spotted there our game would be up. But they may take you for granted—for a time anyway."

"Who's 'they'?"

"That's for you to find out. Maybe nobody now. But *something* happened when Jenkins was on leave. Otherwise they'd have had time to set up a different sort of accident—a more accidental one. But something happened so quickly that they didn't have time to catch up with him, remember? Something so important they had to take the devil of a risk to make sure they shut him up quickly."

"But what makes you think it happened at East Firle?"

"I don't know where it happened. But we have to start there."

Roskill sighed. Alan would most likely have spent part of his leave at home—like Harry, he had had a strong homing instinct. It was unarguably his assignment: he was cornered. But a beastly assignment, for of all places he least relished snooping around that one, where he had once been happy.

"Very well, David. I'll go to Firle. And you haven't the least idea what I'm supposed to be looking for?"

"At this moment not the slightest. But we may pick up a clue or two in a short while."

"From whoever's waiting for us in the Queensway? But they're going to be obsessed with Arabs and Israelis, whichever of 'em had the biggest down on Llewelyn. And that's not going to help us much."

Or was it? He looked searchingly at Audley. Jenkins's death, botched or not, had not been a small-time operation. It had involved manpower and equipment and murderous determination. And information—above all information. There would hardly have been time to acquire the relevant intelligence about Llewelyn and Jenkins simply to set up the operation, therefore the likelihood was that the killers had merely used what was already known to them.

And that eliminated all the jealous boyfriends, wronged husbands and vengeful fathers Jenkins might have left in his wake; it narrowed the field to the professionals, beyond all doubt—the very men who could have killed Llewelyn if they had wanted to do so.

"Let's just wait and see for the moment, Hugh—let's see what they've got in Room 104. But first let's find out what they don't want *me* to know—so you go on up to see them now. I'll give you a few minutes on your own with them."

Roskill frowned at him across the Triumph's bonnet. What the hell was the man playing at now?

Audley's eyes glinted behind his glasses. "One of your little jobs on the side is going to be to keep an eye on me, you know. At least, I hope it will be, because then we needn't worry about anyone else from the department dogging us. So I want them to have time to recruit you."

Roskill tried to immobilise his face. The one and only time he had actually worked with Audley, that had been his job exactly; it wasn't Audley's loyalty that had worried them then either, but simply his unwillingness to explain what he was up to until after he'd been up to it. Secretiveness was apparently the man's besetting sin.

One couldn't blame them, but he hadn't liked the job then and he didn't relish it now, with its insane subdivision of loyalties mocking the real job in hand.

Audley mistook his exasperation for honest reluctance.

"I know how you feel, Hugh," he apologized. "It isn't quite cricket, is it? But we didn't make the rules and we have to play the game their way."

Alan and Harry and East Firle—and now Audley was making a game of it all, damn him! For the first time Roskill almost regretted the chance that had allowed him to escape from flying. The sooner he could pick those tricky brains clean, the better.

IV

OF THE FIVE faces which turned towards him as he
entered the room Roskill recognised only two. Worse, the
friendly one was scowling angrily and the dangerous one
welcomed him with a smile.

"Ah, Roskill," said Stocker. "I'm glad you were able to
come."

Butler's scowl deepened. But that at least was understand-
able: the night before he had loyally obeyed orders he disliked, and had appeared to fail. Obedience, ambition and an
incongruously active conscience had been fighting inside Butler for years, each one baulked by the other two.

Roskill looked coldly at Stocker. What was it Audley had
said they thought him to be—'an overgrown ex-fighter pilot
with a crafty streak'? Best to oblige them then.

He shrugged. "I can't say I'm glad. But Jack's very persuasive when he puts his mind to it."

"And Audley?"

It was the big man sitting in the easy chair in the corner
who spoke. The other two were nondescripts, Special Branch
or Stocker's Joint Intelligence Committee understrappers. But
the big man's rather battered face and unquestionable air of

authority would have identified him even without that faintest
suspicion of Welsh intonation.

"Mr. Llewelyn, I presume?"

"Is Audley coming?" Stocker echoed the question this
time, and he was no longer smiling.

"He should be here any moment."

The smile came back. So it had been Stocker's idea—and
sure enough there was a suggestion of surprise crossing Llewelyn's face. One up to him: he had judged Audley better than
Stocker, even after all these years. Two of a kind, evidently.

"You are very persuasive too it would seem, Squadron-
Leader Roskill," said Llewelyn softly.

"I had moral support from another quarter." They had
counted on Faith so he might as well throw her into the scales.
"But I wouldn't say he's any happier than I am." Casually,
now. "In fact neither of us go much for your methods."

"Needs must when the devil drives, Roskill." Stocker could
afford to be conciliatory now. "And to be fair you must admit
that we wouldn't have got you both any other way. The
situation was not—ah—straightforward, was it?"

"It isn't straightforward even now as far as I'm concerned."
Llewelyn leaned forward. "But you've worked with Audley before. And with quite remarkable success I hear."

"Only once. And I can't claim any of the success—I was
a messenger boy. And there was an RAF angle to that job,
anyway. Whereas this one—"

"This one is different, yes." Llewelyn sat back again,
considering Roskill speculatively. "Do you know anything
about Middle Eastern politics?"

"Very little more than the next man."

"But you've travelled in the Middle East. You were in
Israel just before your leave."

The last thing Roskill wanted was a question and answer
session. Llewelyn must be made to do the talking.

"If you want to know how to avoid a SAM, or whether
the Sukhoi 7s the Egyptians are operating have anything ap-
proaching a Digital Integrated Attack System, Llewelyn, I

can tell you. And I could give you a fifty-fifty guess on the attack system the Israelis are using. And if you pushed me I just might tell you how far I think they've got with laser fire control research—which is further than most people believe. And I could describe three strips of tarmac in the desert for you. That's the Middle East I know about."

Llewelyn grinned. "I take your point. But which side do you favour?"

"Professionally speaking, the combat effectiveness of the Israelis is as near 100 per cent as I've ever seen anywhere."

"*Not* professionally speaking—personally."

"I don't give a damn either way."

"I can't believe that."

"I don't give a damn what you believe, either. But I'll tell you what I believe. I believe that if I'd been born in 1920 I should have flown a Spitfire in 1940—unless I'd been born in Germany. In which case I should have flown a Messerschmitt 109. And just as happily, too!"

"And there's no right and no wrong?" Llewelyn's Welsh lilt was stronger now. A true believer, thought Roskill—and God save us from the true believers . . .

"The Arabs and the Jews? I should say they're both right and both wrong, and I wouldn't trust either of 'em. But neither of them is on *my* side, so for Christ's sake let's get down to business."

Audley would be bursting in any moment, and so far nothing of value had been achieved.

Llewelyn and Stocker exchanged glances, as if to reassure each other that they had the right tool to hand, a crude one, but serviceable.

"Very well, Roskill," said Llewelyn. "It may not interest you to know it, but despite appearances there is at this moment an outside chance of some sort of Middle Eastern settlement. The best chance for a long time, in fact, despite recent events— perhaps because of them even. Just one gesture of mutual trust might tip the balance—and one gesture of mutual hate might tip it the other way."

"Such as your death?"

Llewelyn regarded him steadily. "Strange as it may seem—yes. I've been working behind the scenes—just how is no concern of yours."

Just as Llewelyn had been right about Audley, so Audley had been right about Llewelyn: he had been up to something.

"Who wants you dead then? Who wants the balance tipped that way?"

"That's the difficulty. There are hawks and unofficial groups on both sides. But we'll discuss that when Audley's here. It's Audley I want to discuss now—would you call yourself a friend of his?"

"In as far as anyone is—yes."

Llewelyn nodded, unsmiling. "Good. It's a friend we need to protect him."

"Protect him? I'm not a bloody bodyguard," Roskill demurred. "I wouldn't know where to start—and I've never fired a shot in anger in my life. You need another sort of friend for that!"

"Not from other people—from himself," Stocker cut in. "Audley's a brilliant man, but he's not a practical man and he goes his own way. This time he could run into something nasty if he does that, and we must have early warning of it—from you."

"If there's trouble we want to handle it," said Llewelyn soothingly. "But even if he doesn't run himself into anything we still have to know what he's doing. You kept an eye on him last time, Stocker tells me. We just want you to do the same again, no more, no less."

"Under protest, I did it—did Stocker tell you that? And did he tell you that I wasn't very good at it, either? Audley's not a confiding soul at the best of times."

"But you know him better now—and it shouldn't be more difficult than persuading him to come up here. If you can do the one I'd trust you to manage the other."

Roskill looked at them woodenly, barely controlling the urge to smile: they were all so bloody good at computing the angles—and that went for Audley too—that it was a wonder they didn't disappear up their own orifices.

Except that it was neither a laughing matter nor a game; the memory of Alan Jenkins spoiled the fun and ruined the game.

"So you'll do it?"

Actually it was appropriate that Llewelyn and Audley should each cast him to betray the other, for in a way the whole business was founded on his actions. He, and no one else, had set them on their collision course; how many more collisions would it take to resolve his cowardice?

The knock at the door startled him, and before he could collect his wits he was looking up at Audley in the doorway— Audley who had arrived just ten seconds too early, even though he knew the question and had already supplied the answer.

Not to panic, though.

He looked from Audley back to Llewelyn. "Yes, I'll do that," he answered.

Audley's eyebrows lifted. "You'll do what?"

"My dear fellow, it's good to see you again," Stocker rose elegantly from his chair beside the table. "And good of you to come."

Audley grunted, staring over his spectacles directly at Llewelyn, who stared just as directly back. The pot and the kettle; the Mountain and the Mahomet. Old acquaintances who had forgotten nothing over the years—and learnt a little too much.

"Llewelyn needs no introduction, I know," continued Stocker, overcoming the impossible simply by ignoring it. "But I don't believe you've encountered Yeatman before."

Audley tore his gaze away from Llewelyn and nodded to the smaller of the nondescripts.

"And—" began Stocker.

"Cox," said Audley. "Special Branch."

"We've never met, Dr. Audley." Cox didn't seem put out

by being pinned like a butterfly in Audley's memory, merely curious.

"Rome '68. You were pointed out to me," said Audley, reaching for a chair. Ignoring everyone else he turned back to Llewelyn.

"So someone wants you dead."

"It would appear so."

"Is there a short list?" Audley spoke as though the list ought to be long rather than short.

"Anyone with a vested interest in another Middle Eastern war," answered Llewelyn equably.

"Like the PFLP?"

"It's possible. Or the Sons of Eleazar."

Audley shook his head. "If—" he underscored the word heavily "*if* the Sons of Eleazar wanted you dead you're on borrowed time. But it isn't their policy, anyway."

"Policies change."

"Has there been a change of policy then?"

Llewelyn considered the question for a moment. For a man discussing his own death he was remarkably cool, Roskill thought.

"To be honest—no, not as far as I know."

"Have there been any similar killings in recent months? Or attempts?"

"Not in Europe as far as I know."

"I'd like that checked out."

Llewelyn nodded towards Yeatman.

"And I must have a complete run-down on what you've been doing recently."

"Yeatman will supply you with whatever you need."

Roskill squirmed uncomfortably in his seat. He had never found an upright chair yet that fitted his behind. Worse, Audley seemed to be steering the conversation away from what seemed to him to be the crucial questions.

"Who are the Sons of Eleazar, for heaven's sake?" he asked.

"Second generation of the Jewish terrorist groups—like

the Stern Gang and the Irgun Zvai Leumi, you might say," said Llewelyn. "Another war would suit them very nicely and assassination is part of their tradition."

"Absolute balderdash!" Audley growled. "There's not a shred of evidence to prove continuity. I grant you they were terrorist groups, the IZL and the Stern Gang, but the PFLP's their equivalent today. They were occupied territory phenomena—*Lohamei heruth Yisrael*, 'Freedom fighters of Israel', that's what the Stern gang called itself. The Sons of Eleazar are simply the lunatic fringe of the Israeli hawks, and even they don't think war is desirable—just inevitable."

"It's the same family tree," said Llewelyn. "They don't like peacemakers now any more than they did when they murdered Bernadotte in '48."

"And Abdullah and Nokrashi? My God, man—if it's murder statistics you want I can give you ten Arab ones for every Jewish one. It was the Arabs who gave us the word *assassin*, not the Jews."

"And the Jews gave us *zealot*," said Llewelyn mildly. "But I don't think etymology is going to help us much. The concepts of political murder and fanaticism are somewhat older than our words for them, after all. The point is that in my opinion it could have been either of them, Roskill. What I want you and Audley to try and find out is which one. You can leave the rest to us then."

"But so far your evidence is merely hypothetical. Arabs and Jews have been known to kill people. Some Arabs and Jews don't like peacemakers. You are a peacemaker. Your car blows up. Therefore it was blown up by Arabs or Jews. I don't think my old algebra master would have gone much on that—and algebra's another arabic word."

Roskill looked round for support.

"Aye," said Butler. "And when it comes to peacemakers I could give you the name of two Belgian firms and a Swiss group—and a Czech one, I shouldn't wonder—who'd weep bitter tears the day peace was declared. There's not so much profit in ploughshares these days—small arms shares pay better dividends."

"And some of their salesmen have been known to protect their territory with their product," said Roskill. "So far we haven't got a shred of proof about anything."

"Two shreds—so far we've got two shreds," said Cox. "One from Bicester, one from the car.

"We did Bicester pretty thoroughly yesterday, because there was just a chance someone might have seen the car while it still had someone in it. We drew a blank there, but two people think they saw something very near where it was left at about the right time. One said 'Wog', meaning apparently 'Middle Eastern, inclined to Arab'; the other was more educated— he said 'Cypriot, maybe', which could mean 'Middle Eastern, inclined to Israel'."

"That's a shred, right enough," said Butler.

"Agreed—just a shred. The car's a bit stronger, though." Cox consulted a small red notebook for a few seconds. "TPDX—do you know what that is?"

"At a guess, one of those innumerable plastic explosives?"

"Quite right. A plastic explosive. Russian, very new— and strong medicine. Just the thing for guerrillas, and sure enough the Russians obligingly supplied them with a consignment of it in January. It was the first time anyone received any outside the Soviet Union, as far as we know."

"Well, that pins it on Fatah—if that's what was used in the car," exclaimed Roskill.

"It was used on the car all right, but it doesn't pin it on Fatah," Cox shook his head sadly. "That would have been too easy! Unfortunately they moved it—or a good deal of it—to one of their front line posts in the Ghor as Safi area, south of the Dead Sea."

Roskill groaned. "Don't tell me! The Israelis raided the place!"

"Right again. Softened it up with an air raid on January 20. Then next day what they euphemistically call a 'purging operation' was effected. In this instance they purged Fatah of a large amount of TPDX, among other things of lesser importance."

"So it fits the Bicester evidence exactly—Wog or Cypriot. It could have been either of them."

"Was the Ghor as Safi raid laid on to take the TPDX?" Audley asked.

Cox looked questioningly at Yeatman.

"We rather think it was," said Yeatman. "I'd lay you three to one on."

Audley tapped the table. "Then what you're saying is that they're so damn good they can scoop up the stuff within a fortnight of its arrival, and then so damn clumsy they can't wrap it up properly. Frankly, I don't think they would use it—ever. They just wanted it out of circulation. But if they did use it, it would go off under the right man."

Roskill caught his breath: Audley was tempting fortune now.

"Perhaps it did," said Butler, thoughtfully. "Perhaps—"

"Blow up what's-his-name—Jenkins? In the way most likely to ensure the Special Branch and heaven knows who else would be called in?" Audley ridiculed the idea with a wave of the hand. "Let's stick to what's within the bounds of probability at least. And I think that rules out the Israelis."

"They have been known to miscalculate, you know," Llewelyn protested. "Karameh, for example. The Nahal Diqla business and the Abu Zaabal raid."

"By our standards that's not a very high striking rate," Audley replied. "But don't worry. I'll check out the Cypriots as well as the Wogs."

"When you do, Dr. Audley," Yeatman said, "you might make a special effort in the case of your friend Colonel Shapiro."

Now at last, thought Roskill, they were coming down on the target area. Shapiro was Audley's special Israeli buddy: he had been at Audley's wedding, and at Cambridge with Audley years before. And though the man seemed rather comical, he was top grade military intelligence and hard as nails, blooded in '56 and '67.

"And what has Shapiro been doing?"

"He left town, as the Americans would say, in a sudden cloud of dust the morning of the day Llewelyn's car was stolen. Instead of having lunch with you, Dr. Audley—your regular Wednesday lunch, I believe—"

Audley blinked unhappily.

"—he plunged into rural Sussex and lunched with another friend at Lewes."

"And then, apparently, he drove cross-country," Llewelyn took up the story, dead-pan, "to dine at All Souls, four places away from me."

Roskill strove agonisingly to listen and to think at the same time. Lewes was—what—maybe ten minutes' drive from East Firle?

"One of those little coincidences which make life interesting," continued Llewelyn. "In the terms of personal alibis, Colonel Shapiro has what might be called a watertight one. I can testify that he didn't lay a finger on my car. But in an accessory role, or as a mastermind, I'm afraid he's guilty until you prove him innocent. It does rather look as though he put the finger on me, if that's the correct term. Don't you agree?"

They had ambushed Audley neatly and cruelly. But with Shapiro as their No. 1 prospect, it was no wonder they'd wanted him above everyone else.

"As a matter of fact, I don't agree at all. Jake Shapiro would never set up anything so crude. And since Americanisms are *de rigueur* this morning, I'd say it's much more likely that he's been framed."

Audley spoke calmly, his composure quickly restored. "Besides, he'd be even less likely to miss you than Eleazor's sons—if he wanted you dead you'd be dead. The only surprising thing is that he's in this position."

He turned from Llewelyn back to Yeatman. "And since you're so well posted on comings and goings, where were

all the other possible suspects? The Fatah man, for instance—
I don't even know who the current top man here is now—
did he leave town? And the PFLP man? And that new Egyptian who's got Howeidi's job—what's his name?—Razzak?
He's new in town."

It was Yeatman's turn to look put out, but it was Stocker
who answered.

"You can count Razzak out—unless leaving town on
Wednesday according to plan is a suspicious circumstance in
itself, that is. I happen to know that he went to Paris to see
their ambassador. He asked me on Monday which was the
best early boat train."

A premonition rose in Roskill's mind like a telltale wisp
of smoke from a haystack, catching him unaware.

"Boat train?" he echoed.

Stocker looked at him sardonically. "Unlike, you, Squadron Leader, there are people who are not enamoured with
flying." (How little they knew!) "Colonel Razzak only flies
when he has to, it would seem, and in this instance he was
in no hurry."

"We'll check it out all the same." Audley hadn't missed
it either, evidently. "Dover-Calais, I take it?"

"Newhaven-Dieppe as a matter of fact. A longer sea trip
but a less depressing journey, I'm told."

Roskill stared stupidly at his knee, not trusting himself to
look anyone in the eye. If Lewes was in easy driving distance
of East Firle, Newhaven was almost within easy walking
distance. Razzak and Shapiro were like two bearings on a
map: their point of intersection in time and space could have
turned that peaceful stretch of downland into a place of danger. The coincidence once again was too glaring to ignore.

"You're quite right to suspect everyone, Audley," said
Llewelyn. "The possibility of Shapiro's innocence has occurred to us. You actually favor the PFLP, don't you, Cox?"

"The Popular Front for the Liberation of Palestine as such—
no," said Cox judiciously. "They've been getting more responsible—or maybe more respectable—recently, rather like

the student revolutionaries. But there are one or two offshoots which do frighten the life out of me."

"Such as?"

Cox considered Audley in silence for several seconds. "The one that worries me at this moment in time hasn't even got a name yet. Not a name I can put to it," he said reluctantly. "Or at best only part of a name."

It wasn't reluctance, but diffidence. Cox had never met Audley before, but he would know the big man's reputation well enough. Roskill remembered his own first traumatic encounter with him again: he had been desperately afraid of having his own cherished theories disdainfully shot down in flames.

He looked at Cox carefully for the first time. He didn't look like a policeman—not the bulldog, bloodhound or alsatian varieties anyway. Mongrel with a discernible fox terrier bloodline, unremarkable in any gathering. But that, of course, was the modern Special Branch trend; a hairy hitchhiking student had only recently complained to him that the special fuzz was becoming hard to pinpoint.

What was certain, though, was that Cox's ability would belie his appearance: there'd be no dead wood around Llewelyn and Stocker.

The same thoughts, or something like, must have been running through Audley's head. "Even part of a name is a beginning," he said encouragingly. "A name and a feeling about it. I've started with no more than that often enough."

Cox nodded. "That's about it—a name and a feeling."

"And the name?"

"*Hassan*." Cox paused. "It's a man, or the code name for a man, not a group. The man who gives the orders to a group, maybe an inner PFLP wing, or an off-shoot, or maybe something entirely new—we don't know."

"And what has Hassan done so far?"

"Apparently nothing. The only references we've had to Hassan are in the nature of forecasts. Rather messianic forecasts, too."

"Such as?"

"We've had four, possibly five. And when I say 'we' I mean the joint committee we set up with the Interpol people in '69. The West Germans got the first when they were rounding up everyone after the Zurich air crash. They all add up to the same thing, anyway—*when Hassan gets going he won't make any mistakes.*"

"Then that would seem to rule out Hassan in this instance, Tom," said Llewelyn.

"That depends, sir, on whether he intended to get you or merely to frighten you."

"He's frightened me—no doubt about that. But he could have done that with far less trouble—and without any accidental bloodshed."

Cox shook his head. "I don't think he's fussy about that."

"Which means, I take it," said Audley, "that something unpleasant happened to your five sources?"

Cox looked at him sharply. "Yes—and no. Two of them were released—three if you count the one in France, but we don't really know for sure about him. The French aren't very co-operative these days. All three of them have disappeared, anyway."

"And the other two?"

"They were held on weapons charges. Each of them had a submachine gun hidden in his digs—in each case, oddly enough, it was an Israeli Uzi they'd got, too."

"Not so odd, really," said Stocker. "The Uzi happens to be the best thing on the market. It's standard issue in four or five gentile armies—what you might call an Israeli export triumph."

"Well, the Germans didn't take kindly to it in the hands of a couple of Arab students—one was a Syrian, actually, and the other an Iraqi. They were going to throw the book at them."

"But they didn't?"

"They never got the chance. The Syrian committed suicide—he was in a secure jail in Bonn. But the Iraqi was

picked up in a little town near the Swiss border." Cox paused
for effect. "He was sprung by four masked men armed with
Uzis. It was only a little police station, of course—and they
weren't expecting anything. But it was a neat job all the
same, and the Germans haven't had a smell of him since.
And believe me, they've looked hard."

"All of which is vastly exciting," said Llewelyn, "but
doesn't prove a thing. I've seen your Hassan file, Tom. It's
interesting, even disturbing. But if Hassan exists he doesn't
appear to have reached England. And if he is here we don't
even know what his aims are. You just can't give me one
single, useful, tangible fact to back this 'feeling' of yours."

Llewelyn spoke lazily, only a few degrees from contempt,
his Welsh origins again rich beneath his words—Roskill was
reminded of a mineworkers' union organiser rejecting an ab-
surd wage offer made by a not very bright Coal Board spokesman. For a man under possible sentence of death the union
organiser was admirably cool, but nonetheless exasperating.
The temptation to come to Cox's support was irresistible.

"I don't agree at all." He tried to match the Welshman's
lilt with the sort of public school drawl that would be most
offensive. "I don't know much about your Arab-Israeli feuds,
but I do know that whoever fixed your car was well organised
and ruthless and bloody-minded. And that goes for suicide
and jail-breaking too. It means that this character Hassan
looks after his own—one way or another. Which makes him
a good prospect."

He looked to Audley for support and was disconcerted to
receive a blank stare.

"We'll check him out," said Audley noncommittally.

Like Llewelyn—irritatingly like Llewelyn—he was also
playing it cool now. Roskill shrugged and relapsed into silence, masking his annoyance; this was presumably how the
poor bloody pawns always felt.

Llewelyn smiled at him. "All are prospects and all must
be checked out. Quite right again. But checking takes time
and I can't go on living a—how shall I put it?—restricted

life for ever. It's boring and it wastes a lot of valuable time. So"—he turned to Audley—"just what do you propose to do about it?"

A muscle twitched momentarily in Audley's cheek, as though a boring and restricted life of indefinite duration might be no bad thing for Llewelyn.

"Forty-eight hours," he said. "Give me that long to look up a few old acquaintances and do a little horse-trading. Then I may be able to tell you where you stand."

"Horse-trading?" Stocker looked at him curiously. "I wouldn't have thought you had much to trade with?"

"I haven't. But I've no doubt Roskill has. If you've no objection to his letting slip something here and there I think we might make out well enough."

"Yes, I suppose you might at that." Stocker eyed Roskill. "You must have quite a few marketable titbits about the Middle Eastern air forces tucked away by now—and I've no objection to your disbursing a few in a good cause."

"You haven't?" Roskill looked from one to the other incredulously, dismayed at their calm assumption that he would so easily squander his hard-won capital. It went against all his instincts—and worse, if it ever leaked out it would ruin his reputation. "Well, I bloody well have! I'm not going to play both ends against the middle for anyone, no matter what!"

"Don't worry, Hugh," Audley reassured him. "We won't sour your contacts. In fact I may be able to provide you with a few very useful ones. There's no cause for alarm."

Roskill subsided sullenly. The bugger of it was that playing both ends against the middle just about described what he *was* doing already—and the middle against each end, too. And God only knew what Audley and Llewelyn and Stocker were really up to.

"Talking of contacts, Squadron Leader Roskill, I think you've one exceedingly useful one of which you may not be aware," said Cox. "The Ryle Foundation."

"The Ryle—" A moment earlier Roskill had been halfway

to telling himself that at least there could hardly be any more unpleasant surprises ahead, but evidently there was no limit to them.

"The Ryle Foundation?" He heard his own voice echo Cox uncertainly.

"I believe you know Lady Ryle quite well," said Cox. "And Sir John Ryle."

"I know the Ryles, yes." The voice sounded more like his own this time, no matter how he felt inside. "But I've never had anything to do with the Foundation—and I don't think the Ryles have either." But obviously they did; or one of them did. He couldn't even remember whether it was relief or education or both, for the life of him. "But Lady Ryle does a lot of charity committee work," he concluded cautiously.

"She's an honorary life vice-president, as a matter of fact. And she's on the educational grants sub-committee." Cox sounded as though he had expected Roskill to know much better what Lady Ryle did or did not do.

Education rang a bell. Old man Ryle—or was it the grandfather?—had robbed the Persian Gulf blind in the days when anything within range of a British gunboat was fair game for British mercantile enterprise. And then in a fit of conscience had divided his loot in half, one to buy the family into respectability and one to bring the blessings of education to the Arab world.

It was coming back now, a word here and a sentence there. Grandfather Ryle had been in on the ground floor in oil. But when he'd sold out he'd wrapped the share he gave back to the Arabs so tight there'd never been a breath of either scandal or do-gooding inefficiency about his Foundation; it had been constructed to show solid annual profits in terms of SRNs and agricultural diplomas. No bloody arts and crafts for granddad—the words had been John's. He remembered them quite clearly now.

"You're not going to tell me that there's anything subversive about the Foundation, for God's sake?" Roskill came out of his nose-dive and climbed to counter-attack. "It's as solid as UNESCO—probably a darn sight solider in terms of secure finance."

"You do know something about the Ryle Foundation then?"

Roskill gestured vaguely. "Second-hand stuff—I remember the Ryles talking about it now. They said—"

The penny dropped. Butler had said as much the night before: *They know you got Jenkins in . . . and Audley likes you . . . but I think there's something else behind that too . . .* His connection with the Ryles had been the clincher: what they knew about that—the thought that they knew anything— made his flesh creep. But that wouldn't be what interested them now: there must be something very wrong with the Foundation, whatever its appearance of respectability might be.

"What did they say?" Cox prompted.

Jenkins and Audley and the Ryles, thought Roskill bitterly: no wonder they'd changed their own rules to recruit him! What would have trebly disqualified him under normal circumstances made him the ideal candidate with time pressing them so hard. No time to plant a professional carefully and painstakingly in the Foundation; they needed someone with a ready-made introduction to it. And in him they had the one with the other—the sinking feeling in his stomach told him that they knew it, too . . .

"What's wrong with the Ryle Foundation?" he asked harshly.

Cox looked to Llewelyn.

"I know some of your Arab specialists think the Foundation's clean," he began.

"Elliott Wilkinson swears it is, and he works for them," said Llewelyn.

Audley snorted derisively.

"Well, I don't agree with them," said Cox bluntly. "If Hassan's men are here, I think they could well have come in through it. And frankly, I think they are here."

V

ROSKILL WAS TIRED and uncomfortable and thirsty and bored.

He couldn't quite decide which sensation led the others; as he thought of each one in turn it took over the lead, but they were all jostling one another for a dead-heat.

On the whole the discomfort was probably the most acceptable. The chairs in the lecture hall were plastic and form-fitting, but the form they had been designed to fit was not his, no matter how he tried to rearrange himself. But at least he was accustomed to such a state of affairs and even expected it.

The thirst would have been bearable but for one daunting possibility which had occurred to him three seconds after he had realised he was thirsty: since this was primarily an Arab occasion the drinks promised after the lectures might be aggressively non-alcoholic, in strict deference to the Prophet's ordinance. True, it was an Anglo-Arab evening, but the nature of the refreshment would depend on which half dominated the organizing committee—the Arabs would want to cater for the boozy British, and the British would want to defer to non-existent Arab sensibilities. He could only pray that the Arab faction had come out on top.

At the moment boredom was ahead. The speaker droned on and Roskill looked again helplessly at his watch. Theoretically the fellow should have finished ten minutes earlier, but somewhere along what he had disingenuously called his 'lightning journey through Arab literature' he had taken a wrong turning and had become lost in medieval Persia. It had taken a good—or bad—quarter of an hour to talk his way back to the main road and he was still two centuries behind schedule.

The organizers had unwisely kept their dullest speaker at the end. Or perhaps they hadn't expected him to be so goddamn awful; on paper the opening session on the problems of aid and education had sounded even drearier and in practice only the obvious competence and intelligence of the young, American-trained Arab who conducted it had saved it.

But then the young Arab had been a Ryle man, and the Foundation always paid for the best. Judging by the lightning traveller they needed the best, too: he was an educational stumbling block in himself.

Roskill tried to stretch his legs into another position. His tiredness was not so much the product of his early morning expedition along Maitland's telephone line as the result of the afternoon's Middle Eastern cramming lesson which had followed hard on the morning's head-shrinking conference. The idea had been that he should not betray himself too fatuously at this evening's bun-fight by confusing the National Liberation Movement with the Popular Democratic Front or, the Palestine Liberation Movement with the Palestine Armed Struggle Command, should those mutually hostile bodies crop up casually in the conversation.

But the Foreign Office crammer had waxed something too eloquent for a good teacher. Names and initials had flowed from him: Ashbal, Mapam, Group 62, Friends of Jerusalem, Friends of Arabia, Saiqa, PLO, PLA, PLM, POLP, ANSAR and ALF—as an incantation, repeated quickly enough, it would probably summon djinns from the desert, but it had gone in one of Roskill's ears and out the other.

Unfortunately it had stayed between the ears just long enough to answer the crammer's quiz with deceptive competence.

"Bravo, Squadron Leader," the crammer had beamed at him. "Another two or three afternoons and we'll make an Arabist of you! And a Zionist too if you can spare a morning. The right jargon's half the battle—just string it together with a few slogans and you can pass anywhere...

"In action this evening? Is that the CAABU gathering at the Dorchester? No—the Ryle Foundation one, isn't it? Well, not to worry, Squadron Leader—the Ryle people are as near non-partisan as it's possible to be these days—they don't encourage too much PLO talk. Can't afford to with all that real estate of theirs on the West Bank in Israeli hands, you know. If you don't stick your neck out you'll get by—you can say you're a desalination expert. No one's likely to know much about that... Just remember half of what I've told you and be a good listener—they all want to talk all the time, so that shouldn't be too difficult..."

Boredom and tiredness combined to pull away from thirst and discomfort at last, and Roskill's thoughts wandered back to the morning, when Audley had stood by the Triumph grinning at him triumphantly.

"We got more than we gave away, Hugh—you put up a first-rate show, too. Not too smart to make them think twice— that was just the right note to strike!"

But that not-too-smartness had not been a consciously-struck note, Roskill had reflected unhappily, grinning back at Audley.

"A put-up job from start to finish, of course," Audley had said. "They no more suspect Jake Shapiro than I do. It's this Hassan they're scared of—Llewelyn believes in him as much as Cox. Which probably means they've got more on him than they're willing to admit. They just want to double-check it through me."

"So what do we do?"

"We shall do what they want us to do—today, at any rate. You'd better go and see that Foreign Office crammer of theirs this afternoon—and then you can go to that Ryle meeting tonight as Cox suggested. It might even be useful, you never know." Audley had rubbed his hands. "And I've got a lot of catching up to do to find out what the hell's really happening..."

Very pleased with himself, David Audley had been, like an old warhorse smelling battle on familiar territory.

Roskill had been very much less pleased; it might be a jolly game for Audley, but he sensed that in Audley's game he was becoming something less even than a junior partner. And yet he could see no way of avoiding this downgrading: without Audley he didn't stand a chance of attaining his own vengeance, and the big man was incapable of playing second fiddle to anyone. So all he could do was to follow instructions, keeping his own counsel and never forgetting his objective.

"And first thing tomorrow you can slip down to Firle and scout around," said Audley. "You can reach me at home if you turn anything up. After that we may have something of our own to work on."

Slip down to Firle! Roskill's jaw had tightened at that— so easy to say and so agonising to carry out!

Well, there would come a time maybe when Audley wouldn't find it so easy to control the action...there would come a time...

Roskill started guiltily, catching himself in the very act of falling off his chair. He looked around him, fearful lest he had drawn attention to himself, but the rest of the audience seemed either equally withdrawn or, like the fat Arab with the scarred face in the row ahead of him, unhappily restless. There was a subdued undercurrent of movement—of legs stretching and bottoms searching for comfort.

He looked at his watch again, to find that only another five tortoise-minutes had crawled past. The bloody man was still only at the beginning of the 19th century.

". . . and so we come to what may be considered the dawn of modern times . . ."

The speaker paused to consult his notes. But as he raised his head, his mouth opening to greet the dawn, the fat Arab began to clap vigorously.

For a moment it was touch and go; the speaker looked around wildly and those of the audience who were still with him stirred uneasily. But the Arab clapped more enthusiastically than ever, looking to left and right as though to shame the laggards into action.

The crammer's advice not to draw attention to himself flashed through Roskill's mind, only to be instantly extinguished as his hands came together on their own initiative. The woman on his lift looked at him briefly in surprise and then joined in, followed by the man on her left. Spontaneously applause flared up in a dozen different parts of the hall, those who genuinely thought the lecture had ended rushing to join the dissidents who knew all too well that it hadn't.

Last to join in were the handful who had actually been listening, but when they did so they clapped louder than the rest to hide their embarrassment. There were even a few shouts of 'bravo'—one coming from the Arab himself. Such was the storm of applause that in the end the speaker's chagrin turned to gratification. He had probably never encountered such enthusiasm before.

Altogether, thought Roskill as he joined the stampede towards the refreshment room, it was a notable landmark in Anglo-Arabian understanding: for once the silent majority had co-operated to liberate themselves.

He held back until the worst of the crush along the tables had thinned out, disagreeably aware that the contents of the silver bowls ahead of him was as fruity as he had feared. After carefully scanning the faces of the waiters and waitresses dispensing it he edged his way towards a wizened little man whose magenta nose promised sympathy, even though he was presiding over a bowl in which sliced fruit floated like dead fish depth-charged to the surface.

"Is there any alternative to this—this—" Roskill indicated the bowl "—whatever it is?"

A glimmer of recognition lit the bloodshot eyes. There were some pale, intense English faces among the gathered friends of Arabia he had already seen, but there were also ageing, darkened skins which must have weathered in the forts of trucial levies and Arab Legion messes. There *had* to be something under the counter for them.

The eyes took in Roskill's tan, which had been started under Israeli skies and consolidated in Greece.

Roskill slid a 50-penny piece across the white tablecloth, under the napkin by the man's hand.

"For the love of God," he hissed, "give me a decent drink."

"This is a very thirst-quenchin' drink, sir," said the little man, without looking down but with his fingers testing the coin's heptagonal shape. "For the Arabian gentlemen, that is."

He bent down briefly behind the table, reappearing with a tall glass on the side of which he deftly fastened a sliver of cucumber.

"Window-dressing, sir—merely window-dressing," he murmured reassuringly.

It still looked more like a long drink suitable for the Arab gentlemen, and Roskill sniffed it suspiciously.

It was Scotch. He took a slow sip. And not just Scotch, but the purest, mellowest, most exquisite malt whisky, unadulterated and possibly the largest straight measure he had ever received. The Foundation certainly looked after its own, and with his weak head for spirits he'd have to watch his tongue.

He nodded gratefully and turned away to scrutinize the crowd again for the faces in Cox's file of probables and possibles. So far he hadn't seen one of them, wide though the range at the gathering was: pouchy, easy-living faces; lean, bitter faces; ugly, pitted complexions like the surface of the Moon and the almost feminine beauty which was the inheritance of Circassian ancestry.

The faces reminded him of what the Foreign Office man had said in his enthusiasm: the Middle East had melted down so many races, conquerors and slaves alike, that spotting bloodlines was a game for the expert. Turks, Mongols, Greeks, Albanians, Normans, Napoleon's veterans and Australians of the Imperial Light Horse—the greatest of Islam's admirals had been red-haired.

The historical allusions had been lost on him—the fellow was as bad as Audley—but the roll of honour, or dishonour, had stuck. But with all those in the family tree, he had thought, it was surprising that there wasn't more military talent around.

None of which helped him now, anyway. He swung round to try another segment of the crowd, colliding with the man behind him as he did so. For a horrible second he was fearful lest some of his precious whisky might be lost, only to discover that he'd already drunk most of it.

"I beg your pardon," he apologized quickly.

"No damage done."

A tall, grey-haired man—one of the leathery English. Roskill's eyes dropped: sure enough there was one of the tall glasses in the man's hand, with an identical piece of cucumber window-dressing on its rim.

The pale blue eyes twinkled at him in recognition.

"Havergal. I don't believe we've met?"

There had been a Havergal on the official programme, among the Ryle committee members—a colonel with a string of decorations.

"Roscoe," said Roskill, slurring the last syllable unidentifiably. The collision had brought him into a mixed discussion group from which there could be no quick escape: they were all looking at him. "Desalination's my field," he said. If the crammer was right that should slow them down.

"And is there anything growing in your field?" It was the same fat Arab who had rescued them all in the lecture hall. "Are you going to make the desert bloom?"

"Given time and money," Roskill replied guardedly. All scientific enterprises needed time and money.

"You don't think atomic energy might offer a short cut, then?" the Arab persisted. "Van Pelt's report is premature in your opinion?"

Roskill drained his glass. The only Van Pelt he knew was Lucy, the pint-sized virago in the Peanuts comic strip. He pretended to consider the question, to the obvious irritation of the gaunt young man opposite him who looked as if a banner rather than a glass of fruit cup ought to have been grasped in his fist.

There was a chance there.

"Given time and money," he repeated dogmatically, "we can win enough land to resettle every refugee in the Middle East." He looked the young man in the eye and was relieved to meet the glare of fanaticism.

"The land they need," said the young man belligerently, "is the land that was taken away from them. They want justice—not bloody resettlement."

Roskill saw his own role in sudden perspective: a fanatical desalination man was born inside him—a cutter of political knots with a sharpened slide-rule, as oblivious of reality as the hot-tempered young man and the maxi-skirted amazon who was nodding her head in unison beside him. Once start them up properly and Van Pelt's inconvenient report would be forgotten.

"Crops don't grow on justice—they grow on land. And one bit of land is no different to a peasant from another—" he bulldozed his way over shocked expressions "—providing he can get his plough into it. If half the capital that goes into arms went into desalination research—"

His heretical views were drowned in a chorus of protest; they were suddenly all talking at once about Palestine and Zionism and 'bourgeois city-dwellers'—all except Havergal and the Arab, who had evidently heard it all before.

"Desalination research!" The young man made it sound like a nasty branch of biological warfare. "The *sine qua non* of peace in the Middle East isn't research—it is the overthrow of the economic, political and militarist base of the racist-chauvinist state of Israel!"

"We must cure the moral schizophrenia of World Jewry at the same time," cried the amazon. "That cannot be done until every last refugee has been restored to her homeland."

They all started to talk again, so loudly that people nearby turned to look at them. Roskill felt suddenly like a boy scout who had made a fire with two sticks and set the whole forest ablaze. And he could see no quick way of stopping them before everyone's attention was drawn to him.

It was the Arab who doused the flames—simply by raising a plump hand from which the index finger was missing.

"I think Mr. Roskill isn't denying that there is a refugee problem," he interceded. "He's merely emphasising that our military struggle must never blind us to our long-term aims. As one of your own prime ministers said—Lloyd George, I think it was—'a land fit for heroes'. And doesn't Chairman Mao himself say 'Today's fighter on the battlefield is tomorrow's worker in the paddy field'?"

Roskill mumbled agreement, in confusion not so much because he had said no such thing as from hearing Lloyd George recruited with Chairman Mao to support what he hadn't said.

Christ! The man had called him—'Roskill'!

He couldn't have heard what hadn't been said, which could only mean that he knew already. Which meant in turn that not only had Roskill himself failed to spot anyone, but that he'd been spotted himself—and by someone whose face was not in the suspect file.

"Let's charge your glass again, my dear chap," said Havergal genially.

Sobered, Roskill allowed himself to be steered away from the group. The crowning indignity was that the Arab actually covered their retreat.

"These technological people," Roskill heard him begin

deprecatingly, "experts in their own spheres, but politically naïve . . ."

By God, it was true enough!

Havergal pushed him gently through the crowd to the wizened waiter's corner.

"Same again, Wadsworth," he commanded, conjuring up more of the elixir from under the table.

He handed Roskill back his glass. "Nearly a nasty accident there, Ross—is it Ross or haven't I got it right?"

All the British top brass on the Ryle Foundation were politically respectable—reliable even—except Llewelyn's friend Wilkinson, against whom Audley had warned him. In any case, it was hard to imagine Havergal taking any part in the sort of enterprise he must have fought for most of his military career. And the cat was out of the bag, anyway.

"Roskill."

"Roskill?" Havergal tested the name. "I don't think I've seen you at any of our gatherings before. I take it you're just back from the field. Are you Red Sea or the Gulf or the Med?"

Havergal was far too courteous to say 'Who the hell are you, sir?' but that was what it amounted to. There would be no putting off a wily old bird like him for long, either—it would be far safer to conscript his help. But that could only be attempted after positive clearance, and in the meantime put off he had to be.

"I'm a friend of Sir John and Lady Ryle's."

"Indeed?" Havergal craned his neck and peered over the heads around them. His intention was obvious.

"Lady Ryle doesn't know that I'm here tonight." He had known in his bones that his failure to reach her during the afternoon might turn out awkward.

"She doesn't?" Havergal's tone was neutral rather than disbelieving. "Well, it will be a pleasant surprise for her, won't it? She's coming this way—shall we go and meet her?"

The courtesy was rock-hard now—and the good-mannered gesture allowing Roskill to lead the way was a command.

If you only knew, Colonel, thought Roskill, if you only knew . . .

He saw her first: the dark head so carefully tinted that only an expert might guess the first grey hairs were being kept at bay, her outward air of confidence and breeding tempered as ever by an equally evident inner warmth and gentleness. No wonder all those charities liked to have her on their committees.

"My dear, I believe I've got a friend of yours here," Havergal sounded less assured now, as though he found the prospect of embarrassing her distasteful.

She saw him.

"Hugh!"

"Isobel."

Hints and lies about desalination clogged in his throat, even though he knew she'd be quick to pick them up: practice had made that second nature for them. Already she was covering her surprise with pleasure.

"Hugh—how lovely to see you!" She turned to Havergal. "Squadron Leader Roskill and I are very old friends, Archie—it was kind of you to help him to find me. But Hugh—I thought you were up at Snettisham?"

"Snettisham?" Havergal snorted the name as though he knew it, frowning. The rank and the place name added up to an active profession which had nothing to do with desalination, but the beard and the clumsy deception contradicted the addition. Even the fact that he might connect the Ryles and Snettisham wouldn't account for the reason why someone like Isobel Ryle should be so happy to meet so dark a horse.

"I know your C.O., Roskill—or I used to know him."

"Valentine?" said Roskill. Valentine had flown Hunters in Aden and up the Gulf in his younger days. That placed Havergal appropriately.

Havergal nodded, measuring Roskill speculatively.

"Something came up to change my plans," said Roskill. And to change my plans this evening, too, he thought. However much he hated to involve her it was unavoidable now. "Can I see you later tonight?"

He glanced at Havergal, coming to an immediate decision. "And you, too, Colonel Havergal?"

"Are you going to the dinner after this reception, my dear?" Havergal asked Isobel.

"No, Archie. I've—I've only just got back from holiday. I've got a million things to do."

"I'm not going to the dinner either," said Havergal. "I had a prior engagement." He looked at Roskill. "Which I shall break."

"Can't it wait until tomorrow, Hugh?" Isobel sounded doubtful. "I really do have a lot to do—and I'm awfully tired."

"I don't think it can wait, can it, Roskill?" said Havergal. "And if it concerns both of us, I'm afraid it's something I've been afraid of for a long time."

VI

I T W A S O N L Y after he had actually parked there that Roskill realized he had driven into Bunnock Street from habit, not necessity.

He hated the dingy cul-de-sac, with its blank-faced houses; it always had orange peel and empty cigarette packets in its gutters, a place altogether out of place in what was otherwise a rather smart district. Even the people who lived in it seemed ashamed of it, for he had rarely seen any of them coming or going; presumably there were back entrances which let into what were now more salubrious mews, leaving their front doors to visiting dustmen.

All that could be said of it now was that it looked better by night, by the barely adequate street lighting.

The trouble was that Bunnock Street had three advantages which in the past had always triumphed over his distaste. It invariably offered parking space, as though those of its residents who had cars were unwilling to trust them to it; it was discreetly placed in relation to the Ryles' flat, which was a good five minutes by road, but only an eerie two-minutes' walk through St. Biddulph's churchyard; and, since discretion was all that was normally required, it had a phone box conveniently sited at its junction with King's Row. No adulterer could ask for more.

After he had carefully turned the car round and located it beside one of the lamp posts, Roskill made himself comfortable in the passenger's seat and sat for a time staring down the curving street, as he had done so often before when waiting for Isobel. The waiting then had had a meaning which cancelled out the beastliness of the view, but now it was duty and not even the excellence of the Ryle Foundation's whisky could prevent it from being depressing.

After a time he looked at his watch. It was nearly forty-five minutes since he had left the reception and now half an hour since he had phoned the Department—but that, too, had been depressing, with its odds-against encounter with someone who knew him well—and who now almost certainly knew him even better.

". . . Archibald Havergal? You must be joking!"

Howe's Etonian-Oxonian drawl had packed a world of patronizing incredulity into the words.

"Do you know him?"

"Know him? My dear old Hugh—I can't even believe in him! I didn't know they christened anyone 'Archibald' since Queen Victoria's day—but I suppose he could date from her times—Colonel Archibald Havergal—marvellous!"

"Just get me his record and a security clearance on him, you idiot. And—" he had steeled himself to say the name "—a clearance for Isobel Ryle, too. Sir John Ryle's wife. R-Y-L-E—"

"You don't need to spell it out, old boy. I've seen the Lady Isobel from afar. Strictly Horse of the Year Show, Crufts and Good Works—a dishy piece in a do-gooding sort of way, but a bit long in the tooth for you and me . . . Not to worry, though! Your name's back on the VIP card again, so we'll put a girdle round the world for you in thirty minutes if you like—was it thirty minutes? It'll take us half an hour, anyway, Hugh.

It's not the facts, but the clearance—we have to find the decision makers for that . . ."

Roskill had been squirming by then, and he was squirming still. Even the certainty that Howe himself would probably be vastly embarrassed when what he'd said in jest caught up with him didn't help. It might have been better if he'd tried to get straight through to Stocker, but the evening had been disastrous enough without being quizzed on it while it was still fresh in his mind and before it could be suitably edited on to paper.

But now he couldn't delay the evil moment any later: Howe had had his half an hour and Havergal would soon be at the flat.

He opened the door on the passenger's side to step out on to the pavement, only to discover that it just failed to clear the lamp-post. It was just that sort of night, he warned himself . . .

As he feared, it was a Howe chastened almost into seriousness who answered his call.

"Havergal's straight up-and-down and true blue—absolutely to be trusted. When he came back from Hadhramaut in '64—he'd been somewhere back-of-beyond north of Saywun—they wanted him to work for *us* out there. But he's nobody's fool and he wasn't having any. He said the sun had set on the Empire and he was too old to be out after dark. Also he rather likes the Arabs, warts and all. That's why he agreed to help the Ryle Foundation—though he made damn sure it was above board first: he checked it out with us."

"And it was above board?"

"It was *then*. No doubt you know better now. Apparently you should have been shown the file on it this afternoon, but it was snarled up in the works somewhere. I'll have it sent round to you tonight if you like, together with all the stuff in your in-tray you were supposed to collect this morning."

Howe knew he wasn't at home and was gently fishing for his precise location. Roskill peered down at one of the lines of graffiti on the wall: it was meticulously done in Latin. Home was never like this.

"I shan't be home until later. I'll give you a ring then if I want anything. What about Lady Ryle?"

Howe didn't answer at once, whether from delicacy or a lingering shred of embarrassment it was impossible to gauge. "Lady Ryle is considered a good risk, at your discretion. Nothing's known against her, as far as the Foundation is concerned."

As far as the Foundation was concerned. Howe was relying on his discretion—or appealing to it. Or perhaps he didn't think he had the gall to inquire further.

In ordinary circumstances that might not have been a miscalculation, Roskill told himself ruefully. But as it was it didn't take into account the trauma of the past twenty hours and sordidness of Bunnock Street. Discretion no longer mattered, only the pretence that this could be regarded as a legitimate question. Such an opportunity might never occur again.

"And just what is known about her?"

The delay was briefer this time.

"I wondered whether you'd ask that," said Howe. "I didn't think you would, you know."

"But I have."

"Indeed you have!" Howe laughed shortly. "Well, they know about you, old boy—chapter and verse."

"I never doubted it." God damn them to hell.

"Then I won't bore you with the details. It states that Ryle turns a blind eye for the sake of the children and the better to pursue his own fancies. What might be called 'a civilized arrangement', relying on the good sense of all parties. I congratulate you, Hugh—you appear to have got the best of both worlds..."

Or the worse of both worlds, according to what sort of worlds one found desirable...

* * *

Roskill walked thoughtfully back up the street, pausing only to pick up the slides and the little projector from the car boot before heading for the flat. It hadn't really surprised him that his liaison with Isobel was known. From the very beginning they had been careful, but never secretive—their precautions had been designed rather to avoid embarrassment than to deceive the world in general and John Ryle in particular.

John, of all people, had no cause for complaint: he had virtually propelled Isobel into Roskill's arms, or if not Roskill's, then those of some other member of the squadron. Yet it sounded suspiciously like John who had supplied the chapter and verse on them; perhaps the eye he had turned had not been sightless.

He shrugged to himself as he pressed the buzzer. At all events it would have taken no special investigation to establish that they were more than good friends. More than mere friendship was probably what had decided the Department in its quest for quick results.

He was still testing that probability when Isobel opened the door, more desirable than ever to him now that there was a hint of distress beneath that celebrated composure.

"Hugh, darling—"

"Is Havergal here?"

He pricked his ears and then relaxed before she could answer. It was a question rendered unnecessary by her greeting: he would never be a darling to Colonel Havergal's hearing.

"He's phoning, Hugh—from the box down the street." She searched his face. "I know I shouldn't ask you what you're doing, but when Archie won't phone from the hotel and won't phone from the flat—Hugh, what *are* you doing? And what's Archie doing?"

"Did he ask you about me?"

"Only how long we'd known each other and where we met."

Nobody's fool, certainly. He hadn't bothered to ask her

questions she couldn't answer, and hadn't risked any phone that might be suspect in order to ask somebody who could. And he'd know who to ask, sure enough. The question was—how full would the answer be?

"He was checking on you, wasn't he?"

Roskill reached out for her hand, squeezing it reassuringly. It was enough to discompose anyone, having their carefully segregated public and private lives so suddenly mixed. A mixture like this one could be downright explosive, too.

He smiled at her. "Of course he was checking on me, Bel—and I've been checking on him."

"And I can't ask why, can I?"

"Not really. But it's nothing to do with *us*—or with John. So there's nothing for you to worry about."

"But it has to do with the Foundation?"

The buzzer cut off his reply: Havergal had done his checking quickly enough.

Isobel's eyes were still troubled and her lady-of-the-manor's competence which was a joke between them seemed altogether to have deserted her. Yet Roskill knew instinctively that it wasn't this emergency that had thrown her, so much as his own appearance in it, in the wrong place and out of character. Anyone else, any stranger, she would have taken in her stride.

He squeezed her hand again. "Don't worry, Bel—just be Lady Ryle to both of us. Let her cope."

Lady Ryle was the armour in which the real Isobel lived: beautiful, damascened armour, in the latest style and perfectly fitting, reflecting the wealth and good taste of the wearer but only hinting at the vulnerability beneath it. Poor Isobel! With him at least she had learnt to do without it, and now he was urging her to put it on again.

She looked at him, reading his thoughts. "All right, Hugh—Lady Ryle for you both. But don't think you can pull the wool over Archie's eyes too easily—he's good at seeing through phonies."

This echoed what Howe had said, Roskill warned himself—and it was substantially his own first impression. Havergal might be full of years and whisky, but he was still as tough as old boots and sharp as the bootmaker's awl. It would be as well to stay on his good side.

But the prospect of that dimmed the moment the old man entered the room. Either the check-up had proved unprofitable or it had occasioned second thoughts, for the eye that settled on him was distinctly jaundiced—what it saw it didn't like. Before such an eye a generation of red-necked British subalterns and raw Arab levies had undoubtedly quailed.

"Good evening again, Colonel Havergal," said Roskill carefully. If it was to be war he wasn't going to fire the first shot.

Havergal glanced over his shoulder, making sure that Isobel wasn't behind him—presumably her armour required a moment's fitting.

"Roskill," the Colonel finally acknowledged him, "I've been talking to Fred Clinton about you."

In other circumstances Roskill might have whistled: Havergal had certainly gone straight to the top. Indeed, since Sir Frederick was never available for casual queries, this was an old boys' network operating at an exalted level. It was disquieting, that.

"Despite your bull-in-a-chinashop tactics, he vouches for you," Havergal continued. "I took you for a beginner, but it seems you aren't. It seems I must rely on you."

The soft answer died on Roskill's lips. The only thing that Havergal would ever do with a doormat would be to wipe his feet on it.

"We're rather in the same boat then," he said casually. "He said much the same about you. We shall both have to make the best of it—in the national interest."

"My dear Roskill, that rather depends on how you define the national interest—if there is one in this instance. There was a time when interest and responsibility and honour coincided. Now they don't often seem to do that." Havergal stared at Roskill unwaveringly. "In any case, my concern at the moment is with the Foundation—I don't care to involve myself beyond that."

"And what exactly is it about the Foundation that disturbs you at the moment, Colonel Havergal?"

Havergal shook his head. "You tell me, Roskill."

Roskill considered the Colonel in silence. This was where the man's full file would have been a godsend—it would have given him some clue as to where leverage might be applied. He hadn't asked Howe enough questions, not expecting this hostility.

To Havergal Roskill had signified something he'd been afraid of for a long time . . .

. . . Havergal, who'd retired and been forced to watch his work erased as his country withdrew from the lands it had dominated in his youth. The fact that he liked the Arabs, admiring the uncomplicated simplicity of Islam as so many Englishmen before him had done, only made it worse: the Red Navy ships anchored off Basra and Aden and Alexandria, and the MIGs lined up on the old RAF strips in Egypt, Iraq and now even at Khormaksar, signified that they'd only changed one master for another, and a worse one at that.

But then he'd encountered the Foundation—something useful and above board that fitted his personal inclination and his specialist knowledge . . . something worth living and fighting for.

Isobel came into the room bearing a coffee tray. Typically, her coffee was not in delicate bone china but in enormous NAAFI-style mugs on which Kitchener's portrait and the legend 'Your Country Needs You' was superimposed on a large Union Jack.

"I know you'd both rather have Scotch," she said in her Lady Ryle voice, "but with the way Wadsworth pours drinks I think you've both had more than sufficient."

She set the tray on a low table and motioned them both into chairs. It was the first rule of the experienced hostess to get her antipathetical guests on soft cushions, naturally: stand-up rows were less easy to pursue when sitting down.

"I was about to ask Colonel Havergal about the Ryle Foundation, Isobel," Roskill said quickly. "But perhaps you could answer me—where would you say its special usefulness lies? Compared with other agencies?"

"We're rather unspectacular really, Hugh. We never make headlines."

"What do you think, Colonel?"

Havergal grunted, sensing danger but unable to locate its direction. If he knew his Liddell Hart, though, he'd recognize the strategy of the Indirect Approach.

"I'll tell you what I think," said Roskill with false diffidence. "I think you're right, Isobel—I think it does a very valuable job because it's never been the least bit political—even in the old days it never had any British strings attached to it. It never produced future statesmen or generals—just nurses and farmers and primary school teachers."

It was a mash of snatches of half-remembered lunch conversations at Ryle House—mostly John's remarks, not even addressed to him. It surprised him that they had stuck in his memory, like flotsam left at a freak tidemark.

But it served now to rouse Havergal.

"That's true enough—you've done your homework," he said cautiously. "We've never been a short-cut for the clever intellectuals. We've never sent anyone to Oxford and Cambridge—or to Harvard. Old Jacob Ryle wasn't one of Cecil Rhodes's admirers. He laid it down in black and white—get the good second-class brains and train 'em to do something useful. Work 'em so hard they won't have time to get up to mischief—"

Havergal stopped abruptly, as though he'd followed Roskill's lead one step too far on to dangerous ground.

"But it hasn't worked out like that, has it?"

Havergal remained silent. It was quite clear to Roskill now that he'd come to the flat to get information and not to give it; to get it and use it to purge his beloved Foundation of impurities which now contaminated its down-to-earth aims.

He'd agreed to come because he'd thought—and reasonably enough—that Roskill was a bungling beginner. But apparently Sir Frederick had told him otherwise, and that had put him on his guard.

But that wouldn't serve the present crisis, to which the health of the Ryle Foundation and an old man's peace of mind were secondary. It was enough to know that the Foundation was vulnerable, for that could only mean one thing.

"Let's not pretend any more, Colonel. The Ryle Foundation is being used as a cover for illegal Arab activities. You might as well admit it."

Havergal looked at him coldly. "I don't *have* to admit anything Squadron Leader Roskill. And as to so-called illegal Arab activities—like the national interest, they are a matter of definition. I rather think I am as good a judge as you are of what is illegal and what isn't, and for much the same reasons."

"But Archie—" Isobel intervened, "—we can't have the Foundation used for that sort of thing. Hugh's absolutely right."

"Isobel, my dear, there was a time when I would have agreed with you—and with Roskill," Havergal said patiently. "But the world has changed since then, and if the Foundation's still going to do a worthwhile job it has to change too—just to stay in being."

"Then you condone what may be happening?" said Roskill.

"Condone it? Don't be a fool, man—of course I don't condone it. It threatens the Foundation. But I *understand* it— I know that if I was an Arab I wouldn't be sitting around talking. Do you think the Foundation would last ten minutes in the Middle East today if we tried to crack down on it? We'd be finished."

"So what exactly is it that's worrying you if you know all about it?"

"I don't know all about it," Havergal shook his head. "I wish I knew more, and what I've been trying to do is to keep it within safety limits. But what worries me is *you*."

"I worry you?"

"Not you personally, but what you represent—the stupid, half-baked political shysters who direct you!" Havergal's control of his invective in Isobel's presence was remarkable. "Weak when they should be strong, strong when they should be understanding. Always talking about Britain's responsibilities—they couldn't distinguish a responsibility from a bottle of Worcester sauce!"

It was the ancient lament of the soldier over the politician's incapacity, and it roused a sneaking, service-bred sympathy in Roskill. Except that the soldiers always underrated the politicians' difficulties just as much as the politicians underrated the soldiers'—so that the military dictatorships were every bit as grisly as the civilian variety.

But he was letting his reactions side-track him. What mattered was that Havergal didn't seem to have a clue about the present emergency: he thought the authorities were simply getting nosey.

"Shysters or not, Colonel, they can wreck your Foundation from top to bottom."

"Hugh!" Isobel sounded like a fencing master who'd discovered that her two favourite pupils were using unbuttoned foils.

"It's perfectly all right, my dear," said Havergal. "Threats are part of Roskill's stock-in-trade. Mostly empty threats now, though. The Foundation's too widely based for them to do it any real damage—they might even do it a bit of good in some quarters."

He looked at Roskill shrewdly. "And I don't think they would try anyway. Their hearts aren't really in the game these days—they don't care who kills who in the Middle East so long as the oil flows."

So that was what had nerved Havergal to hold out for information without giving it: he'd reckoned any threat against the well-respected Foundation had to be backed by bluff only. And until two nights ago he'd probably have been right.

But now by giving him the information he wanted Roskill could win the game, not lose it . . .

"In the Middle East perhaps they don't care, Colonel. But at home they do."

Havergal frowned.

"The night before last we lost a man—a friend of mine—right here in London," said Roskill. "And we nearly lost another one. One of my bosses, as a matter of fact—one of your top shysters. I think you could say his heart's in the game this time. Just this once, Colonel Havergal, we mean exactly what we say."

"A friend? Hugh—who was it?" Isobel's incredulous expression mirrored Faith's—to both of them death was always an unforeseen accident on the road or a hushed prognosis in the consulting room, never a deliberate act.

He'd meant to break it to her gently, choosing the time and place, but now he saw that her distress would serve to bring extra pressure on Havergal. In any case he had to tell her now: he could see her already conjuring up in her mind the faces of the friends of his that she'd met and liked—Jack Butler and Colin Monroe, young Richardson who had captivated her, even David Audley, who had rather frightened her. But it would be a worse shock than any of those.

"It was Alan Jenkins."

"Alan!"

With Faith it had been shock, but with Isobel it was at once more than that. For Isobel alone knew about Harry, and being Isobel grasped all the implications of Alan's death instantly—they had talked Harry's death into the ground enough times.

Havergal gave Roskill a look of mingled distaste and curiosity: he knew that the play had been reversed, but he didn't quite know whether it had been deliberate or accidental—whether he was dealing with a cold-hearted bastard who had set the whole thing up, or an officer and a gentleman who had made the best of a dirty job and struck lucky.

Roskill knew the feeling—he had felt it himself about others, Audley among them: you never really knew whether it was luck or cleverness. And now he had learnt that it was possible not even to know the truth about oneself.

Whatever it was, though, it served. Havergal's shoulders sagged half an inch and for the first time he looked his age. Roskill began almost to feel sorry for him, only to check himself before the feeling took root: the old man should have stuck to his retirement—or at least served the Ryle Foundation in a way that didn't play ducks and drakes with his oath of allegiance. Personal definitions of the national interest and the nature of illegal organisations might be all right for debating societies, but those who indulged such fancies in real life couldn't complain when real life caught up with them.

There was no point in doing a victory roll, however. It might even be premature if he failed to handle Havergal with compassion now, of all times.

"We don't want to injure the Foundation, Colonel. That isn't the object at all. And we're not going to let the Special Branch loose on it." Strictly, that might not be true, but it sounded reassuring. "But there are things we've got to know— like how you got wind of what was going on."

He prayed that Havergal wouldn't turn that question against him, because Cox's hunch was based on extremely tenuous circumstantial evidence, and not on anything that was 'going on' at all.

But Havergal's defences were breached. He sighed and squared his shoulders in resignation.

"I'd been expecting it for a long time, if you must know."

"Because you think any Arab worthy of his salt would be up to something?"

"Not just that." Havergal shook his head. "Have you got the Ryle Map, my dear?" he said to Isobel.

Isobel nodded. "It's in the study."

"Would you get it for me?" Havergal turned back to Roskill. "Do you know how the Foundation works?"

"Not in detail."

"Not many people do. And perhaps that's why this has happened," said Havergal mournfully. "We're a pretty unobtrusive lot. We don't turn out top people—or damn students. Just good mechanics and midwives, and that sort of thing . . . You know why old Jacob Ryle set it up like that?"

"Didn't a railway have something to do with it?" Roskill could remember that the disastrous railway, old Ryle's first charitable enterprise, had been a family joke.

"A railway—yes. He built a line as a present for one of his tame sheiks. It cost a fortune. And then he found that there was no freight to run and precious few passengers— the local camel train did the job perfectly well at a hundredth of the cost. He'd simply put the camel drivers out of work— until they knifed the engine driver, that is! They say you can still see some of the track when the sand gets blown away . . ."

He looked at Roskill. "The point is that after that Ryle decreed that we'd work from the bottom. Each area has its own local committee—they set up the projects and they send us suitable young people to train. We arrange for the training at our own technical centres, and then we shunt the trainees round the projects—they work their passage, and that makes the project cheap to run. And the young people see a bit of the world and learn what hard work is before they go back to their own patches."

There was a note of pride in Havergal's voice now. "So we get useful jobs done, and we don't make trouble for the countries we work in. Wherever we're established we're just part of the landscape."

He moved the mugs to one side as Isobel spread a map of Europe, the Mediterranean and the Middle East on the coffee table: a map with a rash of little colored symbols on it.

"It's quite simple," said Havergal. "The green stars are the selection committees, the red squares are the training centers and the blue triangles are the work projects. Do you get the picture?"

Roskill got the picture very well indeed. He had no idea that the Foundation operated on so grand a scale: the green stars were spread thickly over the Middle East, as were the blue triangles. The red shapes were thickest there too, but spread out also into Europe, from Italy to Sweden and Scotland—and behind the Iron Curtain even.

Roskill bent over the map in awe: there were also red squares in Israeli-held Jordan and in the Gaza strip—the ultimate purity test!

As a self-supporting educational foundation in a war-torn world it was a remarkable achievement, and the Colonel had just cause for pride.

But another possibility sprang from the map in red, blue and green: as the cover for an illegal network it was ready-made and perfect—secure in its well-established respectability and accepted without question as part of the landscape, with its members and trainees moving unobtrusively back and forth. No wonder Havergal had been expecting the worst!

But his suspicions had to be founded on more than mere assumption of the worst, nevertheless.

"What actually put you on to them?"

Havergal smiled bitterly. "The failure rate."

Roskill waited patiently while Havergal nodded knowingly to himself, his bitterness fading at the recollection of his cleverness in spotting the reason for it.

"Jacob Ryle couldn't bear the idea that any of his charity might be wasted—particularly after what happened to the railway. So he framed the organisation of the Foundation to avoid wasting money on trainees who wouldn't finish the course—or who didn't do what they'd been trained for."

"Drop-outs, you mean?"

"That's the modern jargon, yes," Havergal nodded. "Not enough intelligence or not enough guts. In the early days some of the local committees weren't too choosy—usually they were just trying to do favours for their friends. Ryle wouldn't stand for that, though; if a committee failed to deliver the right goods he changed the committee.

"After a time everyone got the message. There were still the odd failures, but they were rare—there were years when there weren't any that couldn't be explained."

Ryle had wanted his money's worth, thought Roskill, and quite naturally the old bandit had applied his business methods to his charitable enterprise: shape up or get out. Once the tradition was established firmly all it needed was a competent statistical section to keep an eye on it.

"That was the pattern when I joined the Foundation— even lasted through the decade after Suez," Havergal continued. "But it began to change about six months after the June War."

"You mean the drop-outs began?"

"The drop-outs. I didn't spot them at the time, of course. The figures take time to show up. And even then I didn't smell a rat until I realised that the wrong ones were quitting."

Roskill nodded. The drift of the Colonel's argument was clear enough. The drop-outs of the old days would be due to stupidity, idleness or instability: the new drop-outs would be young men with exactly the opposite qualities, but with other fish to fry.

"And what have you done about it?"

"Nothing at all." Havergal gazed unblinkingly at Roskill. "There's nothing I can do."

"I thought you sacked committees that didn't deliver the goods?"

"We used to, but not any more. Times have changed since Jacob Ryle's days—and particularly since '56. We have to tread more delicately now. And the committees that are up to mischief aren't in my territory, anyway."

The look in Havergal's eye suggested that times had not changed so much in his territory, and wouldn't change as long as he was in charge.

"Where are they?"

"Jordan, Lebanon, Syria and Iraq—we've got fifteen committees in the four of them. According to my reckoning there are only seven doing their proper job now."

"Whose territory would that be?" Roskill fumbled in his memory. "Elliott Wilkinson's?"

Havergal pointed his chin at Roskill, his loyalty to the

Foundation in collision with the plain implication of Roskill's question. It occurred to Roskill that if the Colonel already suspected Wilkinson of chicanery he probably had his own plans for dealing with him. But there was no point in pressing the matter—it would only shut the old boy up altogether.

Roskill hurriedly led him off at a tangent. "But all this is circumstantial evidence—statistical stuff. It takes one hell of a lot of statistics to make one piece of real truth."

He looked at the Colonel narrowly. "If you can supply us with names and details of the drop-outs, that would be a start, anyway. And names of the committee men too. If you can do that there's a fair chance I can get my bosses to cross-check them and leave the Foundation itself alone."

Havergal thought for a time. "If it ever got out there'd be hell to pay, Roskill."

"If it doesn't get out there may be hell anyway. But I tell you what I'll do to prove good faith: I'll give you some of the names we've got. And I'll show you some of the faces we've got that haven't got names."

He reached down beside the chair for the projector. This had been what the man had been after all along, and it was ironic that Roskill had intended from the start to give it to him: the names and faces of the Hassan suspects and every contact of theirs Cox had been able to dig from British files and coax from European ones.

Five suspects and twenty-five contacts: not a great many and most of them looked alike to Roskill anyway. But maybe Havergal, with all his years of Arabian experience, could distinguish them from one another. He might even do more, for as Cox had gently pointed out exactly half of them were graduates or officials of the Jacob Ryle Memorial Foundation Trust.

VII

ROSKILL LEANT GINGERLY against the wall of
the Bunnock Street phone box and listened to the buzz of the
bell on the other end of the line, far away in Hampshire.

He settled down to wait, resigned in the knowledge that
Audley would put off answering as long as possible in the
hope that the noise would pack up and go away. His only
hope of a speedy answer was Faith.

For the second time during the evening his eye was caught
by the carefully inscribed line of Latin: *Meum est propositum
in taberna mori*. 'Meum' was 'my' and 'est' was 'is'—"my
something is". He dredged into his vestigial Latin. 'Mori',
he recalled from the rolls of honour, was 'to die'—Pro Patria
mori. Which left him with "My something is to die in a
something". The nearest work to 'taberna' was 'tabernacle',
but the idea of dying in a tabernacle was plainly ridiculous—
the sort of guess he had chanced in Latin translations so often,
only to elicit the Latin master's eternal complaint: nonsense
must be wrong . . .

The buzz-buzz stopped with a click at last and Faith answered rather breathlessly.

"You want David? Who's calling—who shall I say? Isn't
that—" Faith stopped short, turning Roskill's christian name

into an exhalation of air. It was odd how although she affected to despise the rigmarole of security she was quick to apply the rules.

"I'll get him," she concluded grimly.

Again Roskill waited. She'd probably been in the bath or the lavatory and Audley himself had been sitting in the room next to the phone, obstinately deaf to it.

It couldn't be 'tabernacle', but without knowing what 'propositum' was there was no way of guessing. He rather sympathised with the other anonymous commentator who had scrawled 'Sod the Students' directly underneath the inscription—the authentic voice of Bunnock Street.

"Hullo, Hugh!" Audley's voice rang loud and clear in his ear, disdainful of rules and caution alike.

"Is this a safe line?" Roskill exclaimed, more in surprise than annoyance.

"Safe? Safe line?" Audley repeated vaguely. "I haven't the faintest idea. But if it isn't, then some poor devil's been wasting an awful lot of time listening to nothing. What's up?"

Roskill gritted his teeth. "I think I'm blown, for a start," he said. "Somebody recognised me at—at that meeting I went to."

"The Ryle do?"

Roskill beat his fist against the side of the telephone box. Audley had to be doing this deliberately.

"You're quite sure this line's safe?"

"I tell you—I haven't a clue," said Audley. "But it doesn't matter anyway. All that sort of thing is grossly exaggerated. Nobody's got the manpower or equipment to tap phones just on the off-chance—they only tap when they're sure. And if anyone's on my line, God help them—they'll have had a job breaking the code Faith uses when she orders her groceries. I tell you, Hugh, you're all hagridden with bugging and half the time it's a lot of cock!"

He snorted derisively down the line at Roskill. "And if they've got one of those voice-actuated things clipped on somewhere, how do they know we don't know about it? We could be staging this for their sole benefit . . . So you were spotted. Well, who spotted you?"

Roskill carefully described the fat Arab.

"A Lebanese?" Audley demurred. "No, he's certainly not a Lebanese. Before I was kicked out I'd already been side-tracked there for six months and I know all their top men—he can't be all that new. But never mind: I'll identify him for you tomorrow morning. It shouldn't be difficult. Now—tell me about the Ryle Foundation. Obviously Cox was right about that!"

"Yes, but—" The trouble was that Havergal's memory had proved suspiciously disappointing when it came down to hard identifications. The session had left him with the feeling that the old man had to some extent outsmarted him in the end, and he tried hard to conceal this now in reporting the dialogue.

But Audley merely grunted approvingly as he listened.

"A neat line of reasoning—I think I'd like this Colonel Havergal of yours, Hugh. He was before my time, of course, but I can see why Fred would have wanted to get hold of him—if it was Fred. And I agree with you it might be Elliott Wilkinson he's gunning for. The Arabs would be damn difficult to unseat with things as they are, but Wilkinson's not quite invulnerable."

"You know him?"

"I used to. But I didn't know he was mixed up with the Ryle people. It doesn't surprise me one bit that he's up to no good, though."

"He's pro-Arab?"

"He isn't pro anything—it wouldn't be so bad if he was. He's just old-fashioned anti-semitic. Thirty years ago he'd have ended up behind the wire on the Isle of Man—if he hadn't got to Berlin first. Horrible bloody character. If it wasn't Jews it'd be Catholics or blacks—if he'd lived in the sixteenth century he'd have been a champion witch-smeller. The devil of it is that he's got some very close contacts with our Arab section now—too damn close. And Llewelyn trusts him, the fool."

"But there's still nothing to connect him with Hassan. We've only got Cox's instinct and a handful of names."

"Cox is a good man, Hugh. And we've got more than that now. Things are beginning to come together.

"Things?"

It was all very well for Audley to retire comfortably to his country seat to think beautiful, complicated thoughts while he, Roskill, crouched in smelly Bunnock Street.

"I've been doing my homework, Hugh—catching up on Master Llewelyn."

Llewelyn. Always the Welshman was uppermost in Audley's thoughts. Alan Jenkins's killers were probably a secondary consideration, a mere means to an end, whatever he might maintain. They were still each looking for revenge, but not the same revenge.

"It seems he's one of the errand boys between the Americans and the Russians and Jarring, the UN mediator—strictly an errand boy, whatever he likes to think. But a busy one. I can see how mortifying he'd find being blown up just now, when things are moving."

"He said there was a chance of peace in the Middle East."

"I doubt that. But there *is* going to be a cease-fire, that's certain—the Rogers Plan is definitely on."

The radio that morning had seemed very much less certain, but Audley obviously had better sources.

"It's all cut and dried. The Egyptians will accept first, and the Russians are going to lean on the Syrians . . . Then the Israelis will argue among themselves—that's probably laid on so the Gahal right-wing bloc can be kicked out of the government—but they'll agree in the end. It's all set for early August. Myself, I don't think it'll go as smoothly as—as my informant thinks."

"So what's all this got to do with us?"

"With us? Well, in the long run God only knows what will happen—I've been out too long to make any useful guesses. I suppose it depends on what sort of deal the Americans and the Russians have cooked up . . . and whether the Middle East hawks can queer things . . . But in the short run they're just coming up to the maximum risk period. Once the cease-fire's agreed, maybe it can stand up to a certain amount of double-crossing, I don't know. But just *before*—that's right now— this is the time the guerrilla groups ought to be trying to wreck it."

Audley paused. "And there's one thing that's gingering up the Great Powers—there's a rumour that Nasser is a sick man. The word is that when he was in Russia earlier this year the doctors there told him to take things very easy. But the way things are, he can't, and that's what's got the Russians moving—they don't want peace, but they want to take the steam out of things just in case."

"Whereas Hassan wants trouble?"

"Exactly. In fact I think that's what Llewelyn's been expecting. And not just him either—there's an unofficial clamp-down in Israel at the moment, and Egypt's on the alert too. There are a lot of nervous people in the Middle East just now, Hugh, and that's a fact!"

It was all high-powered, big league stuff and it made Roskill's own research seem a schoolboy enterprise in comparison. But it didn't get them any closer to knowing what to do next.

"There are some bloody nervous people here in London, too, David," Roskill reminded Audley. "It's them we've got to worry about."

"Ah—I was coming to them. There are two men who could really tell us what all this is about—Jake Shapiro and the Egyptian, Razzak."

"Did Razzak get the early boat from Newhaven?"

"If he did it took him a remarkably long time to get to his embassy in Paris. He seems to have lost a few hours on the way somewhere, that's certain." Audley paused. "As a working theory I agree with your reading of things this morning. It's far too much of a coincidence, all three of them being roughly in the same place. It does sound as though Razzak met someone down there, and Shapiro was watching them.

And one way or another your friend Jenkins saw something he wasn't meant to. And if it was big enough to get Jake out of bed that early it could be a killing matter right enough!"

"You still think Razzak met Hassan, whoever Hassan may be?"

"Not Hassan himself—that was never likely. But maybe one of his top men. Razzak didn't go walking on the Sussex Downs for fun—that's for sure. The trouble is that we don't know enough about the man; he's new in London and I daren't go checking on him in records in case someone gets wind of what I'm doing."

"I thought you knew all the brass," Roskill needled him.

"Blast it, Hugh—I do—but—" Audley stuttered for a moment. "That's the whole trouble: he's not really a coming man. Maybe he was ten years ago, but from Suez to the June War he was just a field officer—a tank man. He had a regiment on the frontier in '67."

"Then you do know something about him."

"I do," said Audley rather reluctantly. "But I only know what Jake Shapiro himself told me when we had lunch last week—the day Razzak's appointment came through, apparently."

"Shapiro spoke about him?"

Audley bridled. "It was just—conversation. Jake and I don't talk shop much any more. We haven't got anything useful to say to each other."

"But what did he say?" Roskill persisted.

"He said Razzak was . . . brave."

From Audley it sounded strange, almost a criticism.

"Brave?"

Audley seemed to shrug down the telephone. "When the Israelis were beating the stuffing out of the Egyptians in '67 Razzak was one of those who dug their heels in—apparently he put up a real fight."

One of the hard-faced, bitter ones, he'd be: Roskill remembered the blank, irreconcilable stares he had noticed at the Ryle reception. For men like that any talk of cease-fire would be a betrayal, and that brought Razzak shoulder to shoulder with Hassan.

"But I'll be able to tell you more about him soon," Audley went on. "I'm having breakfast with a man who knows all about him tomorrow morning."

Roskill grunted. That, of course, was half the secret of Audley's success: if he didn't know something, he could usually be relied on to know someone who would.

"I should have thought Shapiro would be your man. He knows Razzak—and he was down there at Firle. If you can get your hooks into him—"

"Nobody gets their hooks into Jake. The best we can hope for is that he'll be willing to trade with you, Hugh."

'You', not 'me'! Roskill groaned. This was the same convenient formula Audley had invoked earlier at the Queensway Hotel, but after his objection to it Roskill had hoped it would be allowed to die a natural death.

"Hell, David—he's your buddy. I hardly know the fellow. You go trade with him."

"I want to keep out of it as long as I can, Hugh. As soon as Jake knows I'm involved he'll be likely to raise the price."

"But you're a friend of his."

"Friendship doesn't stretch this far. But don't worry—he's not likely to ask you anything about aircraft. Missiles, maybe, but most likely tanks, and I can get you that Anglo-Belgian report on the Scorpion and the Scimitar. Offer him the inside information on that welded aluminium armour of theirs. He'll be sure to like that."

Audley sounded suspiciously like the Foreign Office man who thought no one would know anything about desalination.

"But supposing he doesn't?"

"Give him the Ryle Foundation, then—I'm damn certain he'll go for *that*."

It was lamentably clear that Audley was perfectly prepared to see Roskill compromise himself with anybody and everybody in the higher cause of his own tortuous designs, so there was no point in prolonging the conversation. Any moment now Isobel would be arriving beside the car, and he hated the idea of her standing waiting for him in the shadows of Bunnock Street.

"Where do I find Shapiro, then? And don't forget I've got to go down to Firle tomorrow morning, either."

"That's just it, Hugh. You can reach him tonight: he'll be in a fly-blown club called Shabtai's in Silchester Lane—just behind St. Bartholomew's Hospital. He'll be there about 10:30—he's currently wooing a doctor in Bart's."

"A doctor?"

"A female doctor, man—there's nothing odd about Jake. He's ambitiously normal, you might say. His sense of humour's neanderthal, but he's a decent chap if you don't try to double-cross him too obviously. Just don't let him bully you, and whatever you do don't try and keep up with him when he's drinking—he's got a leather liver."

Razzak and Shapiro sounded equally formidable in their different ways, Roskill reflected unhappily. They were both tank men and therefore had to be mad to start with—anyone who chose to enclose himself in a slow, vulnerable steel coffin couldn't be wholly normal, whatever Audley might say.

He could only hope that Audley had guessed correctly, and that he was about to enlist the aid of the right madman.

By the time he had returned to the car he had managed to convince himself that it could hardly be so very far from the mark. If it was based on what looked like a string of coincidences, that was in its favour. Strings of coincidences were like unicorns and mermaids—they simply didn't exist in nature, and sensible men treated them with suspicion.

Alan had been killed deliberately and Alan had been at Firle when Shapiro and Razzak had passed so close to each other. And certainly, if anyone was mixed up with Hassan it would be Razzak—and if anyone had reason enough to spy on them it was Shapiro.

Yet for all that he would have preferred to have met the Israeli after his expedition to Firle, not before it. He had great hopes of Firle: if there had been any sort of meeting there, it had probably been set up in the belief that those wide open downs were a private place. But that was a very typical mistake a foreigner and a townsman might make; in reality there were very often watching eyes in the countryside, ready to note strange faces which would have passed unnoticed in the anonymity of a crowded city street.

Perhaps no one else had seen as much as Alan had, but the chances were at least fair that someone else had seen something.

There was a click from the passenger's door and a rapid tapping on the window—Isobel's characteristic tap.

He reached over and unlocked the door, and Isobel slid hurriedly on to the seat.

"Start the car, Hugh," she said urgently. "Drive off!"

Roskill frowned at her. Isobel was not totally unflappable, but this urgency had the sound of fear in it.

"There are two men in the churchyard watching you," she whispered. "They're just out of the lamplight—I took the short-cut and I almost bumped into them. I'm certain they were watching you—let's get away from here, Hugh, please."

He fought the urge to turn round. If they were watching him from just inside the churchyard, beyond the radius of the last lamp, then he wouldn't be able to see them anyway. Whereas underneath the lamp beside the car his every movement would be clear to them.

He looked ahead down Bunnock Street, which stretched empty and malevolent before him. Isobel could hardly be imagining things: there was nothing else here for anyone to watch. And her instinct for flight was simple common sense— Bunnock Street was not a place to linger in when seventy-five yards and five seconds away, beyond the curve of the terraced houses, was the safety of the main road.

He reached forward towards the ignition, but even as his fingers closed on the key a fearful thought exploded in his brain, paralysing his hand.

Underneath the lamp beside the car.

"Start the car, Hugh!"

Beside the car!

"That's interesting," Alan had said. And he had stared at something for a split second and there had been a white, blinding flare of light . . . torn metal and flesh slapped against the floor and walls of the pit, the crack of the explosion magnified in the confined space of the underground garage, echoing still while pieces of the one-time Vanden Plas Princess bounced from the ceiling and clattered to the floor . . .

Roskill's fingers slowly left the key. He didn't have to look down to see that his hand was shaking—he could feel it shaking.

"What's the matter, Hugh?"

The blind moment passed, and Roskill felt cold and calm—it had been like that when the Provost had suddenly changed from a beautiful little flying machine into an uncontrollable and disintegrating piece of flying junk: the moment of panic and then the businesslike preoccupation with saving himself which was half the battle. Only believe and ye shall be saved . . .

"Somebody's moved the car, Bel," he said gently. "There's just a chance they might have—tampered with it."

"How do you know?"

"I parked right next to the lamp-post, Bel—the passenger's door couldn't be opened when I left it."

"But I got in?"

Roskill nodded. He had been slow, almost fatally slow, sidetracked by his own thoughts and then by Isobel's fear—slow to remember the Vanden Plas Princess.

"Tampered with?" Isobel was calm now, too—beautifully and wholly Isobel, and not to be fobbed-off with half-baked explanations.

"It could be nothing. But if those chaps back there in the churchyard had anything to do with Alan, then they know how to booby-trap cars."

It could be nothing—but to bug the car they had no need to move it. And if they had done nothing but that to it there would be very little point in hanging around to see the fire-works.

But there was no need to spell that out to Isobel.

"I see. And just what do you propose to do about it, Hugh?"

She was sitting more stiffly, but the tone of her voice was still perfectly controlled—altogether much more the experienced charity president questioning her treasurer over an adverse financial report than the female half of an illicit liaison caught sitting on something hot.

"Well, we're safe enough so long as we don't do anything," said Roskill. "I doubt you came into their calculations, but just to make things look convincing I'm going to put my arm along the back of your seat and you can cuddle up to me—just to allay any fears they may have."

Isobel moved towards him somewhat gingerly, as though he was personally wired to whatever might be under the bonnet.

"We always said we'd never do this sort of thing in public," she murmured in his ear. "And certainly not in this disgusting place."

She was bloody well cooler than he was, thought Roskill until he felt for her hand and found that it was trembling.

"What sort of shoes are you wearing? Snazzy or sensible?"

"Sensible. You said we weren't going to eat at anywhere smart."

All the better to run in, if it came to that.

"In a moment I want you to get out of the car, Bel, and walk down the street—walk, mind you—don't run unless I shout. But if I shout then start running."

"And what will you be doing?"

"Christ—I shall be running too, and I can probably run a lot faster than you can."

"Why can't we get out together?"

It was odds on that if the car was booby-trapped it would be the ignition that set it off. They couldn't have had time for anything much more elaborate. But it was just possible that the driver's door was rigged for a second-time opening explosion, a trick that conveniently removed the victim from the actual place where the booby-trappers might have been seen.

"It'll confuse them, Bel. But they probably won't do anything anyway. They'll think we've had a quarrel more likely. Just walk smartly away and don't turn round—and don't worry."

Isobel looked hard at him. "You're not going to do anything noble, are you, Hugh?"

"I'm not going to do anything stupid, if that's what you mean."

"You promise?"

"Promise?" Somehow he had to belittle the danger now, to get her moving. "My darling Bel—you remember the verse Valentine put up over the bar in the Mess at Snettisham— the advice on when to eject—

Some lucky Thracian has my noble shield,
I had to run: I dropped it in a wood,
But I got clear away, thank God!
So f——the shield! I'll get another just as good."

He tried to grin at her. "We've both got to bale out—just do what I've told you. I've no ambition to die for my—"

He stopped as the answer to the question which had been dogging him earlier rose unbidden in his mind: Audley would certainly know what 'propositum' and 'taberna' meant—he must remember to ask him at the next opportunity.

"Hugh?"

"It's nothing, Bel. I've just remembered something unimportant I've got to do. Now, off you go!"

The very irrelevance of what he was saying seemed to reassure her. It even served to calm Roskill himself: it was somehow unthinkable that anything could happen to him until he had the answer to that ancient piece of Latin wit—probably lavatorial wit, too...

Isobel gave him one final look, drew a deep breath and

grasped her bag decisively. Then, with a firm, unhurried movement she opened the door, stepped gracefully on to the pavement—her entrances and exits were always elegant—and set off down Bunnock Street like a swan navigating the town drain.

Roskill watched her progress with one eye on the driving mirror, in which the entrance to St. Biddulph's churchyard was framed.

Ten paces and she was out of the street light's circle and into a patch of half-light . . . and then ten more and she was almost on the edge of the next circle, from the lamp on the other side of the street. Beyond that she was virtually out of reach of danger and it was time for him to move.

With his hand on the door handle he risked turning to get one good, clear look at the churchyard entrance. There was the loom of something darker beyond the pool of light—something that was moving now. In that second it dawned on him that Isobel's door was the obvious one to use. He levered himself awkwardly across towards it, bumping himself painfully on the gear-lever as he did so, and swung himself on to the pavement.

In doing so he had another glimpse of the churchyard: there was a figure, two figures now, there. But in the very instant that he saw them there was the roar of an engine from the other end of Bunnock Street and the glare of powerful headlights which swept over the nearside curve of the street and then over Roskill—and then on to the men themselves.

They threw up their hands across their faces and broke left and right away from the beam of light as though it was a death-ray, leaving Roskill rooted in the shadow of his own car.

The car behind the headlights hurtled the last few yards of the street—a big maroon Mercedes—lurching to a stop within inches of the Triumph, obliquely across its bows.

The rear window slid down smoothly and a swarthy, scarred face peered out of it.

"Squadron-Leader Roskill?"

A plump, good-humoured face he had seen before earlier in the evening—the fat Arab.

The door swung open and a pair of beautifully polished shoes glinted momentarily as the Arab levered himself out. Beyond him Roskill glimpsed Isobel standing irresolutely half-way down the street.

"Forgive me for arriving so—so rudely, Squadron-Leader," said the Arab, limping towards him slowly. "But I don't think your car is fit to drive any more."

"I wasn't intending to drive it."

"You weren't?" The fat man cocked his head in curiosity, and then nodded it. "How very wise of you! Then I can only presume that you are already aware that it's been—is nobbled the word? One nobbles racehorses, so I think one might nobble cars, don't you?"

He patted the Triumph's bonnet appreciatively.

"And those two gentlemen who didn't like the headlights," continued the Egyptian, "I suppose we'd better see them on their way."

He snapped his fingers at his driver and the driver's mate and pointed towards the churchyard. Wordlessly the men obeyed him, like the well trained gun-dogs they were.

The Arab patted the car again. "One of your little electronic gadgets was upset, I suppose," he said conversationally. "Or would that be telling?"

He smiled, and the only thing Roskill could think of doing to hide his doubts about the whole situation was to smile back.

"Nothing so elaborate, I'm afraid," he replied self-deprecatingly. "Let's say I'm just suspicious of cars these days."

"So my journey was really unnecessary after all?"

"Not at all. It's very reassuring to know I've got unexpected friends watching over me."

The fat man chuckled. "You are a most popular person, Squadron Leader. No sooner had my man settled down to follow you, than he noticed that someone else was doing the same thing. And as that made it very difficult for him to follow you, he followed *them* instead—a very sensible fellow."

"And what did he see?"

"He saw them take your car away. And they got away from him then, because he wasn't expecting that. So he phoned me—"

"—And you knew what to expect?"

"When my man told me they'd brought the car back I had my suspicions, certainly."

"But you don't know what's been done exactly?"

It was curious that the fellow was so eager to explain exactly how he'd come storming into Bunnock Street like the US cavalry. It made Roskill want to push him further, to find out what he didn't wish to explain. Like, for example, who the devil he was—which was the one question Roskill couldn't humiliate himself with.

A shrug. "They didn't take it away to give it a wash and a polish, obviously."

"A shot of TPDX in the right place, maybe?"

For the first time the smile slipped a fraction. The Arab cocked his head again slightly and the light from the lamp above them picked out a long whitish scar that ran from his cheekbone downwards, to be lost in one of his jowls.

But before he could begin to reply Isobel appeared beside his right shoulder. The Arab swung half round and faced her, incorporating a little bow into the movement.

"Lady Ryle—I do beg your pardon," he said quickly. "I was almost sure I'd seen you in the headlights..."

"Colonel Razzak," said Isobel in her coolest Lady Ryle voice, "I thought I recognised you too, but in this light I wasn't sure at first either."

Razzak!

No wonder the man had behaved as though Roskill knew him—and no wonder he knew enough about Roskill to be suspicious in the first place.

But—damn it—it wasn't so much Razzak's arrival as his

physical appearance that beat everything. From Audley's brief introduction he had imagined a lean, fanatical Bedouin—a throwback to those great days of Arab empire over which the Foreign Office man had enthused. He had never dreamed that the hero of Sinai would be hidden in the body of a roly-poly Levantine carpet salesman.

"It is a compliment that you should recognise me in any light, Lady Ryle."

In another moment the fat slob would be kissing her hand. Except that the thought was hardly charitable to a man who had just broken the speed limit to stop them both being shredded into little pieces: no matter what his true motives were, and fat and ugly notwithstanding, Razzak's account was in credit.

And that, in itself, was an unforeseen complication. It didn't exactly exculpate Razzak from Alan's death. No sensible man resorted to violence in a foreign and neutral country if it could be avoided, and just because he had avoided it tonight it did not follow that he had done so in Alan's case. It could simply be that Alan had known too much, whereas Roskill knew practically damn all—after the Ryle reception debacle that must have been obvious enough.

But that only made tonight's emergency more frightening: it meant that there was someone else beyond Razzak's control—and that could include both Hassan and the Israelis—who was prepared to turn a London back-street into a shambles for no very good reason.

The door behind him opened suddenly with a crash that made him jump. Framed in it was a Goliath of a man in shirtsleeves and a vast Fair Isle pullover.

The Goliath took in the scene with one slow glance from right to left—Roskill, Razzak, Isobel and the Mercedes with its doors open and its headlights glaring—and then swung his own glare to Roskill.

"I don't know wot your game is, mate," he said in tones in which anger and scorn were carefully balanced, "but you just go and play it somewhere else!"

Razzak stared coldly at the man for a moment, and then turned again towards Isobel.

"Allow me to offer you the hospitality of my car," he said. He turned to Roskill. "And you, too, Squadron Leader."

The Goliath snorted.

Roskill leant into the Triumph and gently slid the keys out of the ignition.

"You can't leave it outside my property," barked the Goliath, gratefully seizing the chance of being awkward. "I'll have the bloody police take it away!"

Roskill was almost relieved that the man had sworn at last; the absence of obscenities in his opening broadside had made his anger more threatening.

"The bloody police will be coming for it very soon anyway," he replied with assumed indifference. "It's a stolen vehicle. You lay a finger on it and you'll be in trouble."

That might at least protect the car from outrage—and the Goliath from sudden death—until he could get the department's specialists to look it over, and in the meantime it took some of the wind out of the man's bellying sails.

He locked the car doors carefully and followed Isobel into the Mercedes. Razzak leant forward and flashed the headlights off and on before settling back beside them.

"You know, I have always admired the independent spirit of the British working class," he said gravely. "But whenever I encounter it myself I have a great desire to kick it in the teeth. And yet I am a peasant myself, and I find my reaction most contradictory."

"I think he had the right of it, Colonel Razzak," replied Isobel, equally seriously. "We were probably disturbing his television and we may well have woken the baby. Those are two capital crimes in England, you must understand."

"The right of it?" Razzak nodded thoughtfully. "He takes us for criminals, and there are several of us and only one of him—but he has the right of it! How admirable!"

The gun-dogs came out of the churchyard and headed towards them, watched closely by Goliath. As he slipped into the driver's seat the younger of the two shook his head at Razzak.

"No one there now, Colonel," he said obsequiously.

Razzak nodded again, and turned back to Isobel and Roskill. "Can I take you now to wherever you were going, perhaps?"

Isobel glanced at Roskill. "I think I'd prefer to go home, if you don't mind, Hugh. I've rather lost my appetite."

"If that's what you wish, Lady Ryle." Roskill was not quite able to keep the relief out of his voice. But her common sense would tell her what he was thinking, anyway: if he was someone's target—and bizarre though that thought was, it appeared to be the case—she would only be a liability to him now.

Isobel reached for the door handle. "I'll take the short cut home, then—don't worry about me. I'm sure you and Colonel Razzak have important things to discuss."

Razzak cut in before Roskill could reply. "Allow me to send Captain Majid with you just in case, Lady Ryle—he would be honoured to accompany you."

"Colonel, I couldn't possibly—"

Razzak held up his hand. "Please! Let us say no more about the matter. Captain Majid will accompany you and make his own way home when you are safely in your house. Jahein here can drive me perfectly well, so long as he remembers it is a car he controls, not a tank."

The driver got out of the car—rather sulkily, Roskill thought—and the older Arab moved behind the wheel.

"It's very kind of you, Colonel," murmured Isobel. "One thing, Hugh—when is the funeral?"

Roskill frowned, perplexed. "The funeral?"

"Your *friend*," she said with a hint of irritation. "I would like to send a wreath, old-fashioned as that may seem to you."

Isobel had known the Jenkins family in Harry's day, Roskill remembered—in the halcyon time when they'd all been equal and innocent recipients of the Ryle hospitality. And

Isobel, who never forgot a birthday or an anniversary, would undoubtedly be an inveterate wreath-sender. It was the side they had not got in common: strange, but he hadn't once thought of Alan's funeral—only of his death.

"I'll phone you when I know," he said.

He watched her walk away beside the Egyptian captain, very tall and straight and entirely Lady Ryle now. It was at times like this that he wondered what the hell he was doing with his life, while knowing that if he could have the same time again he would make exactly the same decisions. A part share in Isobel was worth ten times a whole share of any other girl he had ever known.

VIII

"A REMARKABLE WOMAN," murmured Razzak.

"Yes, she is. And it was civil of you to send your man with her, Razzak."

The man behind the wheel gave a suppressed snort, and Razzak himself chuckled.

"Not civil at all, Squadron Leader—a mere trick to rid me of the noble captain. If I had thought there was any danger I would have despatched Jahein—is that not so Jahein?"

The grizzled head bobbed.

"You see, we are old soldiers, Jahein and I, and the captain is a new soldier set beside us to see that we don't get into trouble. He is like a—what is that shellfish that fastens itself to the rocks?"

"A limpet?"

"A limpet! Yes. Or a pilot fish that swims beside the shark—that might be more like it. But every now and then we give him the slip, don't we, Jahein?"

Jahein spat out a few words of Arabic in a hoarse, almost strangled voice. Their meaning was lost on Roskill, but they sounded so marvelously obscene that no translation was necessary.

Razzak laughed. "Sergeant-Major Jahein has a very low

opinion of Captain Majid—and bad as it is for discipline, I must agree with him. Majid is a nuisance. But fortunately he is an obedient nuisance, so he doesn't get in the way too much—like now, for instance. Let's get out of here before he comes back, Jahein."

Jahein jerked the big car forwards, narrowly missing the Triumph, and embarked on a clumsy turning operation, swearing continuously under his breath.

"A tank driver—I warned you," said Razzak. "And not even a very good tank driver. But there's nothing wrong with his nerve. Slow down, man—I must give a word of praise to the man who had the right of it."

They were alongside the open doorway in which the big man in the Fair Isle pullover was still standing, evidently determined to see them out of Bunnock Street.

Razzak wound down the window and leaned out.

"Bloody Gyppo," the man said loudly and clearly.

Razzak observed him in silence for five seconds. Finally he extended two fingers of his mangled right hand in the universal signal of contempt.

"Up yours, Jack!" he said without heat. "Drive on, Jahein."

Jahein jammed his foot down on the accelerator and his hand down on the horn and shot down the street in a deafening turmoil of noise which ended with a squeal of tyres as he skidded out of Bunnock Street on to the main road without either slowing or looking for other traffic.

"Diplomatic immunity is a wonderful thing," Razzak said happily. "It's a great comfort to Jahein, anyway—he thinks it covers accidental death too."

Jahein shook his head in disagreement and gabbled again hoarsely in Arabic.

"Speak in English, man! I've told you before it is disrespectful to speak so in front of my guests!"

Jahein tossed his head and grunted.

Razzak shrugged his shoulders and turned to Roskill. "It isn't that the old dog can't learn new tricks," he apologized.

"He speaks English perfectly well—though with a slight Australian accent. The Australians taught him all he's ever learned—to swear, fight dirty, drive a tank and hate Pommie bastards. Perhaps that's why I can't get him to talk English, the obstinate swine: you can thank the 9th Australian Division for that. But a loyal old swine—all he was saying was that if the Israelis wouldn't kill me, then I was born to hang and not die in a car crash."

Roskill watched the traffic lights ahead turn from amber to red and prayed that Jahein's instinct was sound as the Mercedes whipped across the intersection.

"And he may be right at that," mused Razzak. "If Captain Majid has his way I shall probably hang sooner or later. But in the meantime, where can we take you, Squadron Leader?"

Meeting Razzak, the unknown quantity, had not been on the schedule for tonight. But perhaps the Egyptian wasn't quite such a question mark since he'd turned up at the Ryle reception: once more it brought him face to face with Hassan. Except that seemed to make nonsense of what had just happened—and not happened—in Bunnock Street.

Unless . . .

Roskill relaxed. "Your driver seems to know where he's going already."

"Jahein?" Razzak chuckled. "Jahein simply likes driving—give him a car and a tankful of petrol and he'll drive nowhere for hours on end. He isn't going anywhere at the moment. Just away from Captain Majid. And he's still learning to find his way round London too."

Roskill watched Jahein slide the big car through a gap in the traffic just ahead of a taxi which had the right of way. Whatever the old dog didn't know, he had nothing to learn about driving; that first impression had been false.

The light from a blue neon sign momentarily illuminated Razzak's face sharply. There was nothing left of the chuckle on it: the eerie blueness stripped away the fat, leaving it hard and serious. That was another first impression gone—there was always supposed to be a thin man screaming to get out of every fat one, and the flash had betrayed a lean bedouin inside the carpet salesman.

"Well, if you could drop me near St. Paul's, that would do very well," said Roskill. "It's not very far from here."

"I think Jahein can manage that," Razzak murmured, settling back comfortably, his hands interlocking over the bulge of his stomach. The gesture transmitted itself to the man behind the wheel as if by telepathy; as Razzak sat back the car's speed dropped to a sedate crawl. Getting to any destination too quickly wasn't part of the action.

"I suppose you're curious about my having you followed tonight," the Egyptian began conversationally.

"Under the circumstances I think I should be grateful."

"My dear fellow! Think nothing of it! I'm sure you would have done as much for me. Besides, I owe you an apology—I couldn't think what there was to interest you in the Ryle Foundation. But there obviously is something, that's quite clear."

Razzak was evidently prepared to be disingenuous. But it was a game two could play.

"You owe me an apology for the Van Pelt report, certainly."

"The Van Pelt—?" Razzak began to laugh. "Yes, that was rather naughty I must admit. The Van Pelt report—quite unforgiveable!"

The hands across the stomach shook as he laughed. 'Naughty', with its nursery and pansy connotations, struck Roskill as both inadequate and out of place in Razzak's excellent vocabulary. Unless—a second thought arrived almost simultaneously—unless it was literally accurate: that saying of Chairman Mao's hadn't struck quite true either.

So the inconvenient report had simply been a figment of Razzak's imagination—a mere joke at Roskill's expense, damn the man!

"And you really don't think there's anything to interest us in the Ryle?"

"Not nothing of interest, Squadron Leader, but nothing to interest *you*. I thought weapons and guidance systems were your specialities, not—" Razzak paused momentarily "—countersubversion. I thought that was the Special Branch's job."

He sounded perfectly matter-of-fact and only mildly curious. Far too mild and matter-of-fact to be true: they both knew that this was the opening bid.

"You know about the Foundation then?"

"My dear fellow—I know it's being used by someone, if that's what you mean. You don't think I'd be interested in good works for their own sake, surely?"

"And who would 'someone' be?"

"That would be telling, wouldn't it! Can you tell me what's happened to make it so interesting?"

"Is that the basis for an exchange, Colonel Razzak?"

"It could be."

Roskill thought furiously. Of all men, Razzak probably had most to offer and would give least. But even what he didn't give might be of interest. And after Bunnock Street it was possible that the Egyptian's role might not be quite what they had imagined...

"Didn't you know the heat was on?"

"The heat?"

"Someone—possibly your 'someone'—tried to kill one of our civil servants a couple of days ago. Didn't you know?"

"Civil servant?" Razzak sounded surprised.

"A rather top man. And you haven't heard?"

"I only got back from Paris this afternoon. Who was it?"

"A man called Llewelyn. I think you know him."

"*Llewelyn!*"

"Does that surprise you?"

Razzak didn't reply immediately. It looked very much as though the news had genuinely surprised him. And that, Roskill thought grimly, was significant in itself, because it hadn't surprised Llewelyn. Yet what seemed to have thrown the Egyptian was not the deed itself, but the target.

"Llewelyn!" Razzak muttered to himself. "The fools! The stupid, criminal fools!"

"Which fools do you mean?"

Razzak turned towards him. "You say they failed though? They didn't get Llewelyn?"

Roskill blessed the semi-darkness of the car which concealed the anger he felt burning his cheeks: *No, you bastard, they didn't get Llewelyn—they got Alan Jenkins. Is that what you want to hear?*

The flare of irrational rage died down, dowsed by the knowledge that it was dangerous—that hot emotional involvement was always to be avoided because it betrayed both men and judgement. Only cold, professional anger was permitted, and not too much of that.

Razzak had had one chance of incriminating himself. Now he could be given another.

"Oh, they missed him all right." Not too casually, now: that would spoil it. "They killed some poor devil of a technician who was checking out his car, though."

Again Razzak fell silent, giving away nothing this time.

"It was a bomb in the car?"

That was another good feel line. It would be worth finding out just what sort of job the Egyptian could make of throwing them off the scent of Hassan and on to that of the Israelis.

"They used TPDX."

Razzak whistled softly. "Ah—now I see why you were so quick off the mark back there at your car. It's tricky stuff, that TPDX—I don't blame you being nervous! A very little goes a long way."

"And you know who might use it?"

The Egyptian shrugged. "The Russians flew in a load of it to Amman a few months ago, the idiots. By now every fedayeen group between there and Mount Hermon has some. You aren't going to learn anything from that."

There was a note of exasperated contempt in Razzak's voice which embraced both the Russians and the fedayeen. And he was being damnably slow off the mark.

"And the Israelis?"

"The Israelis?" Razzak seemed mystified. "So what about them?"

"They've got some too."

"Got some?" Another shrug. "Probably they have—the thieving swine have got plenty of other people's property these days. You're not going to tell me—" he stared at Roskill in the flickering light of the passing shopfronts "—my dear Squadron Leader Roskill—you're not going to tell me the Israelis fixed that car?"

"It happens that Colonel Shapiro was damn well-placed to get it done."

"Shapiro?" Razzak exclaimed incredulously. "You must be joking!" He continued to stare at Roskill in evident disbelief. "But you're not, are you!"

"He had the opportunity," Roskill said defensively. This wasn't how the fat man was meant to react.

Razzak shook his head. "I think you're being less than frank with me. If Shapiro had the opportunity—if that's what you really believe—you can discount him. Whatever he is, he's not a fool. And if he wanted to do it he wouldn't make such a goddamn mess—it would be done properly while he was lying on the beach at Tel Aviv."

That familiar tune! It was reassuring to have Audley's assessment confirmed—but disconcerting to have the confirmation from this source.

Unless Razzak was on the level. Unless, unless, unless—there were too many snakes in this game, and not nearly enough ladders . . .

"Then if not Shapiro, who do you favour?"

There was a bump and the painful hiss of tires rubbed callously against the kerb. Roskill glimpsed the bulk of St. Paul's ahead.

"You weren't looking for Colonel Shapiro at the reception this evening, Roskill. Who were you looking out for?" Razzak turned the question back to Roskill.

"I thought we made a deal just now, Colonel. Who were *you* looking for?"

"I wasn't looking for anyone in particular. I was—how shall I put it—showing my face. Showing it where it isn't often seen. Showing it where I wished it to be seen."

Razzak paused, then touched Roskill's arm and pointed across the street. "Who do you see over there, just on the corner?"

"The policeman?"

"The policeman. He isn't doing anything. He's not hunting anyone. But if there are any criminals walking in the street they can see him, and he is saying to them 'I am here. I've got my eye on you. So don't try anything!' He doesn't have to say a word, but they can hear him just as well as if he shouted.

"And he is just an ordinary bobby. I am a lot more than an ordinary bobby, my friend. For those I wish to be seen by—I am a Scotland Yard chief of detectives."

"And who would that be?"

"The fools, Roskill—the fools! The ones who throw the grenades and shoot up school buses. The ones who try to play soldiers in the dark while it is safe and then run away before the sun rises. The ones who kill the wrong people at the wrong time."

"You don't approve of the liberation movement?"

"Liberation my arse!" Razzak snorted contemptuously. "They couldn't liberate the skin off a rice pudding. They can't even agree what they want to liberate for more than ten minutes, never mind how it's to be done."

He shook his head vehemently. "I know what you're thinking too—that we Egyptians aren't liberators either, because the Zionists have kicked *our* backsides three times since '47." Razzak pounded his knee. "But it doesn't matter how many times we get beaten by them—we are still their real enemy and they'll still have to come to terms with *us*. Not the Syrians or the Iraqis or the Jordanians—and not the Liberation Front."

"You don't rate guerrilla warfare at all?"

"When it works inside a country—yes! In Vietnam—or the way the Zionists fixed you British in Palestine. But not hit and run from across a border. And not by stupid terrorism in foreign countries—that just makes things worse for us. That's what ruined us in '67. The bloody Syrians called the tune, and we did all the dancing! *Next time* we're going to call the tune!"

And maybe they would at that, thought Roskill—with the Russians committed and the Americans weary of pulling chestnuts out of the fire. Llewelyn seemed to think there was a chance, anyway—even if Audley was as cynical as ever.

But that wouldn't extract payment for Alan—and by God someone was going to dance for that! The high bloody politicians could pursue their high bloody policies to their hearts' content. Only this once he had his own private score to settle.

"If you wanted to nip trouble in the bud, you've started too late, Colonel," he said harshly.

"But they didn't get Llewelyn."

"Not this time they didn't."

"There won't be a next time, Squadron Leader. I'll see to that."

"No good. This isn't the Gaza Strip, and they don't get one free shot here. We want these chaps, Colonel—and if you won't give 'em to us we're going to get them ourselves, no matter who they are. Whatever you may hear, that's how it's going to be."

"I see." Razzak considered Roskill's angry words in silence for a moment. "Well, I can tell you this, Squadron Leader: there is a—a new group that may be mixed up with the Ryle Foundation. I didn't know they had reached London, but if they have this might be their work. If you can hold off for forty-eight hours I could probably pinpoint them. But you must hold off."

"Hold off?"

"That's right. Do nothing—and whatever you do, don't phone me at the embassy, or I shall have someone like Majid breathing down my neck and getting in the way. You can phone Jahein at his flat—he can stay home and watch television—he'll either have a message, or he'll know how to get to me." He fished a crumpled envelope from his pocket and laboriously wrote a number on it. "Phone him there. But whatever you do, don't start stirring things up in the wrong places."

Roskill took the envelope. Either Razzak had been scared into making a genuine offer, or he was simply trying to buy time.

"And just what are the wrong places?"

Razzak looked at him steadily. "The Ryle Foundation for a start. And I don't want the Israelis breathing down my neck either—don't start chasing them. It's bad enough having to put up with Majid."

"That's asking one hell of a lot, Colonel—you're asking me to sit twiddling my thumbs. I'm not sure I can do that without knowing exactly what you are supposed to be doing."

The Egyptian took a deep breath. "Does the name Hassan mean anything to you?"

Roskill cocked his head—it had to be the right note of interest now, with no hint of the surprise which tightened his guts.

"Hassan who?"

"Hassan will do for now—it doesn't matter whether it's a real man or just a murderous bloody-minded idea. But that's what I'm after, Roskill—that's what I'm after."

"And if you find him you'll give him to us."

"Give him to you?" Razzak growled. "If I find him, you can rely on that. And just you make sure of him, by God. Because if it was Hassan who bombed Llewelyn's car and he finds me sniffing around, he'll put my name to the top of his list!"

IX

HOWE HAD GONE off duty when Roskill finally got through to the department again; a much younger voice answered him, making no trouble—as Howe undoubtedly would have done—when he asked to be put straight through to the technical section stand-by man.

He had toyed with the idea of asking for further details about Razzak, until he remembered what Audley had said earlier: it was vital that Llewelyn should be kept in the dark about what they were doing, and any official request they made would go straight back to him.

So the bugger of it was that they were thus effectively cut off from their own information services and thrown back on their own resources. Which was fine for Audley, but rendered Roskill himself almost powerless—and, damn it, that might well be just what Audley was counting on!

Even calling the technical section was a risk, but it was one risk that had to be taken. The Triumph was probably safe enough in Bunnock Street—it always had been in the past. But if any hopeful car thief tried his hand on it the results might be catastrophic. And *that* was the risk that could not be taken.

Roskill sighed. At least the car was a loose end that could be tied up, a tangible object that could be tested and made to produce facts. It belonged to the world he understood, not to Audley's world of possibilities and theories and hypotheses.

There was a soft Highland voice on the other end of the phone. So Alan's senior partner, Maitland, was no longer on duty; it was a cold, sad thought that by routine it should have been Alan himself who answered him now.

"You've a little trouble with your car?" The man softly rolled each 'r': it was a comforting, competent sound—the sound of the ever-reliable Scot, resigned to getting the English out of trouble.

Roskill explained the Bunnock Street nightmare as simply as he could.

"That was verra smart of you, sir."

"It was lucky, certainly."

"Aye, lucky too," the Scot conceded. "And that would be a two-year-old car of yours?"

"Three-year-old, actually. How do you know?"

"The new Triumph has a steering lock—it would be a verra difficult car to move, and you say they didn't have much time."

"I don't quite see why they had to move it at all."

"Well, it depends on what they've done to it. But likely they preferred to work in a more private place. It's surprising how much people notice. But no matter—it's enough to know that they moved it and we shan't be wasting our time."

Roskill cleared his throat. The Scot would be wondering why he'd insisted on getting through to him directly when a message would have served well enough.

"I think I ought to warn you—" he began awkwardly. "I feel I must warn you personally that there could be a connection between my car and—the car that killed Alan Jenkins. There may not be, but there could be."

There was a pause at the other end of the line.

"Thank you, sir. I had that in mind, verra much in mind.

I'll not forget it—and you'll have your car back in one piece as well, never fear."

The smell that greeted him as he entered Shabtai's took him directly back to the mess tent under the netting beyond the baking runway where the Israeli Skyhawks had been poised: a Jewish cooking smell that was strange rather than exotic, and exciting as everything on that airstrip had been exciting.

He pushed through a curtain of beads—there was no other way to go—and came to the head of an ancient wrought iron spiral staircase which looked as though it had been extracted from some Victorian garden. Below him was a brick-arched cellar, with dim lights and crowded tables and a hubbub of conversation. There was a smoke haze and a whole range of further smells, each of which seemed to predominate at a different level as he descended the staircase, like the strata in an exposed cliff face.

As he reached the bottom step a girl started to sing in the furthest corner. She sang loudly and uninhibitedly, unaccompanied except by rhythmic clapping from people at the tables nearest her. Presumably she was singing in Yiddish, but Roskill couldn't make out the words anyway—it was the sort of singing that always embarrassed him because it seemed to insist on audience participation.

He stopped a perspiring waiter and inquired for Jake Shapiro. The man grinned and nodded, pointing to the far corner opposite the singer.

He threaded his way between the jammed tables. In a purely British establishment—at least one with a widely mixed collection of age groups like this—his passage would have been marked by blank looks and murmured apologies on both sides; but here he was received with smiles and left with the impression that he would have been welcome at most of the tables he disrupted.

Audley was wrong, he thought. Caricature or not, Shabtai's atmosphere was genuine. Or perhaps it was simply that Audley was a born loner who couldn't take crowds of people in any form except between the covers of a book, so that his judgement betrayed him in their presence. It would be the idea of Israel, not the Israelis in the flesh, which would attract him.

"Colonel Shapiro."

His vision had adjusted to the dimness, but there was no mistaking the man anyway: the bushy, ragged Stalin moustache and the broad, heavy shoulders—where Razzak was deceptively fat there was nothing deceptive about this hard-muscled bulkiness. It reminded Roskill of one of his father's prize bulls, amiable but unsafe.

Shapiro looked up at him—a confident, unhurried look. The mouth was hidden in the moustache's shadow, but the complex of lines on each side of it suggested that he was smiling.

"Ah! I wondered who it would be." Shapiro set down the heavy pewter tankard he'd been nursing and brushed back the lick of black hair from his forehead. "Roskill, isn't it? One of Sir Frederick's band of brothers? We met at poor old David's nuptials—you were one of the zoot-suited ushers, weren't you?" He gestured with a large, hairy hand. "Take a seat, Squadron Leader, take a seat!"

"It's nice to be expected," Roskill drawled. "I was afraid I might be disturbing a private party."

"Not at all! Any friend of old David's is welcome—even on business. You must have some of my beer, now you're here." Shapiro raised his tankard in one hand and snapped his fingers at a waiter. "I've got my own little barrel—special strong ale, a firkin of it. Not a bit like the pressurised nat's water they flog everywhere now—a *real* beer, this is."

He drank deeply.

"To be honest, I didn't expect *you*, though, Roskill. One of the SBs like Cooper or Cox, I thought it'd be—or if Sir Frederick was in on it, maybe Jack Butler. I thought you were strictly airborne these days—in fact, you've just been over to pick old Hod's brains, haven't you?"

"A flying visit—yes," Roskill said carefully. "Your chaps were very hospitable."

"You asked a lot of sharp questions, so I hear. The feeling

is that you got more than you gave." Shapiro wagged a finger. "I shall have to look out now, shan't I!"

Roskill grinned at the incongruous idea of anyone outsmarting an alerted Shapiro. That, as 'old' David was fond of saying, would be the day!

"But you have been expecting someone?"

"Someone was asking for me this afternoon, I'm told. And I've been waiting for something to happen ever since I heard about Llewelyn's car." Shapiro gazed frankly at Roskill. "I suppose you already know I was dining with him that evening?"

So much for security . . .

"You've got good hearing. Colonel Razzak doesn't seem to have heard so quickly."

Shapiro shrugged. "It's my job—and you can't blame me if Razzak isn't up to his. But that's hardly fair to the poor bugger—he's been enjoying a dirty mid-week in Paris, hasn't he. Is he back yet?"

Roskill watched their waiter maneuver his way towards them bearing a tall glass jug of beer and another tankard. He set the tankard before Roskill, filling it exactly with one graceful, practised movement, and then did the same for Shapiro's without bothering to find out whether it was empty. Presumably it was more often empty than not.

"There now!" said Shapiro with a growl of satisfaction. "You'll not find a better beer than that in London—it's as near as you'll get to the old London strong ale. Man I get it from swears it's all in the fining and filtering and dry-hopping, but I think it's just got more malt and less water. All the rest of it's bullshit."

Good beer it might be, Roskill reflected unhappily, but on an empty stomach lined with whisky it was likely to be disastrous. Yet the laws of hospitality and the honour of Britain demanded that it should be drunk, and drunk properly. 'Open your throat and pour it down' had been the first boozing rule he'd learnt: there was nothing he could do but obey the rule.

He took the tankard, opened his throat and poured it down

in. Surprisingly, it descended very easily—smooth, heavy and only moderately cool.

"Bravo!" Shapiro regarded him with enthusiasm. "The same again?"

"With what I've had already tonight I think that'll do very well. I shan't be fit to drive—" Roskill stopped in mid-sentence, sobered by the thought that as of the moment he had no car; for the time being it was the dangerous property of the soft-voiced Scotsman.

"Ah! The breathalyser!" Shapiro nodded regretfully. "I never use a car in London, and I forget that some people still do. You should use public transport, my friend—it's like they say on the posters: car free, carefree. There are too many cars in London anyway."

"So one blown up here and there doesn't matter?"

Shapiro stared in silence at the check tablecloth in front of him. When he raised his eyes to meet Roskill's, there was no longer any amusement in them.

"Now that was a bad business—a sad business," he said heavily. "Not the car—the car is nothing. But you lost a man, didn't you?"

"A good man."

"All men are good when you lose them. We know that in Israel better than most, because we can't afford to lose any-one. There are too few of us as it is."

"Then you'll understand that we want to know why we lost him."

Shapiro raised his eyebrows expressively. "Doesn't Llew-elyn know?" He paused, and then went on, nodding to him-self. "Obviously he doesn't know, so because I was having dinner with him he thinks I might have set up the whole thing—is that it? Does he think that? Do *you* think that?"

"I think—" said Roskill slowly, searching for the right answer, and finding it in Audley's own words "—I think it's not quite your style."

"My style?" Shapiro smiled a rather sad, twisted smile. "There's no style in killing. You either do it, or you don't do it. But I'm glad you don't think I did it. You see, I haven't any reason for killing Llewelyn. I don't like him and he doesn't like me. But he's working for peace in the Middle East, and frankly I'd rather have any sort of peace, on almost any terms, than what we've got now."

It sounded an honest answer, thought Roskill. It was just a pity that it wasn't an answer to the real question. But the time to put that one had not yet arrived.

"So if it wasn't me, who was it? Is that what I'm supposed to tell you?" Shapiro grinned again, some of his good humor returning. "I'm sure you didn't come slumming down here just to put my little mind at ease."

"I did rather think you might be able to tell me about Muhammad Razzak, for a start," said Roskill.

"Razzak?" Shapiro frowned. "You don't mean to tell me that old Razzak's a suspect? I doubt whether he knows Llewelyn from the Earl of Snowdon. He's a soldier, not a terrorist, anyway."

"Plenty of soldiers have changed their jobs, Colonel Shapiro. Like you, for instance."

"Huh! Like you too, Squadron Leader," Shapiro murmured ironically. "And I don't doubt we shall both live to regret it. But Razzak's been in Paris—is that supposed to be a suspicious alibi?"

What was downright odd, if not suspicious, was that these two old enemies each discounted the other's guilt. At the very least, and whatever they might think privately, they ought to be doing each other as much mischief as they could.

"Being in Paris doesn't clear him any more than being on the spot makes an assassin of you, Colonel. You've both got dogs to do your barking for you."

"And you think Razzak may have loosed his dogs?"

"I think I don't share your low opinion of Colonel Razzak. And I don't really know what his style is."

Shapiro waved his hand impatiently. "Style—I tell you, that's a lot of balls. I *know* the man, and I tell you he's not—"

He broke off abruptly as the waiter materialised in front

of them, beer jug at the ready. Roskill reached forward to cover his empty tankard with his hand, but this time the man spoke instead of pouring.

"Phone in the back room for you, Jake," he said familiarly, indicating the back room's direction with his thumb. "Urgent."

"It's always bloody urgent," Shapiro complained. "Thanks, Shabby. Look after my friend."

Before Roskill could protest, a slender stream of beer frothed into his tankard. Shapiro eased himself out from behind the table, but turned back towards him before he had taken two steps. He looked down at Roskill.

"You're way off target about Razzak—and me. I don't have a low opinion of him at all. For a Gyppo he's quite a guy—he's quite a guy by any standard. You wait till I get back."

Roskill watched him bulldoze across the room. Everyone seemed to know him and on his triumphal progress towards the back room he contrived to kiss the two prettiest girls along the way. They appeared to enjoy it, too.

The waiter smiled at Roskill and shook his head. "That Jake—he's a bad man," he confided happily. "I am glad my girls are out of his reach, safe at home."

He filled Shapiro's tankard—Roskill hadn't seen it being emptied, but empty again it undoubtedly was. "Say—do you want something to eat? The egg and aubergine's special tonight—or the stuffed tomatoes, maybe? On the house, anything you want, yes?"

Roskill was torn between hunger and a faint queasiness deep down which told him that he'd already drunk well but not too wisely on an empty stomach.

"Cottage cheese fritters—or if you're not really hungry, maybe a slice of honeycake?"

The mention of fritters and honeycake reinforced the shrinking feeling. In any case, if he started to eat now the night would develop into a carouse, and the morning after would be a purgatory when the clearest of heads was required.

He shook his head with feigned regret. "It's tempting, but I've already eaten."

"Well, if you change your mind, just sing out."

Roskill stared down into his beer and tried to concentrate. For whatever reason, Razzak and Shapiro were each concerned to make no trouble for the other. And Razzak had even offered to get him information about Hassan. So perhaps Shapiro could be prevailed on to make an even better offer.

And yet Hassan, who was everyone's bogeyman, was still a completely nebulous figure. There was absolutely nothing concrete so far to link him with East Firle, and consequently with Alan Jenkins. It was Razzak and Shapiro who were surely involved there—the bastards *were* involved somehow, no matter how clean the bills of health they advertised for each other.

He nodded his head angrily. As usual, everyone was giving everyone else the runaround, and he couldn't even think straight any more with the liquor and the noise and the heat.

He picked up his tankard, glanced around to make sure no one was watching him, and then quickly tipped most of it among the bright plastic blossoms arranged in a long display box on his right. If it was as good as Shapiro said it might bring them to life; at least it couldn't do them any harm.

He was only just in time, for a moment later the Israeli loomed up in front of him just as he was ostentatiously draining the last swallow of beer.

"Sorry about that, Roskill—my date got hung up at the hospital. She loves her work far more than me, that's the trouble. But she'll be here any minute now."

"Then perhaps I'd better be pushing along."

"Before you've got what you wanted? Man—don't be silly. Besides, Rosie Halprin could tell you a thing or two about Muhammed Razzak. After we took him apart she put him together again, back in '67."

"Put him together again?"

Shapiro drank, lowered his tankard and carefully wiped the froth from his moustache.

"How much do you know about Razzak's little war?"

"He was a hero of some sort, wasn't he?"

Shapiro shook his head. "Not the half of it, friend—not the half of it. He was a special sort of old-fashioned, cold-blooded hero."

He stared out into the smokey room, and then back at Roskill.

"You know what happened in Sinai? The first two days were the fighting days—the third day was Grand National Day. There was nothing wrong with their defences, they had perfectly good Russian linear system positions. It's just that the Russians would have smacked us with counter-attacks once we were through the forward lines, and the Egyptians didn't do a damn thing—there weren't more than a couple of attempts at counter-attacking.

"On the second night I was picking up strays—tanks we reckoned we could put right quickly enough for the other fronts if we needed them. It was all over the bar the shouting, the odd mishap.

"And then I got a call that someone was hitting the junction of the roads from Abu Agheila and Bir Lahfan, just south-west of Jebl Libni—there'd been some sniping there earlier, but this was kind of determined. And inconvenient, because next day we were going flat out for the Canal, as I say.

"But I had a few patched-up Centurions with me, and we picked up a few more en route, and we sorted it out. And that's where we took Razzak."

"You mean Razzak organized a counter-attack?"

"It wasn't much of a counter-attack—more a forlorn hope. He'd scratched together a handful of T 54s and one or two SU 100 tank-destroyers, and there were some infantry and engineers on the run from Abu Agheila he'd cobbled together. But that wasn't the point—the point was how he'd got there."

Shapiro paused. "I pieced some of it together from a talkative lieutenant we picked up with Razzak, and some of it afterwards. It's quite a story—quite a story..."

"I thought Razzak commanded a tank unit on the frontier?" That had been what Audley had said.

"He did—in their 7th Division forward area. But he wasn't there when we attacked on June 5th—he was in Cairo having his balls chewed up for defeatism!"

The Israeli showed his teeth in a wolfish smile that had no honour in it.

"Razzak's no fool. He reckoned we were coming, and he sent back a report saying that they ought to pull all their armour back from the frontier and dig in deep round the places that really mattered—like El Arish. Leave the Gaza strip to fend for itself, he said apparently.

"Hell—I'm not going to give you a lecture on his tactics! We would have licked 'em anyway, but it wouldn't have been a walkover and we'd have lost even more good men than we did.

"But as it was, they didn't like it and they had him back in Cairo on the Sunday to tell him so in no uncertain terms. And he got up early on the Monday morning to hitch a lift in a light plane back to one of the forward strips. Not quite early enough, though—the field he was taking off from was one of our priority strikes.

"So the poor old sod was grounded two hundred miles from where his command was getting pasted—the sort of situation every commander has nightmares about!"

"But he did get to his regiment?"

Shapiro shook his head. "His unit was mincemeat before he even reached the desert, and I don't doubt he knew it would be. No—when most of the regimental brass was heading for home, old Razzak was just steering for the sound of the guns. He knew damn well what would be happening—he knew what our air strike meant because he'd seen it himself. He set out simply to try to hold us up somewhere so that some of the army could escape as it did in '56—he didn't reckon anyone else was going to do it.

"God alone knows how he managed to get as far as he did. A Fouga strafed his staff car sometime that first day and creased him a bit—but he just went on walking until he met another car coming in the opposite direction, making a break for it. He took that one at gunpoint—left a brigadier standing by the roadside in the middle of nowhere. And when that ran out of fuel he just went on walking.

A special sort of old-fashioned hero indeed—the paunchy, pockmarked sort, obstinately trying to salvage something from the ruin achieved by the fools and the loudmouths...

"He never had a chance, of course. If he'd reached the front that first night he might have knocked some sense into someone, but I doubt it. The second night was too late—it was just a gesture, that's all. But it was quite a gesture: you know what he said when we finally picked him up?—which was when he'd fired off everything he'd got, I can tell you."

"What did he say?"

"He'd been hit several times, actually. He was a real mess by then. But he just lifted up his hand and said—in English, too, he said it—he said: 'You've shot my bloody trigger finger off—look what you've done!' Cheeky old sod!"

Shapiro wagged his own trigger finger at Roskill. "And that's the man you're suggesting had a bomb plugged into Llewelyn's car! Friend, I'm not a great admirer of Egyptians in general, but I'd stake my last shekel that Razzak wasn't in on it. That handsome side-kick of his—Majid, is it?—*he* might do it if he had the know-how. But not Razzak. If that's what you mean by style, then it's not his style. With him it'd be face-to-face or not at all."

He spoke with a sudden passion which was not really out of character; some of the biggest comedians became like this the moment they stopped playing to the gallery, and there had never been any question that Shapiro was a hard man under his clowning.

What was out of character was not only that he was going out of his way to give Razzak an unsolicited testimonial, but that he now seemed inclined towards Audley's contention that there could be any recognizable style in killing.

But Razzak's self-sacrificial tactics in Sinai certainly didn't prove that he was incapable of removing opponents by any available means. It almost suggested the very opposite—that under the layers of fat lay an iron determination unshaken by odds, difficulty and danger.

"Do you get my point?" said Shapiro.

"I'm not at all sure that I do, no," said Roskill slowly. Perhaps it was the opposite point the crafty sod intended—to damn the Egyptian with praise. "But I think your admiration for Colonel Razzak is—touching—to say the least."

Shapiro grimaced. "Ah! The authentic supercilious voice of England—the lesser breeds shall not show unfitting qualities of sportsmanship towards each other! I do beg your pardon, Squadron Leader. But it isn't simply admiration, I assure you. I *know* Razzak, that's all I was attempting to show in my clumsy way. I don't underrate him, but I know how his mind works. That was what you wanted to know, wasn't it?"

"You think we should look elsewhere?"

"I'm quite sure you'd be wasting your time on Razzak." Shapiro gazed at Roskill quizzically. "Does it surprise you—my advice?"

Roskill nodded. "It does rather."

"I ought to be stirring things up, eh?" Shapiro grinned. "If I thought he could be properly saddled with it I might be tempted. Then again, I might not—there's no real percentage in playing 'Wolf, Wolf'. It weakens one's credibility."

He leaned forward towards Roskill. "You're wondering why I'm being so nice to old Razzak—and helpful to you. But to be honest I wouldn't cross the road for either of you, any more than you'd cross it for me. But look at it from my point of view, friend—*I* know I didn't do it and I don't reckon Razzak did. But I know some dimwitted Arab did, and it'd suit me fine to see you nail him—and if it suits me I'll see he gets plenty of publicity when the time comes."

"Not with a D Notice, you won't."

"D Notice?" Shapiro blew a derisive raspberry. "No D Notices in the States—or in Europe. They lap up D Notices, in fact—makes 'em see the fire under the smoke. And with my contacts in the Commons I'll make your D Notice look pretty sick, too. If you get your man I just can't lose—that's the way I see it."

That was the way Roskill was seeing it too—and seeing it very clearly. The newspapers had got very fair mileage out of the bomb explosion at the Zim office in Regent Street and the Marks and Spencer's fires the year before—and even from the crazy plan to kidnap Clore and Sieff. And the air liner bombs had been a far greater disaster for the Arab cause. But an act of terrorism directed against a foreign, non-Jewish Government official would unite official opinion against the Arab cause more surely than any of these crimes.

Except that the killers hadn't been after Llewelyn at all; he kept almost forgetting what only he and Audley—and the killers—knew: that this was no deliberate act of misconceived policy, but something much simpler—the hurried elimination of a witness.

But a witness to what?

He met Shapiro's eyes. The agonizing thing was that even if the man didn't know who the killers·were, he might very well know why they had acted. And that was the one question that couldn't yet be asked of him.

Shapiro evidently misunderstood his expression; he shook his head sadly.

"I'm sorry you had to lose a good man to give me this on a plate, Roskill. It's a bloody waste, that's what it is—like this whole rotten situation we're in. Nobody gains, not us and not the Egyptians, and not those poor devils in the camps across the Jordon."

"Only the Russians."

"Them?" Shapiro waved a hand. "Not them either— you wait and see. The Arabs hate their guts."

That was what Audley was always saying. In the long run meddlers in the Middle East only found trouble as the reward for their pains.

"So Razzak says you're innocent, and you say Razzak's

whiter than snow," said Roskill softly. "But if not either of you, then who?"

"Does old Razzak say that? That's white of him!" Shapiro brushed his moustache thoughtfully. "Well, I would say the only good reason for knocking off Llewelyn would be if he was the kingpin of the cease-fire negotiations—which he most certainly isn't. But of course he may *think* he is, in which case somebody may believe him . . . so we want someone dotty enough to believe it and fanatic enough to kill . . ."

"With TPDX."

"Indeed?" Shapiro raised his eyebrows. "Then we want someone who knows his way round explosives too."

"It's as tricky as that, is it?"

"Not tricky—just powerful. If you only lost one man, then they only used a very little of it. A beginner would have used too much and blown up the whole block." He began to count off his fingers. "Not official Fatah—they're down on foreign jobs after the last mess-up. Not Saiqa—their London man's hot on good public relations at the moment." He stopped, frowning. "Of course they could have hired some freelance white talent—there's enough money floating around to tempt some of the bad hats. They wouldn't like doing it, any of the groups. It would make 'em feel reactionary and inadequate. But for a once-only job they might stretch a point . . ." He stopped again, gazing into space. "On the whole I don't think so, though. If it ever leaked out there'd be tremendous loss of face. Besides, with all the training Moscow's been giving, there must be plenty of them around who know how to handle the stuff . . . So where does that get us?"

He looked at Roskill. "There's the Chinese-orientated wing of the PFLP that's never been brought into the fold. But they wouldn't know about Llewelyn, and if they did they probably wouldn't be interested in him. So not them either, I reckon." He grinned. "Don't rush me, though. We'll get ourselves a short list in the end, never fear."

If he was going to work his way painstakingly through the possibilities it might be hours before he reached the vital one, and he might never reach it at all. There was no real point in prolonging this process of elimination, anyway.

"How about Hassan?"

Shapiro looked at him quickly, like a teacher faced with a suspiciously sharp question.

Then he nodded to himself slowly—the teacher smugly satisfied that he had seen right through the question and the questioner to the instigators.

"So that's what it's all about, then!" he murmured, still more to himself than to Roskill. "Hassan's really got off the ground at last!" He whistled softly. "That's a thought to conjure with, and no mistake. We shall all have to fasten our safety belts now, shan't we?"

"You know about Hassan?"

"Know about him? My friend, until you just mentioned him I hoped he was only a nasty rumour. But if you British are worried about him, then I'm worried about him too!"

"What *do* you know about him?"

"Very little. I tell you, I thought he was only a crazy rumour," Shapiro spread his hands.

"We don't think he is."

"Indeed?" The Israeli looked directly into Roskill's eyes. "Well, in that case I should move very carefully, Squadron Leader. Very carefully and slowly. What did Razzak have to say about him?"

"He said very much the same thing, Colonel Shapiro."

"Then for once I agree with him. He's giving you good advice."

One thing was certain now: neither Razzak nor Shapiro wanted trouble. And as the threat of trouble had moved the Egyptian to offer a deal, it might serve equally well to get something out of the Israeli . . .

"That's one thing we can't do, I'm afraid. This time we're not going to take things lying down." Roskill fumbled for the right formula. "Llewelyn may not be as important as he thinks he is, but he still pulls a lot of weight. So if you can't give me a line on Hassan, we're going to have to take this city apart hunting for him."

He carefully kept his voice casual. Even as it was it sounded bloody thin—all Shapiro had to do was to tell him to go ahead and do his worst. The Israelis had nothing to lose—and the proof of that sat across the table: while Razzak had been seeking him out, Shapiro had been boozing contentedly!

The Israeli sat silent for a moment, doodling with a fingernail on the tablecloth. Finally he looked up again at Roskill, a conspiratorial glint in his eye.

"Very well . . . then if you want to play it the hard way I'll tell you what I'd do if I were you"—the finger wagged at Roskill—"I'd have a word with David Audley, that's what I'd do."

"David—!" Roskill had no need to feign surprise. "But David isn't even in the Middle Eastern section now."

"You don't need to tell *me* that!" Shapiro gave a short, bitter laugh. "But in or out, he's still the best man you've got—and you're a friend of his. He's not in quarantine, is he?"

Roskill frowned. The best man—maybe; but this hadn't been in the best man's calculations!

"Look, Roskill"—the finger pointed at him like a pistol—"you don't want to go at this half-arsed. You need someone who can calculate the angles. You go to David, and tell him I sent you. Tell him about Hassan—and Llewelyn. And tell him that what's scaring the pants off everyone is the Alamut List."

"The Alamut List?"

Shapiro nodded. "Alamut. He'll know exactly what it means when he hears it—in fact, he'll probably know better than any of us!"

X

E AST FIRLE WAS its eternal, unquestioning self, tucked comfortably in the shadow of Beacon Hill.

As Roskill steered the hired MG carefully round its blind corners he felt unreality pressing in on him. It was impossible to relate feuding Arabs and Jews to privet hedges and japonica; outside the pub only four years since—a lifetime's four years—he had sat with Harry and an old man who had spent his working life making wagon wheels. They had talked for an hour about the war, and it had been fifteen minutes before he had realised that the war the wheelwright was remembering was the Kaiser's, not Hitler's.

It might just as well have been Napoleon's, when the old chap's grandfather had probably done his duty with the other beacon watchers on the hill, serving his turn beside the great pile of furze and pitch and damp hay, waiting for the French as other lads had once waited for the Spaniards and the Normans and God knows how many other invaders down the ages. The past still ran deep and strong in East Firle; it was the present that was blurred.

Unchanged, it was all unchanged. Even the immense wooden gates were still immovably open for him at the bottom of the Old Vicarage drive, decrepit, but too expensive to replace four years ago and now far beyond a widow's pension. The tattered white paint had flaked a bit more perhaps, and the straggling lilac thicket behind had grown wilder. But it was the same old place exactly, run down yet welcoming.

The neat electric button on the front door buzzed confidently, though. That would be some of Alan's work; in the old days the house had always been full of his electrical enthusiasm, from shaving points in unlikely places to a complete internal telephone system, all beautifully installed—to the chagrin of visiting electricity board experts.

"Who is it?"

The disembodied voice caught him by surprise, coming from just above his head.

"Speak into the mike above you," said the voice—a young female voice, apparently rather weary of explaining to idiot callers how they could communicate with her.

Roskill stared up at the apparatus. More of Alan's work. It was skillfully done, too. Made to last—and it would probably outlive the family's tenure of the house, to become a curiosity for future occupants: Alan's memorial.

"Speak into the mike over your head," the young voice commanded him sharply. "Who is it, please?"

"It's Hugh Roskill," he projected upwards.

"Hugh Roskill," repeated the voice, perplexed. "Hugh Rosk—*Uncle Hugh*! Good Lord—come on in, Hugh! The door's open and I'm coming down."

'Uncle Hugh' could only mean that it was the baby of the family, the unprogrammed late addition that had always mooned around in the background, clad in the hideous uniform of the English schoolgirl and hero-worshipping the godlike Harry from afar. Poor kid, the last four years had taken Harry and her father from her, and now Alan too.

He pushed open the door and walked hesitantly into the hall. It was bigger and barer than he had remembered, with no clutter of shoes and gumboots on the red polished tiles, carelessly hung coats and school scarves on the row of wooden pegs.

That was only to be expected, though: there were fewer wearers now, and those who were left were older and tidier. Only to be expected, but saddening. It was as though the house was dying round its occupants, and he, the killer, was returning to the scene of his crime.

"Hugh? It *is* Hugh, isn't it! I hardly recognized you in that beard—I didn't know the RAF allowed that sort of thing."

Gone the school uniform and the pony tail; instead a shockingly disreputable shirt and trousers and the long straight hair. Harry's little sister had become indistinguishable from the millions of nubile teenagers who had sprung up like buttercups and daisies in the last decade.

"I don't fly these days, so they don't really mind. Sorry to disappoint you, Penelope."

"But it doesn't—it doesn't at all! I think it looks madly *cinquecento* and sexy."

The beard, thought Roskill grimly, would have to come off, and the sooner the better. It had never occurred to him that little girls would find it sexy.

Penelope looked at him. "I suppose you've come down about Alan," she said. There was neither grief nor curiosity in her tone. It was a simple statement of fact.

"Something of the sort," he replied gently.

"Well, Mother's gone to Lewes to shop, but his room's open and you can poke around it if you like. I don't mind."

"Why should I want to poke around his room?"

She tossed the hair out of her eyes. "Well, it was all hush-hush, what he was doing—bugging people with his electronic things, I suppose. So we've been expecting someone to come down and sort out his what's-its." She regarded him with a trace of truculence. "Now that you don't fly, do you bug people too?"

It was the rebel generation, of course, and hardly to be wondered at. But in this house it was surprising somehow, nevertheless; and there would have been a pretty tug-of-war in her loyalties if Harry had been still alive.

"I don't bug anyone. Navigation's my line—radar and

that type of thing," he said neutrally. It wasn't the conversation for which he'd mentally prepared himself, and it made the sympathy on his tongue taste more than ever like hypocrisy. "I'm sorry about Alan, Penelope. It was rotten luck."

"Yes, it was." She paused. "Or I suppose it was, because they didn't tell us much about it, except that there was this explosion in the laboratory where he was working. Do you know what happened? Is that why you're here—to tell Mother all the ghoulish details?"

"I just happened to be passing by, actually. I don't know anything about the explosion."

"Oh." The flicker of interest faded. "Well, Mother won't be back for a couple of hours. She may not even be back for lunch if she meets up with anyone. Aunt Mary's in, naturally—you can go up and see her if you like."

Aunt Mary was in, naturally. Always in, or at least no further than her wheelchair could go. But it was nevertheless Aunt Mary he had come in to see, for she of all people saw almost everything and heard in the end what she had not seen. If there had been anything to see or hear around Firle that day, Aunt Mary was as good a bet as any for the information.

"I'll do that. I'd like to see her again."

"Okay then—just go straight up. She's in the end room, the usual one." She turned on her heel towards the kitchen. "I'm on lunch duty today, so I won't come with you. But you can have a bite with us if you like."

"I'll have to get on my way soon."

"Suit yourself."

She left him standing.

The room on the end—that had been Mary's ever since she had finally surrendered to the wheelchair. It was the best room in the house and the whole family had united to force her to accept it. They had united, too, to overcome its one disadvantage, labouring through one long, hot summer to build a miniature lift from the first floor to the ground floor. Not that there had been any shortage of volunteers; relays of guests and neighbors had willingly lent muscle-power and technical assistance—fifteen courses of the brickwork were Roskill's own: for everyone who knew Mary it had been a sad labour of love.

So the room had become her base rather than her prison, catching the sun the whole day to warm her and giving her a great sweep of landscape as well as the curve of the downland on which to focus the German naval telescope her father had brought back from the Zeebrugge raid.

If she had seen anything on *that*...

"It's Hugh!" She was awaiting him, already facing the door; she would have heard the distant murmur of voices and no visitor to the Old Vicarage ever left without visiting the end room.

He had forgotten how beautiful she was. There had been some old general—he had read a book about him way back—of whom it was said 'he made old age beautiful', and the same was true of Mary. Except that sixty years was not old and it was the crippling arthritis and the pain which had aged her, though without tarnishing that beauty. Isobel would age like that, exactly.

She held out her hands to him. "It's been such a long time, Hugh—far too long. We've missed you."

It wasn't a complaint; somehow it implied that the fault was hers, not his, and that she wanted to make it up.

"Mary..." He took the cold, twisted hands.

"It *is* good to see you, Hugh!"

Her unashamed pleasure cut deep into him. This was the darkest treachery: *dearest Mary, I haven't come here to see your eyes light up. I've come to ask you what they saw up there on the hill. Did you see anything, Mary? Did you? And did Alan tell you anything?*

"It's good to see you too, Mary darling."

The truth, but what an empty, guilty truth it was!

"I hadn't the heart to come after Harry was killed," he heard his voice say in the distance. "I think—I somehow felt I was to blame. It ought to have been me that time."

"What a very silly thing to think!" She underlined the word 'silly'; for Mary silliness was the venial sin and only wickedness carried a heavy penance. "And Harry would be the first to tell you so. You were each promoted, and you weren't to blame for that."

"It wasn't quite as simple as that, Mary." He could hear himself still, as though he was listening to a tape. "I didn't take that promotion because I really wanted it—I took it because I was losing my nerve. I could feel it running out of my boots every time I flew."

It sounded strange, blurted out just like that, unasked, the thing he'd kept hidden from everyone but Isobel. And he'd never intended to share it with anyone else, either. Yet telling it to Mary now seemed perfectly natural—it was the curious effect Mary's charisma had on everyone, from the milkman to the vicar. She had never sought confidences, they simply tumbled out in her presence.

Perhaps that was really why he had never returned to East Firle: it was too easy to talk to Mary.

"Hugh! Now that's the silliest thing of all! If you felt like that, then you were right to do what you did, not wicked. If you hadn't you might have killed someone else as well as yourself. But you certainly didn't harm Harry."

The plain facts in black and white, sensible and honest. But that wasn't how the scales of guilt were balanced: guilt was always the might-have-been that could never be out-weighed by good sense and honesty.

"Perhaps you're right, Mary."

"Of course I'm right. And it's all past and done with now—there's no sense in remembering bad things in the past unless they help to make the present better. And I'm sure your present doesn't need any helping." She patted his hand. "Are you happy, Hugh? And are you doing a useful job?"

Roskill smiled at her. Happiness and usefulness had always been Mary's criteria for the good life.

"I sometimes wonder whether what I do is useful, Mary. But it's certainly interesting enough."

She nodded, smiling at him. "And are you married yet?"

It was on the edge of his tongue to tell her: *no, Mary, not married. But I love a married woman seven years older than I am, with two sons at boarding school and a rich busy husband who doesn't give a damn provided she doesn't rock the boat. And what the hell am I to do about that, Mary? Just tell me what . . .*

But one slipped confidence was enough for one day.

"No, Mary—not yet, anyway." He smiled back at her. "And you—have you still got your finger on East Firle's pulse?"

"Shame on you, Hugh! You make me sound like a nosey old woman, and I hope I'm not that."

"Not at all. It's a sympathetic ear you have, not a nosey nose." He looked at her affectionately. No elaborate lies now, for she would see through them. And no excuses either, for she deserved better than that; if he couldn't trust Mary's good sense, there was no sense left in the world. "And I need your ear now, Mary."

For a moment she regarded him in silence, searching his face. And there was sadness in her own face now as she identified his purpose: he was no longer her special visitor, redeeming a long absence, but a duty caller like the meter reader and the postman, just doing his job.

"It's Alan, isn't it?"

"Yes."

She held his gaze steadily. "What is it you want to know about him?"

"He spent his last leave here." Roskill felt a muscle twitch in his cheek. If he'd ever wondered why one was never normally assigned to a job involving one's own friends and relatives, he had the answer in full now. "I want—we want to know what he did and where he went. And who he met, and anything he said or saw out of the ordinary."

He could see from the stricken look on her face that he'd bungled it ridiculously: he'd made Alan sound like Philby and Burgess and Maclean rolled into one, and the report of his accidental death transparently the offical lie that it was. How could he have been so clumsy?

"Alan hadn't done anything wrong, Mary. But we think he may have had some information for us—something important. And we don't know what it was. What I'm doing now, asking you these questions, is really just routine."

"But it was important?"

"It might be very important."

"Well, I'm surprised he didn't tell you."

It was an oddly stupid thing for someone as sharp as Mary to say. Unless the years really were beginning to tell.

"We never saw him, Mary. The accident was on Tuesday night. He wasn't due back on duty until the next day."

"I mean in his letter to you."

Letter?

"His letter?"

"Haven't you had it? He wrote it on Tuesday morning— he borrowed a fivepenny stamp off me for it. It had to be a fivepenny because he wanted it to go first class."

"To me?"

"He said it was to you. Because in return for the stamp he said he'd send my love. I thought that was why you were here—because of his letter. The Ice Maiden posted it from Lewes, to make sure of the London post."

"The Ice Maiden?"

"Sorry—it's the family name for Penny. And you haven't had it? That's really too bad of them, even though it is usually reliable."

A letter from Alan. So he had seen something, and knew he had seen it. Or at least wanted a second opinion on what he had seen—that made sense. For Alan had never sent him a letter before, but he was the most obvious contact for advice inside the department.

And a letter somewhere in the GPO pipeline, since it had so far reached neither the department nor the flat . . .

Mary swiveled her chair round and lifted the old-fashioned phone beside her.

"I'll just make sure Penny really did send it," she said. "I know she did go to Lewes that morning. But—Penny? That letter of Alan's on Tuesday, the one he wanted to get the next London post—did you take it in?"

She watched Roskill over the receiver, listening. "You didn't . . . you did *what*?" She frowned in puzzlement. "I think you'd better tell Hugh about that."

Roskill took the receiver from her.

"Penelope—what did you do with that letter?"

"Haven't you got it? Well, you can blame Alan's friend if you haven't. He was the one who posted it."

"Which friend was this?"

"Good Lord, I don't know. He turned up on the doorstep about twenty minutes after Alan disappeared in a cloud of blue smoke—he wanted Alan urgently, but I told him Alan had cleared off."

"You didn't tell him where Alan had gone?"

"I couldn't very well do that, because I didn't know— he'd just shifted his flat, but he went off in such a rush he forgot to tell us where his new one was. At least he didn't write it in the book, anyway, the clot."

"What did you tell him then?"

"I told him Alan would be back at work next day, so he'd have to make do with that."

Yes, they'd made do with that all right . . .

"And the letter? You gave him the letter?"

"The letter? That was just lying on the hall table—I was going to take it in to Lewes for him. I said to him—to Alan's friend—that the new address might be in there, but he said it'd be a bit much to open it because it was marked 'private'."

Roskill closed his eyes. The room seemed still and airless and close, but there was a chill down his back. She had killed him. She had killed him in innocence, but as surely as if she'd planted the TPDX with her own hands.

"Hullo, Hugh—are you still there?"

He blinked. "Yes, Penelope. So you gave it to him."

"Well, he said we shouldn't open it. But he was going

straight back to London and he'd post it there. So I gave it
to him, of course. I suppose the clot's forgotten all about it.
I'm sorry if it was important, but he seemed a sensible type."

A sensible type of killer, certainly. And lucky too.

"What was he like?"

"The friend—he was dishy. Dark hair and a super tan—
very Mediterranean. But dressed like a bank clerk, all grey
suit and striped shirt and cuff links, you know."

If it came to the pinch he could take her up to the gallery
in Records, but the fellow might not even be in them, not if
he was one of Hassan's men, and in any case was probably
long gone by now.

More immediately, Penelope had turned their suspicions
into fact. And not only fact, for she had given the killers the
solid motivation they had needed to take such risks and to
plan so elaborately: they had known what Alan had seen and
what he planned to do about it. So they had moved to elim-
inate not a risk, but a certainty.

"It wasn't an accident, was it?"

Mary was staring at him.

"An accident?"

"I'm not blind, Hugh. The look on your face a moment
ago—you looked as though someone had read your death
sentence. But it was Alan's, wasn't it—that letter the man
took away—it was Alan's."

The risk had been there from the start, that she would
suspect there was more to Alan's death than mere accident
the moment he started asking questions. But now she too had
more than suspicion on which to work.

"Hugh, I know very well that Alan worked for some branch
of security. I knew it because he never talked about his work,
when he always told me about everything else. But I didn't
know it was dangerous." She looked at Roskill questioningly,
almost pleadingly. "I accept you can't tell me *why*—if that's
your job, I do understand it, Hugh. But at least you can tell
me how he really died."

He said softly: "Does it matter, Mary?"

"It matters to me. Of all of them, Hugh, Alan was my special one. Betty was ill when he was little, and I practically brought him up." She paused. "I'm not bargaining—I'll tell you everything I know. But I'd—I'd feel better if I knew that he died to some purpose, and not because of a silly mistake he made in his work."

The rules said 'no'. The rules said he must always wear a double face and tell outsiders nothing more than was needed to make them co-operate. But the rules were not ends in themselves, just as the interest and security of the realm was not an end in itself.

So to Mary the rules must say 'yes', or go straight out of the window: her peace of mind was what it was all about.

"It wasn't an accident." He put his hand over hers. "It looked like an accident, but it wasn't. And I don't believe it had anything to do with his job, Mary. It wasn't a particularly dangerous job. But he saw something, or maybe heard something, while he was down here on leave, and he was killed before he could report it. And he didn't feel a thing—I promise you."

Mary remained silent for a moment.

"Thank you, Hugh," she said at length. "I'll never tell anyone what you've told me, not even Betty." She drew a deep breath. "And now you must ask me your questions—you want to know what Alan did on his leave."

"I think it's just that Tuesday morning that matters—the day he left. He left in a hurry, didn't he."

"In a frightful rush," Mary nodded. "He was going to go after lunch, but when he came back from the Beacon he'd changed his mind."

"He'd walked up to the Beacon?"

"He rode up on Sammy—Penny's horse. She's half his horse, actually. She was, I mean . . . He paid half Sammy's bills on condition he had first choice during his leaves. He always used to take Sammy out on the hills first thing in the morning. Then he used to spend the rest of the day pottering.

He was fixing up the two-way speaker in the porch this leave, so that I could answer the door from here when the family was out. I don't believe he went out anywhere else during the whole time he was here."

Like Harry, Alan had always used home for relaxation and family life: his London existence had been frenetic, and Firle was where he recharged his batteries.

"He rode up to the Beacon, then."

"He walked Sammy up the steeper parts—he liked to get to the top as quickly as possible. I used to watch him through the telescope—he'd wave when he reached the top."

"And you watched him on Tuesday."

She looked at him in despair. "Hugh, I didn't—not on Tuesday. I had a bad day on Tuesday—I try not to take the pills the doctor gives me. They make me woozy and I want to keep them for when I shall really need them. But I just had to take one that morning, and I didn't feel up to anything after that. I'm sorry."

Roskill couldn't hide his disappointment. It had been a black Tuesday indeed—not only because Alan had chosen to ride to the Beacon at that fatal moment in time, but because twice thereafter the chance of learning what he had seen had been lost.

"But you saw him when he came down."

"Only very briefly. I was resting and he only came to borrow a stamp, and then to say goodbye. He was always very considerate when I had a bad day, and I'm not very good company then."

"Did he say anything?"

"He said he was writing to you. He was excited, Hugh— he certainly wasn't frightened. I do remember asking him why he wasn't staying for lunch, because Penny was cutting the asparagus for him. But he just said 'The sooner I'm off, the better'—I think he said . . ."

Like Harry, Alan had a broad streak of ambition in him. And if he'd had some idea of what he'd seen, he might also have had an inkling that it might be dangerous as well as important. And that would account for the letter, and for his leaving it to Penelope to post, as well as for the quick getaway. It might even account for his not leaving his new address.

But it all added up to nothing new, except that what he'd seen had been on the Beacon itself—and that the only lead lay in Penelope's identifying the dishy young man.

He stared forlornly past the shining brass case of the telescope to the hillside beyond. But looking wouldn't turn the clock back four days to betray what had taken place up there, six hundred feet above him.

Yet the hill drew him. It was hard to imagine that Alan had unwittingly seen his death up there, if that had been how it had been. There was nothing up there but the birds wheeling and diving over the grassland. On warm, windy days the gliders joined the birds, and in summer there were wild strawberries—he'd picked them with Harry and had brought them down here to this very room.

He got up and began to move towards the window.

"Don't go near the window, Hugh," Mary said suddenly. "There's something else."

Roskill froze in mid-step.

"Go directly behind the telescope," Mary ordered him. "Now look through it at the Beacon."

Obediently he focused the telescope on the top of the hill. It was a splendid instrument, heavy yet moving smoothly and freely on its mounting. The hilltop came up sharply, every feature of it clear even though no direct sunlight came through the grey clouds above it. But there was nothing to see on it except the grass shivering in the wind.

"Come right along the skyline, away from the long barrow towards the tumuli—the tussock of grass on the right at the base of it. Do you see anything?"

As a fire order it left something to be desired: there were a whole series of mounds up there, most of which were not visible at this angle, or at least not visible to Roskill's eye except as slight irregularities in the grassland. Mary knew this landscape like the back of her hand and she could—

But there *was* something up there, snug down beside the trailing edge of one hump. And not something, but someone.

"Have you got him? Deerstalker hat and binoculars. I spotted him more than an hour ago, just after breakfast—it was the flash of the binoculars that gave him away. A bird-watcher I took him for."

A bird-watcher? Well, there were birds up there right enough.

"And I thought what a very silly bird-watcher he was."

"Silly?" Roskill turned his eye away from the hilltop towards her.

"He can't see much ground from there. The hill falls away too quickly in front of him. And even if he could see enough ground, the Beacon is the last place I'd go to bird-watch. Far too many people go tramping over it—quite enough to spoil it for him, anyway."

Roskill squinted through the eye-piece again. Deerstalker and binoculars, and the suggestion of a dark jacket.

He turned back to Mary again. "You think he's watching us?"

"I thought he was watching the house an hour ago, but I thought I was imagining it because I couldn't think why anyone would want to do that. But now—" she trailed off. "Now I don't know what to think."

No one had tailed him to Firle—the MG had seen to that. So whoever was watching up there had to be directly connected with Alan's death—and that meant Hassan.

He stared back up the hillside longingly now. So near, and yet so impossibly far! Ensconced up there, on the highest point for miles around and with tracks leading away in at least three directions, the bastard was laughing. He could see from afar who was coming, and could stay or go as he chose.

He shook his head in a mixture of resignation and frustration. It wasn't as if he could call up assistance, even if there was time to do so: the Firle trip was strictly off the record.

"You'd like to know who it is, wouldn't you, Hugh? To see whether it really is a bird-watcher?"

"I'd have to be a little bird to do it."

"Not necessarily."

Mary met his gaze, so she wasn't kidding him, evidently. Again he looked up towards the skyline. She could hardly envisage a breakneck cavalry charge by car; it wasn't that the MG couldn't do it—the West Firle approach was easy even for sedate family saloons, and the mile of trackway along the ridge was perfectly usable if the farm gates were unlocked. But he'd never get up close unnoticed: the watcher would have spotted the MG already.

"How, Mary?"

"Go straight up, of course—the way Alan used to."

The way Alan used to?

She swivelled the chair and propelled it into the shadow to the left of the curtains.

"Come here, Hugh, by my shoulder . . . That man up there, he thinks he can see everything, but he can't—he can't see what's right in front of his nose. Look—"

Roskill followed her pointing finger. Five, six years she'd been a prisoner of the chair, and for the years before that increasingly handicapped. But she was born and bred to this countryside, had walked and ridden it before he was born and knew every inch of it.

"—You go out of this house at the back past the stables and into the spinney. Then the hedge beyond is in full leaf now, and it hasn't been laid for years. After that there's the patch of woodland, and you come out just *there*." The finger stabbed decisively.

"And from where he is he can't possibly see you beyond those last trees, because the slope of the hillside in front of him blocks the view. There's the little path up the side of the hill there, that Alan used—it's steep, but Alan used to lead Sammy along it, under that bit of furze. So you'll come up away on his left."

She was right. If he followed that little worn path he'd

end up on the very shoulder of the ridge, little more than a hundred yards, maybe only fifty, from the deerstalker hat.

Except that he didn't fancy even those last few yards if the watcher really wasn't watching birds. He'd be as obvious and out-of-place—and as vulnerable—as a fox in the stubble. The very suddenness of his appearance would make his position doubly dangerous: it might panic the man into doing something frightful.

But Mary was looking at him fiercely, and he could hardly admit just how cold his feet were.

"You don't think it would work?"

"It'd work all right—up to that last hundred yards. And then he'd spot me." He shook his head. "I don't want to run him to earth or to scare him off—I just want to get a good look at him."

"And he'd recognize you?"

"I'm afraid he would."

The truth was he was altogether too distinctive in his neat grey city suit to go tramping over the hill, apart from the damned beard. They'd tagged him at the Ryle reception, and by now the word would be out on him for sure. Even if by any remote stroke of luck it hadn't reached the bird-watcher, those field-glasses would have caught him walking from the car to the house. He'd been in full view of the hill there— he'd even paused to look up at it just to make the job easier.

Mary sighed, and then gave him a small understanding smile. "You're quite right, Hugh—I'm afraid I'm just a silly old woman who watches too much television. From this chair everything always seems to look either too easy or too difficult. He's probably just a bad bird-watcher anyway."

Her understanding only made it worse. He rubbed the beard, scowling at himself in the gilt mirror on the wall behind her. He'd secretly been rather proud of it, at least until Penelope had found it sexy. Now, the sooner it came off, the better.

The sooner it came off!

He stared at the reflection in the mirror intently, no longer scowling. The beard and the suit were mere trappings, not integral parts.

"Mary—is there a razor in the house?"

She looked up at him in surprise. "There's an old cut-throat of Charlie's—?"

"And some old clothes of Alan's? And a rucksack or something like that?"

But now she was already ahead of him. "And Charlie's old hat and an old pair of spectacles too, with clear glass in them." She paused for breath. "But don't take a rucksack, Hugh—take Sammy!"

Roskill frowned at her, perplexed for a moment.

"The horse, Hugh—nobody would look twice at a horse-man on the hill. There've been riders up there already this morning. They went straight by him."

He looked at her doubtfully. He'd not been in a saddle since heaven only knew when. But if he could stay on top it would double his mobility, never mind his credibility...

"I'm not much of a horseman, Mary."

"Sammy's not much of a horse."

He couldn't disappoint her now, and—damn it—he didn't want to. Besides, it might actually work."

"Hell, Mary—I'll give it a try," he said.

XI

TWENTY-FIVE MINUTES LATER he wasn't quite so sure the horse had been such a good idea.

She was a docile enough creature, undeniably, easy to ride on the flat and tolerably sure-footed on the hillside. But however many times she had been up the sheep-track—he supposed it was a sheep-track, though there was no sign of any sheep—she hadn't learned to traverse it willingly: he was already sweating with the effort of dragging her up and he suspected that only the near impossibility of turning round kept the beast going. In fact there was now no turning back for either of them—they were saddled with each other.

He scanned the escarpment above him for movement. At least Mary's memory of the lie of the land had been exact, and only the skyline of bare turf was above him.

And one thing was established, anyway—he felt it in his bones: this had been how Alan had unwittingly created the necessity for his own death. He had ridden out innocently for his early morning exercise using his favorite route, and had set up his own appointment in Samarra.

It was a thought that turned the sweat on his back clammy. Moreover, the deerstalker might even be the man Alan had seen, in which case he might recognize the horse, even if he failed to recognize her new rider.

He looked critically at the mare. No, that was hardly possible: Sammy—it was an unlovely diminutive for Samantha—was a most anonymous horse, a very common, brown, ordinary horse without a single distinguishing mark.

He toiled on up, past the wire fence with its strands conveniently looped for easy passage—Sammy knew the drill of old and waited patiently while he refixed them—and then on under the furze patch. Beyond it the going was easier and the skyline was still empty.

He looked back down towards the village, to the house and to the window from which Mary was watching his every step. Far beyond it he could see an electric train racing silently towards Eastbourne, flashing sparks from its wheels. And beyond that a great blue-black column of rain and raincloud spreading slowly like the wrath of God across the miniaturised landscape.

The rain was five, maybe seven miles away—and how fast did rain travel?

He reached the end of the furze, the jumping off point and a suitable resting place for the horse. He could wait here for the rain to reach him, and then go on in with it, or go straight in the moment Mary gave him her signal.

He looked back towards the house again, and as he did so he saw the white bath towel flap over the window sill—that was the signal that Deerstalker was still in position.

Wait or go?

Roskill realised suddenly that he was very close to being frightened, and the longer he waited, the more frightened he'd get.

Go then!

He held the reins carefully in his left hand and using the advantage of the hill swung himself into the saddle. Sammy backed nervously, sensing her rider's fear, and for one brief, blind second of panic Roskill felt he was losing control of her.

He urged her forward and felt her gears engage. Up the last few yards on to ground that was only gently sloping, and turn—*now walk, Sammy . . .*

The burial mound stood out against the grey sky—*now trot, Sammy . . .*

Jingling harness, horse snorting and spluttering, landscape jumping—musn't lose stirrups . . .

He approached the mound directly, uncertain until the last moment whether to veer to the left or the right of it. The right would be safer, as the man wouldn't get a direct look at him, but equally he wouldn't get a direct view either and the whole point of this crazy ride would be lost.

Left, then—

Sammy thumped stiff-legged past the burial mound, at the last moment turning slightly crab-wise against the hillside's slope and so giving him a perfect view of his quarry, deer-stalker, field glasses, open mouth and all.

And then, in a second of total confusion, he was past and tugging savagely at the reins, fighting to stop Sammy from breaking into a canter which would take them all the way to Alfriston.

Jack Butler!

He was fifty yards on before he managed to turn the mare and quieten her to a walk. And by then Butler was no longer lying prone, but was sitting staring at him in the midst of a small pile of belongings, the wind riffling the pages of a foolscap notebook beside him.

Butler!

But if Jack was down here—up here—eyes glued to the Old Vicarage, what price Audley's—and his own—so clever scheme to make a fool of Llewelyn? Damn it, it looked as though Llewelyn was making a fool of them . . .

He let Sammy amble back towards the mound at her own snail's pace, covering his doubts with a grin. Whatever the truth, this wasn't the time to admit anything incriminating.

"Hello there, Jack," he called out. His eye caught the cover of a book beside Butler's hand in the grass—a Golden Eagle, it looked like, perched on Tennyson's crag—at the very moment Butler plonked the notebook on it. "Spotted any interesting birds?"

Butler knew about as much about birds as he knew about desalination, most likely.

"I shan't spot anything queerer than you today." Butler rose stiffly to his feet. "Where the devil did you spring from, Hugh. And looking like—" words failed him "—like that?"

Belatedly Roskill remembered he was wearing the plain glass spectacles, the relics of some East Firle amateur dramatic society's production, not to mention the dilapidated pork-pie hat. But he resisted the temptation to whip them off, which would only be to admit that he realised how comical he looked.

Except that Butler certainly wasn't laughing; if at the best of times that pale, freckled face rarely smiled, it was composed now in an expression of deadly seriousness.

"You don't expect me to go riding in my best suit, do you?" Roskill chided him.

"I don't expect you to go riding at all at a time like this. What are you doing up here?"

"I was going to ask you the same question. Doesn't Fred trust me? Or is it Llewelyn who gives the orders?"

Butler swept the deerstalker off his head and ran his hand through his short carroty hair. Then he looked up at Roskill, his eyes angry.

"Neither of them knows I'm here. And I shouldn't be here if I wasn't daft." He shook his head bitterly. "But I guessed you and Audley were up to something, and I'm afraid you're bigger fools than I am even."

Roskill smiled. "My dear Jack—some joker fixed my track rods last night. You don't need to tell me how to add two and two. Do you think I've forgotten what happened to Alan?"

"I think you're a fool to keep whatever it is you're doing to yourselves—you and Audley," Butler said harshly.

"Maybe so. But then you've kept it to yourself too, apparently."

"I said I was a fool. But then I'm not supposed to be in on this business any more—I was only brought in to make sure you two reached the briefing yesterday."

"Then what exactly brings you to Firle?"

"David Audley did yesterday at the Queensway—he couldn't resist telling them to their faces, could he?" Butler's lips curled. "And I remember how quiet you went when I told you about Maitland."

"So you checked."

Butler nodded. He wasn't the fastest man alive, but he was very, very sure. And if he'd checked, he'd not have missed anything.

"Which still doesn't explain why you're here, Jack."

Butler looked down at his highly polished boots, then slowly raised his eyes to meet Roskill's. "To teach you that two and two can be made to equal minus one, lad, that's why. Do you know who you're up against? If you'd just get off that creature I might tell you something interesting."

There were times when Butler's almost fatherly concern for him irritated Roskill unbearably. But also there were times when the man's caution paid off, and this could be one of them.

Roskill disengaged his feet from the stirrups and slid awkwardly off Sammy. Over her back, away to the north-east, he saw the great dark rain column, which now blotted out half the scene below them.

"You'd better make it quick, Jack, or we're both going to get wet."

Butler looked carefully round the naked hilltop, ignoring the rainclouds, before answering.

"I don't know why they asked me to the Queensway yesterday. Just to put you at ease, I suppose—as I said, my brief was just to hook you both, no more, no less." Butler still wasn't apologizing, merely stating facts. "Only I got there a shade ahead of time."

He watched Roskill. "You can claim what you like for your electronic toys, Hugh—but there's nowt to beat the human ear. Listen before you knock, that's what my old Dad always used to say!"

Butler's father had been a printer—a head printer, as Butler liked to remind people—in darkest Lancashire, Bolton or Blackburn. Roskill had always suspected from the way Butler spoke of him, half proud, half rueful, that the old man had considered his son's preference for the army instead of an apprenticeship the equivalent of a daughter's choice of prostitution rather than the mill.

"They were arguing," said Butler. "Llewelyn and Stocker were arguing over just how expendable you were. The Welshman said that Audley musn't be risked, but you could be. And Stocker said you were one of Fred's kindergarten and there'd be the devil to pay if you were damaged."

Butler had an exact memory as well as a good ear; if he said 'expendable', then that was the word Llewelyn had used. The bastards had discussed him as though he was a piece of fairly expensive equipment!

"And Llewelyn asked the Special Branch man how he rated the risk—"

"How did he rate it?"

"He said if they were right about Audley he'd pretty soon find the right hole and then he'd put you down it like a ferret. Only you weren't a trained ferret and Hassan was no rabbit."

"So I'm an untrained ferret now!"

Butler shook his head sadly. "You're a bright lad, Hugh—with your weapons systems. But you're being used for something different this time."

"They warned me, Jack—you were there when they did it. You're forgetting I'm supposed to go running back to them every time David blows his nose."

"But you aren't, are you?"

Roskill shrugged. "It doesn't happen to suit me."

"Aye—it doesn't suit you!" said Butler, scowling. "Man, they've got Audley summed up properly, and you too, I'm sorry to say. He's a bloody genius at research, but when he has a job of his own to do he goes his own sweet way, and they know it. When they warned you they were just covering themselves with Sir Frederick, that's all."

He paused for breath, running his hand through his hair again. "Have they bothered you at all? Have they tried to get in touch with you?" He didn't wait for an answer. "They bloody haven't, have they? I tell you, Hugh, they're just waiting for you two to get things really stirred up. And you'll do just that, if I know you!"

"We haven't done anything exactly spectacular yet, you know, Jack," Roskill protested mildly. It was odd—he'd never seen Jack so vehement, at least not since the cancellation of the South African cricket tour.

"Enough to get your track rods fixed."

Roskill gazed at Butler, overwhelmed suddenly with curiosity.

"What's all this got to do with your sudden urge to come bird watching here?"

"I knew I could pick you up here as soon as I found out about Jenkins. It was the one place I was sure you'd turn up."

"But why, Jack? It's not your affair any more—you ought to be home with your girls, or watching the cricket."

Butler glowered at him. "Aye, but somebody's got to watch your back for you. And in my book you don't send anyone out without telling him the score..."

He clipped off the sentences abruptly, as though their implicit criticism of his superiors went against the grain of his character. Roskill eyed him with astonishment: he'd always regarded Jack as a fundamentally simple man, who did his job and minded his business, sustained only by a rather old-fashioned patriotism, the three small female Butlers and the latest cricket scores. But now it looked as though his loyalties were rather more complex.

"Besides, if I want to go bird-watching in my own time—" the hint of Lancashire broadened as Butler gestured to the darkening landscape "—I can watch where I bloody well please, and—"

He stopped suddenly, his freckled, hairy hand frozen in midsweep and his attention snatched away from Roskill by something which had caught his eye below them.

"Blue and white Cambridge saloon in the drive beside your car. Isn't that—?"

"One wing mirror?" Roskill cut in. "And there'll be a patch of rust on the white strip, forward of the door?"

Butler lifted the field glasses.

"Aye—it's Audley's car, isn't it!" Butler turned back to him. "Did you expect him to come down here?"

They both knew well enough that Audley never strayed abroad on business from the department or his home if it could be avoided. And in this instance Audley had even spelt it out: *If I were spotted there it might give the game away.*

"He'd only come here in an emergency, Jack."

"Likely there's an emergency, then. Or maybe he's not as thick as you are."

"It's simpler than that," said Roskill. "Before I came down here I phoned him up—he wasn't in and I left a message with Faith."

"A message?"

A big raindrop spattered on Roskill's cheek, rolling down to the corner of his mouth. He brushed it away.

"I told her to ask him what Alamut was."

XII

"JAKE'S QUITE RIGHT," said Audley. "I probably do know more about Alamut than he does. But the Alamut List is something different."

Roskill looked at Mary doubtfully. It was typical of David to shoot his mouth off in front of civilians; it wasn't so much lax security this time as that calculated and deliberate amateurishness of his—the flouting of the rules to prove that he was a gentleman rather than a player. Except that this time David might not be wholly to blame—if Mary had crooked her little finger at him.

Audley caught his look and waved his hand airily.

"Miss Hunter and I have already had a talk, damn it— she already knows enough to ruin us, thanks to you."

Mary's eyes rested on the big man approvingly, as though he had already been compacted into her inner circle. So the charm had not been one-way, Roskill thought with a twinge of jealousy: when Audley put himself out, which wasn't often, he too had a way with him.

But having blabbed already himself, Roskill knew he was in no position to protest, even though he could sense Butler's disapproval. It would be interesting to see how long it took Mary to crack Butler's shell wide open too.

"Who is he, then?" Butler asked. "Hassan?"

Audley shook his head. "Let's get things in order first, Butler. I want to hear exactly how Hugh got on to him."

Settled in the huge leather armchair, Audley was a good deal more relaxed now than he had been when Roskill had arrived. But then he had seen Butler through the telescope and had feared—as Roskill had done—that he'd been taken for a ride. The good news that they were still in business had rather taken the edge off the bad news that the business was nasty: he seemed to have expected that.

They listened in silence while Roskill gave them his edited account of the previous evening. The trick, as he knew from long experience, was to practice the ancient and dishonourable art of British understatement. He had learned from a wise American years before that most people instinctively assumed that understatement concealed courage and competence. Used properly it rendered both cowardice and incompetence alike invisible, and long years of exposure had not rendered the British themselves immune to it—if anything they were more easily deceived than foreigners, who sometimes mistook it for inarticulateness.

At the end Audley nodded sagely. Mary was gazing at him in rapt attention, which would have been very gratifying if he had not felt such a charlatan.

"So the Ryle Foundation is Hassan's cover?" said Butler.

"I think it's very likely. Not exactly a cover, though—or not just a cover. A ready-made framework as well."

"The ivy on the oak tree," murmured Mary.

"That's it. Only not so obvious—more like a tape worm."

"And we still don't know what he's up to here," growled Butler. "Except he's quite ready to kill just to keep us in the dark, that's the only thing we know. And he's damned efficient at doing it."

"Efficient," Audley repeated thoughtfully. "But not so efficient with your car, was he, Hugh?"

"I'm not so sure about that now, David. To be honest, I'm not at all sure that it was Hassan at all. There was something

not quite right about that whole business—and that's what
the technical chap seemed to think when they phoned me this
morning, too—"

That reassuring Highland voice:
"McClure speaking, Squadron Leader—I'm sorry, Squad-
ron Leader, but we can't let you have your car back yet."
"For God's sake, why not? What's wrong with it?"
"Nothing—and that's what's wrong. Or almost nothing.
The nut on the track rod had been removed, that's all."
"The nut—? Christ, man—do you call that nothing?"
"Och, I can see well it might have been awkward on a
motorway—"
"Damn right it would have been!"
"But it needn't have come to that, Squadron Leader. With
the track rod, you know, it takes time to free itself and jump
out. It could have killed you or it could have no more than
dented your bumper."
"So what?"
"So it's a verra chancey way of putting a man down. It's
something and nothing, if you take my point. It'd be an
amateur or a man who didn't know his own mind who'd do
such a stupid thing...Or it could be a wee cozenage."
"A what?"
"A deception, Squadron Leader—a red herring. A cover
for something else much smarter. You told me to mind young
Jenkins last night, and I do. And you'd do well to do as much
yourself...But if that's the way of it, we haven't been able
to find it yet, though we're still looking. And the while, I
cannot let you have the vehicle..."

"—Then he offered me a department car. But as I was
coming down here I thought it wiser to hire one for myself."
No need to labor that point; cozenages could be attempted
by friends who wished to keep track of him just as easily as
by foes.
"And then I got to thinking about it," said Roskill, watch-

ing Audley—this was Audley's technique, after all. "If Hassan wanted to stop me, he didn't need anything as crude as the track rod. And if he just wanted to follow me, there'd be no point in fixing it at all. He doesn't fit, that's what it amounts to."

Audley raised an eyebrow. "Razzak?"

Roskill nodded. "I've got the feeling that Razzak wanted to meet me. And he wanted me to believe he was on the side of the angels."

"Well, he chose one hell of a risky way of making friends," said Butler. "He could have broken your neck for you—then you'd have been on the angels' side yourself."

"I don't think he'd ever have let me get out of that street, Jack. I think he was parked just round the curve out of sight, waiting for me. In fact I'm damned sure he was waiting for me, now I come to think of it—his lights went on and his engine revved up the moment I got out of the car."

"It's tenuous, Hugh," said Audley critically. "I agree with Butler. Why bother with the car at all?"

"Because—" Roskill frowned, searching in his mind for the thread of reasoning he was certain was there, somewhere. He shook his head helplessly. "Look, David—I think Razzak's quite a chap, but he's a dark horse. We know he was here, at Firle, almost for sure. Hassan's being here is just guesswork, but in any case it could just as easily have been Razzak who had that car fixed for Alan—and that gives him one damn good reason for wanting to have a quiet talk with me."

"Which is—?"

"Alan's letter. It was addressed to me, remember."

"And your turning up at the Ryle reception would have shaken him?" Audley smiled disconcertingly. "I can see the drift of it now. It's not a bad theory in its way, I suppose."

"It's more than that, David. Razzak was maybe a bit too keen to give me a lead on Hassan last night—he even tried to clear Shapiro in favour of Hassan. And that makes me wonder now whether Hassan's not just a very convenient scapegoat—and what was done to my car was to keep up the illusion that Hassan has a fixation about cars."

"Very neat, Hugh. And I think I go along with you as far as Razzak's fixing your car. But for the rest"—Audley paused—"you're rather off the mark, I'm afraid."

Roskill checked himself from replying. By Audley's standards that was a mild, almost apologetic warning that he was talking nonsense. And he seemed very sure of himself.

"Shapiro didn't buy your theory, did he?" said Audley gently.

"With the cease-fire coming, neither of them wants trouble for the other."

"Of course they don't want it. The trouble is they've already got it."

"But—"

"No buts." Audley looked over his glasses at Roskill. "They told you a great deal last night, Hugh—about that business in Sinai—but there was one thing they didn't tell you. A rather significant thing, really. It was Jake who saved Razzak out there. Transfusions, battlefield surgery, then airlifted out—the lot. If it hadn't been for Jake, Razzak would have died there in the desert. Did they tell you that, either of them?"

Audley stared away from them towards the hillside, which was suddenly bathed in a great shaft of sunlight.

"Maybe Jake saw something of himself in Razzak, I don't know. But he's not a sentimentalist—he's a very subtle man. A man who looks ahead. It may be that Razzak's just a marked card he put back in the Egyptian pack, but I don't think so. I think he wanted to make a contact for the future."

He turned back towards them again, staring directly at Roskill.

"You can take my word that Hassan's here, or his men are. But we had the picture wrong all the same—Razzak didn't meet them up there on the Beacon—he met Jake Shapiro."

Razzak and Shapiro!

"If you hadn't been so close to it, you'd have seen it for yourself, Hugh," said Audley soothingly. "It was staring us both in the face. In fact there's nothing exactly new in the Israelis and the Egyptians having secret meetings—they've done it here before, and in the States. But what is special this time is it was these two, of all people."

Razzak and Shapiro! Roskill was vexed at his own obtuseness: it was so simple and logical an explanation to the two men's identical reaction. So simple that he hadn't had the wit to see it!

He frowned at Audley.

"But that doesn't change anything, David. It still leaves us with Alan and Razzak—if Alan saw Razzak and Shapiro together—"

"Hugh, Hugh!" Audley held up his hand, frowning, as though Alan was an extraneous element in the pattern, best forgotten. "What if he did? It would have been awkward for them, but it wouldn't be a killing matter. He couldn't have heard anything. If he'd have reported the meeting—and if it had leaked out from us, as I suppose it could have with Elliott Wilkinson around—that wouldn't have been enough to have him killed."

"Then what would have?"

Audley shrugged. "I can only guess, Hugh. It seems to me that they met here because they wanted to make sure that somebody in particular didn't follow them or listen in. They could each get up to the Beacon from a different direction and you can see for miles from up there. But if somebody *did* follow them—and if Alan saw who it was and recognized him—"

"One of Hassan's men, do you mean?" said Butler.

"And he was murdered just for that?" Mary said softly. "Just for that?"

Audley blinked at her. It bore down on Roskill with absolute certainty that Audley really didn't care either way why Alan had died, or by whose hand. It didn't even matter any longer than Llewelyn should be humiliated. What absorbed the man now was what had passed between Razzak and Shapiro, and only that.

"If he was a danger, Miss Hunter," Audley began didactically, "—if Hassan's man wished to keep his cover—it may be he thought Alan was our man on the spot. We just can't tell." He paused. "But I think he really died because killing is what Hassan's men do best. It's their business."

"Their business?"

"I sat up half the night trying to puzzle it out." Audley smiled to himself. "I had most of the bits already actually— it was only your bit I needed, Hugh. When Faith passed on your message about the Alamut List it wasn't very difficult.

"You see, there's nothing in the files about Hassan, because he hasn't done anything. Even what Cox told us—that was negative material. Hassan's never claimed to have shot up an airline office, or hijacked an airliner. He's never even raided across the Jordan. You'd almost think he doesn't exist."

"But Razzak was scared of him—and so was Shapiro," Roskill interrupted.

"And so was Llewelyn. But he wasn't *surprised*—that's what was so odd. And what's much more surprising is the way Cox assumed that if anyone wanted to kill Llewelyn, it would be Hassan. Razzak did the same, apparently—Hassan was his first choice too."

"That's right." Roskill nodded. " 'A murderous bloody-minded idea,' he said. And—Christ!—" the Egyptian's words came back with a jolt "—he told me to play it cool, otherwise Hassan'd move his name up to the top of the list. My God! The list!"

"The Alamut List," Audley repeated. "The Alamut List is the difference between Hassan and all the other guerrilla leaders, Habash and Gharbiya and Haydar. They believe in terrorism, sure enough—and liberation and revolution and all the rest. But Hassan's special subject is going to be assassination, no more and no less. The very name gives the game away—"

"The name?"

"Alamut. It was the name of the *Hashashin* castle in the Elburz Mountains in Northern Persia—it was where the original sect of the Assassins started, back in the eleventh century. It's all in Joinville's 'Life of Saint Louis'—*Make way for him who bears the lives of kings in his hands*."

Butler rolled his eyes at Roskill, for Audley's knowledge of medieval Arab history was at once the pride and the despair of the department. It had been his cover in all his Mediterranean and Middle Eastern journeys in the old days, with learned articles to his credit to back it. Indeed, there were those who had suggested that the cover had always been his real preoccupation, for which his job was the real cover. So Shapiro had meant exactly what he'd said, though perhaps with his tongue in his cheek.

"But I won't bore you with a history lesson." The tightness of Audley's voice indicated that he'd picked up Butler's look. "What it suggests is a program of selective political assassination. The removal of the inconvenient doves for the benefit of the impatient hawks."

"That's the devil of a lot to build on a name." There was a sparring note in Butler's words, almost a touch of disdain at Audley's intellectualism. "One name and a botched killing."

Audley measured Butler coolly. They were chalk and cheese, thought Roskill, and neither of them would ever meet the other's mind. Unconsciously they would always goad each other by overplaying their chosen roles of the omniscient, donnish theorist and the practical, plain-speaking soldier, even when they were in basic agreement.

"I grant you they're frightened," went on Butler. "I can smell the fear on them. But if you're right, then Llewelyn and Stocker have got a damn funny way of going about things—letting you and Hugh loose with only half an idea of what you're up to."

Dear old Jack! Roskill felt a rueful affection for the square, pugnacious face, the very pattern of the British military countenance—except that old time scarlet would have clashed

hideously with the freckles and the hair. And except that this
very morning had proved that appearance to be deceptive:
when he disapproved of his masters' behaviour, Jack was
ready as Audley to intervene on his own initiative.

"I don't think so at all, Major Butler," said Audley mildly.
"To my way of thinking, the name substantiated the fear, and
the fear produces the action. I said to Hugh yesterday that
Llewelyn knew more than he was saying—I think he knows
about the Alamut List. And I think he's got enough self-
regard to believe he'd be on it at the top—that's why he
never gave a thought to Jenkins. He was half expecting it to
happen some time."

"Well, why the devil didn't he tell you from the start?"

"Ah, now I can only guess at that," said Audley, peering
over his glasses. "Just how good an assassin Hassan is I don't
know—though I wouldn't describe what he's done so far as
a botched job. But I rather think he's a good propagandist."

"A propagandist?"

"Yes. After all, he hasn't really done anything yet, but
he's spread the word where it matters. When you think about
it, the Alamut List is just a piece of theatre—like Robes-
pierre's black book that put the fear of God up all his col-
leagues. He's using fear as his fifth column—before long,
whoever dies, he'll get the credit. Without lifting a finger."

It was true, thought Roskill. Hassan was as nebulous as
morning mist, but already his name was doing his work for
him. Fear and uncertainly emanated from it—it was a mist
in which men saw dead men's faces, and looking closer saw
the faces were their own.

He shrugged off the nightmare; in another moment he'd
see his own reflection in his mind if he let his imagination
work.

"So they all think this is the beginning of a massacre," he
said harshly. "But we know it isn't, because it was Alan they
were after, not Llewelyn."

"But Razzak and Shapiro met, Hugh. And as everyone's
already said, with the cease-fire coming up now's the time

Hassan has got to make his play. God knows whether the Americans and the Russians can make the cease-fire stick, but if Hassan really is the hardliner they say he is, he's not going to wait and see."

It was all circumstantial evidence, just one or two degrees from bluff. But Razzak and Shapiro weren't fools to be stampeded by mere suspicion, and neither was Llewelyn. And although Audley's knowledge of what was really going on in the Middle East was rusty and out-of-date, he had always had an uncanny instinct for distinguishing reality from illusion.

"But what I don't see—" Butler frowned fiercely "—there's nothing new about assassination in the Middle East. Or anywhere else, for that matter. These last few years—damn it, the precautions are routine now."

"True. But if the name Alamut means what I think it does, there's never been anyone like Hassan before either—not in recent times, anyway. All the other Palestinian groups have had much broader aims..." Audley sighed, and shook his head. "It's plain madness, but there won't be any shortage of volunteers."

He looked at them bleakly. "In the old times they used to promise paradise to assassins, but they don't need to do that now. I was in the camps across the Jordan in '68. They were full of flies and dirty children and automatic weapons even then—and no hope. God knows what they're like now. But even then I could have gone into any of them and sworn in a hundred fedayeen—it's practically the same word as the Assassins had for their killers. Not with a promise of paradise—just to get them out of the hell they're in already, poor devils."

He stopped abruptly as his eyes reached Butler, as though embarrassed at this descent into emotion.

"Which means we've got to crack down on Hassan hard—and quickly," said Butler. "Poor devils or not. Mooning over this Alamut List won't do a ha'porth of good—if we wait for them to start we've already lost half the battle!"

"Christ, Jack—!" The insane image of Butler in chain-mail, kite-shaped shield on his shoulder, swinging a great Crusading sword in the midst of a crowd of howling Arabs, rose in Roskill's mind. "Who do we crack down on, for God's sake? We don't even know who they are!"

"The girl downstairs has seen one of 'em," snapped Butler. "Start with him, and to blazes with diplomatic immunity and kid gloves! Then move in on the Ryle Foundation—one good shake there, and something should come to the surface. And get in touch with the Arab governments—if Audley's right this is one time when they won't play awkward. It's their *necks* on the block even more than ours this time—they'll have their security wallahs moving like blue-bottomed flies.

"You've got to get things moving! I don't know what you and Audley have been up to, but you're both sitting tight on a keg of gunpowder, and any minute now it's going to blow you both to kingdom come!"

"I see." But Audley's face had a blank, obstinate cast to it which Roskill recognized: if there was any force in Butler's argument there was evidently a more powerful force which moved him in the opposite direction. "And what do you think, Miss Hunter?"

Butler's jaw tightened as he followed Audley's invitation to Mary, who had sat mouse-like through the exchange, her hands clasped on her lap. For one second Roskill thought Butler was going to explode—it was hard to imagine an appeal better calculated to make Jack see red; an appeal made on a violent issue of state security addressed to a grey-haired, crippled maiden lady. Women were Jack's blank spot at the best of times, and in this instance he could hardly be expected to penetrate that gentle expression to the uncrippled intelligence beneath.

But his control asserted itself in time—this might not be Jack's best day, when he'd lost a day's cricket in order to save fools from the consequences of their folly and ended by crossing swords with Audley, but bullying sweet old ladies would clash with his image of himself, however much he was provoked by circumstances.

His subsidence was not lost on Mary, however.

"I don't really think I'm qualified to pass an opinion," she said diffidently, placating Butler, but watching Audley.

Roskill saw that this time at least, Audley had not set out deliberately to niggle Butler. It was far more in character that he would wish to use Mary's unclouded judgement; if there was one thing Audley did superlatively well, it was to identify brains and then to pick them clean.

"I'd still very much like to hear what you think," said Audley. "Spectators have a way of seeing some things the players miss."

Mary bowed her head, studying her hands briefly. Then she looked up directly at Audley.

"Very well, David. I must say I don't really understand why you don't want to tell anyone what happened here—I do see Major Butler's point . . . But"—her voice gained in determination—"if the men above you already knew about this Hassan and his list, they certainly don't need you to tell them what they already know. They must want you to do something—or find out something—particular. Something only you can do, possibly."

Roskill glanced at Butler out of the corner of his eye. Good for Mary.

"Quite right, Miss Hunter," said Audley encouragingly. "I think they wanted me to make contact with Jake Shapiro again. If anyone can give the lowdown on Hassan it'll be Jake, but he wouldn't stop to give our friend Dai Llewelyn the time of day. That's the whole trouble—they kicked me out once for being too close to Jake. And with things as they are, they don't want to get involved with Israeli Intelligence. But if I happened to go back to my old ways off my own bat, unofficially—that would be different . . ."

"Yet it can't be this Alamut List that they want," Mary said, frowning.

Audley perked up. "Why not Miss Hunter?"

"Well . . . if I've understood what you've been saying, it would be a list of all the moderate men—people like nice young King Hussein—the people who really want peace."

"That's right. And Eban and Allon and Abu Khadra and all the others."

"That's what I mean—you already know who'd be on the list, so it can't be that . . ." Mary trailed off. "Of course, I only know what I read in the papers, but I always think the Israelis are great *doers*. I mean, they've been putting up with things, and having things done to them for so long, and now they've found out that they can do things just as well. Not just the wars they've fought, but the way they captured that Nazi—Eichmann—and the way they fought back against the guerrillas who tried to take their airliners—while other people talk, they *do* things . . ." Again she stopped uncertainly.

"Go on, Miss Hunter."

"So—" Mary rallied "—so I'd want to know what they're planning to do about Hassan, because they're the ones who wouldn't sit down and wait for him to start shooting and murdering. And they wouldn't expect anyone to help them. Unless—unless—" she stared hard at Audley—"unless that was why Colonel Shapiro met Colonel Razzak. Is that too stupid?"

Too stupid?

Not an exchange of information and a friendly word of warning between honest enemies, but something more: an alliance!

An Egyptian-Israeli entente!

It could be temporary, and must be unofficial and highly secret, with nothing on paper. But was it feasible?

Roskill glanced at Audley, and saw that he was smiling. So this, or something like it, was what Audley had been after all along. And given that Shapiro and Razzak were the only ones of their kind in that sea of hatred and distrust, who better than them to make the contact? They could be enemies still, but facing a more dangerous common enemy—with the Nazis at the gates, even the Russians and the West had made common cause once, without relaxing their deeper enmity.

"Now have I said something silly?"

"On the contrary, Miss Hunter," Audley laughed, "you have said what I hoped to hear. What drew Hassan's men wasn't so much the meeting as its subject. And that's why Razzak and Jake were both so keen to keep us from breathing down their necks just now: whatever they're negotiating has to be dynamite. And the moment you said you weren't going to give up, Hugh—even after Razzak had promised to find out about Hassan—that was when Jake thought of me."

"But why you?" Jack Butler sounded humbler now. "You're supposed to be out of the Middle East."

"Out of the Middle East—but not out of favor with Sir Frederick," said Audley quickly. "If it came to the push I could still pull some strings, and Jake knows it. And he trusts me, that's the point. He may even suspect I'm already involved—he knows Hugh's a friend of mine, anyway. And remember, all he wants is to get the heat off for a day or two, if what Razzak said is anything to go by—"

"But is it?" Roskill interrupted. "I still don't quite know what makes Razzak tick. You were going to find out about him, David—I haven't even seen the official file on him, damn it!"

"But I have," Butler said shortly. "There's not a lot in it either. He's peasant stock, with a dash of Turkish or maybe Albanian. Cairo military academy. Two tank conversion courses over here—that's why his English is so good. He did one on Shermans back in '46, and one on Centurions a few years ago, with attachment to the RTR—they thought he was pretty sound. And he's been blooded three times: he was in the Irak al-Manshia siege in '48, where Nasser won his spurs. Then in '56 he broke out of Um Katef—it took him fifteen days to walk home. And then the '67 business."

"What about his politics?"

Butler nodded. "I'm coming to them. He was in the Free Officers movement by the end of '49—he was one of the

group that captured Farouk's palace. Then Nasser put him in
Intelligence, and he was in the special squad that smashed
the Muslim Brotherhood after they tried to kill Nasser in '54.
Went to Russia next year and put up some sort of black
there—he was sent home in disgrace, anyway—"

"He broke a Russian officer's jaw in an argument," said
Audley. "Officially it was a professional argument. Actually
it was over a girl—a bit of uncomradely racial prejudice. He
doesn't like the Russians much."

"Well, it certainly stopped his promotion dead," said Butler. "He was shipped back into the army and it took him ten
years to get his battalion. And the rest you know."

"Not quite," said Audley. "Those are just the bones of it.
What it adds up to is that Razzak's a patriot—and not an
Arab patriot either. An *Egyptian*."

"So that's why he doesn't like the guerrillas much?"

"If they were Egyptian guerrillas he'd like them, Hugh.
Egyptians—yes. Palestinians, Syrians, British and Russians—all damn foreigners to him. And when you think that
Nasser's the first real Egyptian to rule Egypt for a couple of
thousand years you can see his point. In fact Razzak's more
an Egyptian than an Arab in just the same way Shapiro's
more an Israeli than a Jew—maybe that's what they've really
got in common! Anyway—"

The phone beside Mary overwhelmed the rest of his words
with a shattering burst of sound, startling them all.

Mary picked up the receiver. "It's all right—it's only the
house phone. We haven't got a proper one any more. It'll be
Penny about lunch—yes, Penelope?"

But as she listened her eyebrows lifted in surprise, and
her eyes fastened on Audley. She put her hand over the mouth-
piece.

"We've got another visitor—and for you, David!"

Audley pursed his lips. "So soon? I'd rather expected Jake
to wait for me to come to him. But it seems I was wrong."

"It isn't Colonel Shapiro," said Mary. "It's the Egyptian—
Colonel Razzak."

"Razzak!" Audley frowned and blinked. *"Razzak?"*

"For you? But how the devil did he know where to come?" Butler snapped. "I made sure no one tailed me, and the driver's not born who can keep up with Hugh—"

He stopped dead as his question answered itself: any toddler in his pedal car could keep up with Audley's driving, and with Audley none the wiser—if he even bothered to look in his mirror.

"Well, don't look at me," Audley said defensively. "I'm not a field man used to peering backwards all the time, blast it. And no one but Faith and Hugh—"

Audley stopped too, for once one second behind everyone else in making the connections, and laughably put out by it. Roskill couldn't help grinning at him: that celebrated incompetence in practical matters was at last paying a practical dividend.

"And *Jake*," he said. "So at least we don't have to test your theory about Shapiro and Razzak. You've proved it yourself, David. The real question's why Razzak's coming out into the open now."

Audley sucked his lower lip, glaring at a point in space two feet in front of his nose. "The real question is why it's Razzak and not Jake. Damn it—I was depending on Jake."

"Will Razzak know enough to connect young Jenkins' death with Firle?" Butler asked.

"What are you getting at, Jack?"

"Well, if he does he'll be scared stiff we're going to pin it on him. The very fact we're here means we know one hell of a lot. It's logical."

"So why's he making contact with us now?"

"To stop us doing anything," said Audley quickly. "From what he said to you, Hugh, I'll bet it's time he's trying to win. Anything to get us off his back until whatever he and Jake are doing is completed. And that gives us a club to hit him with—let's get him up here, Miss Hunter."

"A club to hit him with?"

"A lever, I should have said, Miss Hunter. If it was Jake

it would be different. But Razzak doesn't know me, and he's not going to tell us more than he has to."

"But he wants your help."

"He wants us to delay doing anything. And that's a risk I'm not going to take unless I know exactly why, down to the last detail. Which means we're going to have to throw a scare into him."

"What I've seen of him, that isn't going to be easy," said Roskill. "He doesn't strike me as the scaring type. And we haven't got much to scare him with, when it comes to the crunch."

"I'm afraid I shall just be in the way," Mary said diffidently. "He's certainly not going to be scared of me."

Audley focused on her. "Now you could just be wrong there, Miss Hunter—you could just be wrong. If I've got it right Jake wanted me involved because he knows I feel the same way about the Middle East as he does. I'm a dove from conviction, not necessity."

He looked from Mary to Roskill. "But you two are different. You've each got a score to settle with someone. Razzak won't have allowed for that, but it's something he'll understand when he meets it. The Koran says that Allah rewards those who forgive—but then it lays down that those who avenge themselves when wronged incur no guilt!"

"But, Dr. Audley—David—I don't want vengeance. It won't bring Alan back."

"Hugh doesn't feel that way, do you Hugh?" Audley nodded at Roskill. "You've wanted an eye for an eye from the start. Now's your chance to force Razzak to show you how to get it. I'll give you a cue, don't worry."

Roskill studied Audley suspiciously. The tricky sod was up to something for sure; his very eagerness betrayed it. But so far their objectives still seemed to coincide...

Mary watched them both for a moment, reluctance written plainly on her face.

"We can't keep him waiting any longer, Miss Hunter," Audley said. "Ask him up, please—and trust me!"

XIII

CHARACTERISTICALLY, PENELOPE DID not show Colonel Muhammed Razzak where to go; from the tentative way he put his head round the door it was clear that she had given him the same vague directions that she gave to everyone else.

The liquid brown eyes—Omar Sharif's eyes set incongruously in that battered face—passed over each of them uneasily before finally settling on Mary. Already this was something less than the jolly, confident Razzak of the previous night.

"Madame," the Egyptian bent courteously over Mary's hand, though he was too well-versed in English protocol to kiss it. "Your niece informs me that you are holding a levee and that I may join it. I hope I am not intruding."

"Indeed you are not, Colonel Razzak. You come most carefully upon your hour. We were talking about you only a few minutes ago."

Marvellous—she was bloody marvellous, thought Roskill proudly. Not even Audley could have scripted her better!

"You have the advantage of me, Madame," Razzak was holding himself very straight now. "You make me nervous!"

"Oh, surely not, Colonel. I've been hearing how gallant you are."

"Madame—?" Razzak spread his hands speechlessly. He had been so very much the master of the situation the previous evening that it was immensely morale-raising to see Mary floor him now, unintentionally or not. Roskill felt his own confidence and resolution hardening.

"This is Dr. Audley, whom you wish to meet, my niece said. And this is Major Butler—and Hugh you already know. And I am Mary Hunter...Do please sit down, Colonel."

Razzak nodded to each of them in turn before easing himself down into the leather armchair which Audley had vacated.

"And just what exactly are you and Jake Shapiro up to together, Colonel?" Audley said conversationally.

Razzak's eyes were opaque, but he was unable to stop them shifting between Audley and Mary. It struck Roskill that he was now watching one of the Audley techniques from the inside—the very technique that had been used on Butler and himself, God damn it! Mary's intelligence probably was only a bonus; for Audley she was at once a catalyst and an inhibiting factor, to be used in either role as necessary.

"Don't worry about Miss Hunter," Audley went on smoothly. "Miss Hunter has an interest in what we're going to talk about. And she knows far too much to be left out of things now."

"Far too much?" Razzak's tone was controlled. "And exactly how much is far too much?"

"She knows *Hassan* was responsible for her nephew's death." Audley underscored the name heavily. "The man we lost was her nephew, you see, Colonel."

It was Roskill's cue, unmistakably.

"And he was a friend of mine—a good friend," said Roskill menacingly. "So this isn't just routine for me. This is personal."

"What Hugh means is that he's not so concerned with diplomatic niceties, whoever else may be. And you know how rough the Anglo-Saxons get when they take the law into their own hands." Audley smiled suddenly. "In fact you could say he's taking a very old Anglo-Saxon law into his hands. A thousand years ago in these parts the family of a murdered man had a choice of justice. They could ask for *wergild*, which was paid in cash, or they could take vengeance, which was paid in blood. Hugh's very old-fashioned—he doesn't want *wergild*. And as his friend I have to go along with him."

The Egyptian stared at them in astonishment. Whatever line of approach he'd prepared for, it wasn't this!

"And as for me, Colonel Razzak," Audley continued, "it comes down to this: I know Llewelyn wasn't Hassan's target. And now I know that you met Shapiro up on the hill there somewhere. But *Llewelyn* doesn't know either of those things yet, because we haven't told him. All you have to do is to convince us that it's worth our while to sit on what we know for a time. It's up to you."

"Up to me?" Razzak said softly. "My dear Dr. Audley, I came down here to help you, not to be threatened by you with—" he searched for words "—with Anglo-Saxon laws!"

"To help us? Colonel, I'm not so naïve and nor are you! You came down here to find out how much we knew and then to buy some more time with some more promises. But promises aren't good enough. I want the whole story now."

Razzak squirmed forward and began to maneuver himself out of the chair. "I was told you were a man of sympathy, Dr. Audley. I was told wrong. As far as I'm concerned you can tell Mr. Llewelyn what you like—"

"Llewelyn?" Audley snorted. "I can see you haven't got the message at all. Llewelyn would settle for *wergild*."

Razzak stopped on the very edge of the chair. "And just how would you get blood from me?"

Audley pointed towards the telephone. "By picking up that phone and dialling a man I know in Fleet Street, Colonel Razzak. And I'd say 'Larry, old man, I've got a little story for you'—"

"You wouldn't dare—"

"—'about the British security man who got himself killed because he happened to come upon an Egyptian and an Israeli who were having a private chat down in Sussex last Tuesday.'"

"*They* wouldn't dare."

"Tomorrow's Sunday—and I'm a very reliable source. I tell you, the Sunday papers would eat it up—and you with it!"

Razzak considered Audley in silence for a moment, then shook his head. "No, Dr. Audley. Perhaps *they* might after all, but *you* wouldn't."

"*But I would*," said Roskill.

"Hugh—" Mary began doubtfully.

"No, Mary darling!" He felt the anger welling up in him now, and there was no need to simulate it. "They think they can fight their private wars here, and we won't dare lift a finger because it would be undiplomatic. But I don't give a damn! Some bastard fixed that car so it'd kill Alan, and by Christ if they think they can sweep it under the carpet they're wrong!"

He turned to Audley. "You don't have to stick your neck out, David—I'll stick mine out. And it'll be a pleasure!"

Audley's bluff had been too coolly mounted ever to sway a man like Razzak. Perhaps it had been calculated to give Roskill himself another cue—it didn't matter; what mattered was that hot blood was something different. Even before he met the Egyptian's eyes he seemed to feel the man's resolution weakening—it was like sensing victory across a chess-board in the moment before the decisive move was made.

"That's how it is, Colonel," Audley murmured. "I told you Hugh was after blood. Now perhaps you believe me."

"I see!" Razzak nodded to himself as though some inner truth he'd doubted had of a sudden become plain. "Well, I was warned you were hungry. But it seems you're greedy too..."

"Greedy?" Audley leaned forward as the Egyptian sank back into the armchair. "Believe me, Colonel, I'm the best friend you and Jake Shapiro have got—I'm the only thing that stands between you and trouble. And trouble is something you don't need just now, isn't it!"

Razzak looked at Audley sardonically. "And this you are doing for old time's sake—because Jake's an old friend? Can I believe that now?"

Jake—it was no longer Shapiro, but *Jake*. And it was a more eloquent flag of truce than any formula of words. Except they now had to meet the bill for the threats they'd made: somehow the Egyptian's confidence had to be won.

"No, Razzak," Audley's voice deepened. "But you have to believe that I'm taking a risk of my own in holding out on my own people. If it gets out, I'm not going to be very popular, am I?"

"True," Razzak conceded. "Very true."

"But it isn't just a matter of friendship. I may be out of touch, Colonel, but I can still work out why Hassan's in a different class from the PFLP."

The Egyptian said nothing.

"Hassan's plan is to pick off the moderates—right? And the cease-fire plan means he can't delay any longer?"

An impassive nod. The olive branch was recognized, but not yet accepted.

"But you're not really worried about that, are you, Colonel? Not in the wider sense, anyway. It's Egypt that matters to you. Not Jordan or Syria—or Israel." Audley took a breath. "And we both know that in the wider sense Hassan will *fail*."

Not utterly impassive now—a flicker of interest.

"He'll fail because he's trying just another short-cut, and there aren't any short-cuts in the Middle East any more—just the long haul. Peace or war, the long haul's still the only way."

Razzak's eyes glinted again now.

"All Hassan can do is add confusion," went on Audley, "and this is the one time when Egypt can't afford it, isn't it? *Not after Nasser's heart-attack last year.*"

The shutters came down again. "Heart attack?" Razzak said carefully.

"Influenza, they called it. But we don't have to pretend now, Colonel Razzak," Audley shook his head. "How long do they give him if he doesn't pack things in? A year? Eighteen months? Not more, I think..."

The Egyptian watched him warily.

"It's quite simple, Colonel. You're one of his old soldiers—one of the men who took the tanks to Farouk's palace in '52. You weren't an assassin then, and you aren't now. You were one of the men who broke the Moslem Brotherhood. He trusts you."

Audley paused. "All Hassan will do is maybe kill a few men, and if Nasser wasn't a sick man himself it wouldn't matter—the balance doesn't matter while he's there, because he can handle it, and Hassan wouldn't dare move against *him*. But time's running out, and he can't afford to lose any of the old guard now—when he goes they have to balance each other. Egypt needs them *all*."

"So—?" Razzak interrupted him at last. "So—?"

"Why, so I agree with him," said Audley. "I think the odds are against him—and you. But the least we can do is to shorten them as much as we can. Which means we treat Hassan as a mad dog. And mad dogs have to be put down quickly."

The Egyptian's lips twisted. "Even by dog-lovers?"

"Especially by dog-lovers." Audley took the jibe on the chin. "Quickly—and painlessly if possible. And without hate."

For one long-lasting moment the Englishman and the Egyptian stared at each other, oblivious of everyone else.

"Especially by dog-lovers," Razzak echoed him suddenly, but this time without any irony in his voice.

This, Roskill realised, was as far as Audley would ever go towards admitting what his wife said he felt for the poor bloody Middle East, snarled up now in a quarrel as impossible to resolve as an Escher engraving—with its little men trudging forever up a staircase joined to itself... Conscience or idealism—or exasperation—whatever it was, Audley was offering it to Razzak now in exchange for the man's trust.

"And Squadron Leader Roskill—and Major Butler?" said Razzak softly. "Dog-lovers too?"

"Hugh is with me. He wants what we both want—"

"—And I want nothing," said Butler. "Except my head examining . . . I'm on my own time here. So if this country isn't involved you can trust me. If it is, you can't."

Razzak considered them.

"Very well, then," he shook his head, as if to emphasise the folly of his decision. "It seems we have to trust each other . . .

"But you weren't quite right just now, Audley—nobody trusted me specially to do this dirty job. I won it by right of my own stupidity!" He tapped his chest. "I'm the man Hassan once told all his plans to. And I let him walk away—I let him simply walk away."

Razzak took a deep breath before continuing. "I suppose it wasn't altogether my fault. It was the first night of the June War, and I had other things on my mind." He closed his eyes for an instant, as though to refresh his memory with darkness.

"We were taking a rest about fifteen kilometers from Jebl Libni. There was a truck bogged down off the road—crew gone, but it gave us some shelter from the wind. It gets cold in the Sinai at night . . . In the daytime you've got the heat and the dust, and half the flies in the world—but at night you can't keep warm sometimes. That's the Sinai for you . . ."

Razzak shivered, then caught hold of the thread again.

"I heard the scrape of his boots on the road—if I hadn't I might have shot him, but he was wearing his boots so I didn't."

His boots?

Razzak answered the question before it was asked. "You know, they throw away their boots, our soldiers do, when they're running away . . . First their rifles, then their boots.

But he'd still got his boots—he'd got four water bottles, a machine pistol and his boots, so I reckoned he was maybe an officer or a technician, and I thought he might know how things were up front. But he knew even less than I did. All he knew was that we were finished already."

Razzak couldn't keep the ache of bitterness out of his voice. Roskill was suddenly put in mind of old Havergal the night before: to know one's own honour was still whole, but to be ashamed of one's own country—what sort of trauma, what sort of deviation, that might produce was outside his experience. But it might well put a man outside the normal rules.

"He didn't need to have it spelt out for him. He'd seen their planes, and he hadn't seen ours. He knew, Hassan did."

For a moment he was lost again.

"You're sure he was Hassan? He called himself that?"

"He called himself nothing, Dr. Audley. He never said who he was or what he was—he was just one ice-cold angry man. I've met some angry men these last three years, but never one as cold as that—he was like burning ice that strips your skin off. I think if I'd been on my own he'd have shot me—not to get my water bottle, but just because he thought I was running away!"

"But you weren't—and he was, damn it!" Butler cut in.

Razzak shook his head. "Who was running away and who wasn't? I've never been quite sure which I was doing— maybe I was running. And Hassan certainly didn't think he was running away from *his* enemy; I believe he felt he was running towards him for the first time in his life!

"You see, when I saw how angry he was—he was spoiling for a fight—I asked him to join us. But he said I was a great fool . . . and he asked me to join *him* . . ."

" . . . to kill a few Jews and then be killed yourself—where is the purpose in that? Any street urchin can do as much with a grenade in the market place, to no purpose. But if you're set on dying, I can show you how to die usefully. These

Jews—they are the last enemy, not the first. We Arabs must root out the enemy within first—the selfish ones and the cowards, the little men in the big uniforms. The men who put their countries' politics before the Arab destiny..."

"I asked him how he proposed to do what even Gamal Abdul Nasser hadn't been able to do. He said: 'The same way the old *Hashashin* did—you kill those men who stand against you or in your way, so that your chosen friends can step into their places.'

"And then, when I'd turned him down, he talked to me—or at me, if you like. I suppose he thought he was talking to a dead man, so it didn't matter. But I think he needed to talk to someone very badly at that moment—to tell just one person about his great new idea for uniting all the Arabs, and just how it would work. And by the will of God it was to me he talked!"

"But you weren't tempted?" said Butler.

"Tempted?" Razzak stared at Butler. "Would you have been tempted, Major? Politics by assassination?"

"Bloody nonsense," grunted Butler. "I beg your pardon, Miss Hunter, but that's what it is. I agree with Audley—you'd likely get a worse lot, and then you'd have to make a habit of it."

"I agree! That's just what I thought it was. The pity of it was that I didn't take him seriously—I thought the sun had touched his brains...but then he thought I was crazy too, and when he'd talked himself out he went off on his madness and I went off on mine. It never occurred to me to put a bullet in his back—he didn't seem that important."

That had been quite a meeting under the bogged-down lorry in the desert, thought Roskill: two angles of the Firle triangle. And the third angle not so very far away either—somewhere to the north-east Jake Shapiro's tank recovery team would already have been in action.

But the drama of the occasion seemed to have escaped

Audley. "And just when did you start to take him seriously? When the Alamut List turned up?"

Razzak gave him a crooked smile. "It wasn't I who took him seriously—I forgot about him. But he didn't forget *me*, Audley: he was fool enough to take *me* seriously. You know, the funny thing is that I let him go and he came back to me of his own free will—it's enough to make you weep!"

"How—?"

"Let me tell it my own way. It'll amuse you, I promise you." Razzak lifted his maimed hand. "When I came back with *this*—and my stiff knee—they said I was no good for a soldier any more. So they gave me back my old security job—except it was a sinecure now because I had one of Sabri's bright young men to do the work. Huh!

"And I also had another bright young man—a Palestinian—to keep an eye on me, just so I wouldn't tangle with any more Russians. Huh! But a good boy in his way all the same . . .

" . . . A good boy with a hot-headed little sister in the Gaza strip. A hot-headed little grenade-throwing sister, whom the Israelis promptly picked up with their usual efficiency.

"But when my boy went to all his clever friends to try and spring his little sister, he found they couldn't help him—or they wouldn't help him. Or they thought another martyr for the cause would be a good thing. So in the end he came to old Razzak as a last resort. And I fixed it for him. No, Audley, not through Jake Shapiro. There are other ways such small things can be done . . . judiciously . . .

"And that put my young watchdog in an awkward position, because he now had an obligation to me."

" 'He that doeth good shall be rewarded with what is better,' " murmured Audley.

"Ah! The devil quoting the scriptures!" Razzak grinned. " 'And shall be secure from the terrors of that day. But those that have done evil shall be hurled down into the Fire.' Very good, Audley—and my young man paid his obligation by telling me a story. But it happened to be a story I'd already heard once—in the Sinai.

"Only *then* it was just a mad idea, and now it had turned into reality—and my story-teller was part of it."

"Part of it?"

"I thought he was Sabri's man. In fact he was one of Hassan's 'Watchers'—*Al-Rukba'n* he calls them. They're the ones who have been drawing up the blueprints for the kills and keeping an eye on people like me."

"I would have thought there was a simpler way with people like you," said Butler. "And you particularly."

"Ah—that's because you think Hassan's like all the rest of them, just one more indiscriminate killer. But he's not, and that's what makes him strong! He's a *discriminate* killer— what makes his men believe in him is that he says too many Arabs have died already. He sees himself as a surgeon, not a butcher—believe me, Major, I know."

"You *know*—that's just it. You're a danger to him."

Razzak shook his head.

"Major, I don't propose to bore you with Hassan's organization—it's only his version of the 'cell' system. No single cell knows enough to be dangerous and Hassan himself is the only link between them—it's a very small set-up."

"But the Ryle Foundation—" Roskill began.

"He uses it certainly. But it's also part of the illusion he meant to build. Rumors—but when you grasp at them they vanish; incidents that don't lead you anywhere. Squadron Leader, Hassan's like a conjuror who makes a great play of concealing something that wasn't ever there in the first place!"

"Then what *is* there? Is there anything at all?"

"What is there?" Razzak's expression hardened. "There's a precision killing machine that was all ready and waiting before the conjuring tricks started."

Roskill stared at him. It was just as Audley had said: the psychological warfare was a preparation—the fear of the assassin that had turned his knees to jelly in Bunnock Street. The fear that Cox and Shapiro and Audley had each echoed.

The bomb wired to the ignition and the rifleman crouching in wait on the roof-top...

"So what have you done about it?" Butler said.

"Until this week, Major—nothing."

"Nothing!"

"Major, the one new thing my Watcher told me was that *our* security system was penetrated. And not just by him either." The Egyptian sighed. "Now—you tell me how you'd move against someone who'd already got you staked out— you tell *me*."

He looked around contemptuously. "The only reason I'm alive and here now is that I've done *nothing*—I've sat on my arse for four months biting my nails and pretending to be even more stupid than I am."

"Until now," said Audley quietly.

"Until now. And I'll tell you for why—"

"Because sooner or later Hassan has to make contact with his Watchers. Or they have to make contact with him. And that's the moment when he's vulnerable. If his security is as good as you say, it's the only moment."

Razzak looked at Audley approvingly. "Very good, Audley—"

"Not very good at all, merely logical. Without the Watchers, Hassan is nothing—he's the will, but they are the brains. The killers are nothing too—ten a penny in the bazaar. And your problem isn't new, Razzak."

"My problem?"

"You can't trust your own service. We had a section in one of the Gulf states that went sour on us in—it doesn't matter when. But there was a job to do there, and we couldn't trust them to do it. So we gave it to someone else altogether— someone who wasn't exactly friendly, but who had the same interest in this case."

Mina al Khasab—the oil refinery affair! It had been department scuttlebutt that Audley had used the Russians to evict the Chinese...

"There's nothing new under the sun, Colonel Razzak.

Somehow you know where Hassan's going to meet his Watchers. The new Alamut. But you can't get at it yourself *and Jake Shapiro can.*"

Roskill frowned—if that was it, then the risk Razzak was taking was enormous. But, by God, once he'd taken it—once he'd argued the Israelis into taking his chestnuts out of the fire—the picture changed altogether.

It wasn't just that he was bypassing Hassan's Watchers—and with men whose efficiency far surpassed the Arab intelligence services—but that if anything went wrong it would be the Israelis who carried the can: to Hassan and to the world at large it would be just another instance of the Jews slapping at one of the terrorist gadflies with their usual heavy hand.

Either way, with any luck, both Razzak and Egypt would be in the clear—

Out of this nettle, danger, we pluck this flower, safety . . .

He looked at the Egyptian with new respect. A dove—maybe; a patriotic Egyptian—beyond doubt. But above all a cunning bastard after Audley's own heart!

"But wait a moment!" Butler exclaimed. "If you know where Hassan's meeting his people, why do you need the Israelis? You don't have to use your security men now. A squad of paratroops could do your work for you."

"It isn't as easy at that, Major," Razzak shook his head. "Alamut—if we can call it that—isn't a *place* any more, not a secret hideout I can point to on a map and say 'There—that's Alamut!'" The second finger that did service for the lost trigger finger tapped the arm of the chair, and then was lost in the fist that struck down on the place it had been tapping. "I can't say 'Bang—that was Alamut!'"

He waved Butler down. "I don't even know what Hassan looks like—medium build, medium height, mustache maybe, dark glasses perhaps—I only know where he will be at a point in time. Alamut is not somewhere—it is a time, not a place . . ."

"It can be on Cloud Nine for all I care," Butler snapped.

"They meet there and you want to hit them for six. But you can't get at them. Is it in Israel?"

"Israel?" The disbelief in Razzak's voice was answer enough.

"Not Israel then. And obviously not in Egypt. So one of the others, where your writ doesn't run—but neither does Israel's either. So why Israel? Why not your Russian allies—they don't want trouble either—" Butler's eyes settled for a second on Audley "—and they've been known to do other people's dirty work?"

"Major Butler—" Audley began.

Butler cut him short. "No, Audley. Maybe it feels right to you, and maybe history repeats itself—but I have to have facts to swallow. I want a plain answer."

"And I will give you one." Razzak held up his hand. "I accept Major Butler's disbelief. Six months ago I would have agreed with him—and even now it's not something I'm doing willingly."

Razzak lifted his chins and stared down his squashed nose at Butler. If it had been a lean face and a hawkish nose it would have been a proud look, even an arrogant one. So that, thought Roskill, was probably what it was.

"Major, this man Hassan is very confident of himself but he is also very careful. If anything happened now—anything—to make him think that maybe he's not been so clever, then there will be no Alamut tomorrow."

"Tomorrow!"

"Less than thirty-six hours from now. And I'll never get another chance like this—not a chance to take Hassan and Watchers in one bite."

Razzak sat forward. "But you are right, Major—I could ask the Russians. Or the Syrians—and even the Iraqis too, though as things stand between us that would hardly be wise. But all of them are better placed to take Alamut if I offered it to them. But having taken it, would they destroy it? Or I wonder—would they use Hassan for themselves?"

He grimaced. "I think they would be tempted. But even

if they weren't I think they're no more secure than we are. I think they'd scare him off, Major."

The Egyptian's tone was carefully controlled: only the words themselves conveyed the distrust and contempt he evidently felt for his allies and fellow-Arabs.

"So you prefer your enemies?"

"When my enemies have identical interests—I'd make a treaty with the devil himself, Major."

A slow smile cracked Butler's face. Whether by accident or intuition, Razzak was speaking Butler's language now— the language of pragmatic patriotism which measured friendship neither by blood nor past history, but by the calculation of mutual benefits.

"The same interests," said Audley, "but not the same opportunity for temptation perhaps?"

"Hah!" Razzak chuckled. "There you have the answer in a nutshell—but less than that even. The Israelis have no opportunity at all! They can do what I want or they can do nothing at all. What you call a Hobson's Choice."

"It seems that you've managed things rather well, then, Colonel."

"No, Dr. Audley. It's simply that Alamut has left us only a Hobson's Choice to make."

Razzak nodded at Butler. "You guessed very close actually, Major. 'Cloud Nine' you said. You see, Hassan is meeting his friends on tomorrow evening's Trans-Levant flight from Aleppo to Mosul."

XIV

"TOMORROW EVENING'S ORDINARY, scheduled flight." Razzak showed his teeth, beautiful white even teeth, as incongruous in his ugly face as those liquid brown eyes. "But if you had ever tried to book a seat on this particular flight you would have failed. And I'd guess the regular crew won't be flying tomorrow either, for one reason or another. It might even be hard to find out which of Trans-Levant's fleet it'll be, too, until the very last moment. But otherwise—an ordinary flight, yes!"

"Good God Almighty!" Butler exploded. "Man—are you *sure*? Because if you're wrong—"

"Because if I'm wrong, what I propose to do would be a crime?" Razzak raised his eyebrows eloquently. "The thought had crossed my mind, Major Butler. But I am not wrong. That flight will be Alamut, believe me. The final briefing before the kill. But it must be our kill, not Hassan's."

An ordinary flight . . . And yet there was method in it: if Hassan had one or two men strategically placed in Trans-Levant's operation—if he had it penetrated like the Ryle Foundation—then it wasn't as crazy as it sounded. The problem of organizing any secret convention was that the delegates had to converge on a place. They had to meet *somewhere*, and in meeting they maximized the danger of discovery.

But if the crew and the passengers could be hand-picked, an airline flight solved this problem dramatically: quite simply, the meeting would be over before anyone knew it had taken place. What seemed a random collection of travellers would come together naturally and disperse naturally. If by any mischance any individual delegate was being followed, the pursuers would be baulked at the departure point and then led straight home when they picked up their quarry again.

Razzak was watching each of them speculatively—watching each of them test the plausibility of what he had told them and, as each found it not so implausible, waiting for them to react to it.

"So you want the Israelis to sabotage it?" Butler was frowning and there was doubt in his voice.

Razzak shook his head. "No, Major Butler. If I thought they could sabotage it, then I'd have done it myself without their help. But sabotaging planes isn't as easy as it used to be—and sabotaging this one just isn't possible, believe me."

"I was going to say"—Butler said brusquely—"Hassan's a fool to put all his eggs in one basket so they can all be broken at once. And him too. But why isn't it possible?"

"Many reasons, Major. The men he has in Trans-Levant will be his most trusted ones, that's certain. And even if we knew which plane they were going to use, which we don't, no one's going to get close to it at Aleppo—not now, anyway."

"Why not now?"

"Because Aleppo airport is at this moment sealed up as tight as a camel's—as tight as Fort Knox. By Hassan, I believe—and at no cost to himself."

"How the devil has he managed that?"

"Very simply, Major. At this moment Aleppo airport already has a bomb scare of its own. Someone phoned up yesterday to warn them that the Kurdish extremists—the ones who haven't accepted the settlement with Iraq—are going to blow up one of the Iraqi flights. It was in the newspapers this morning. Not a plane moves until they've checked it out thoroughly."

The Egyptian shrugged. "It could be just Hassan's good fortune. But I don't think it is. The Kurds have denied it and for once I believe them. You see, Major—it has the *feel* of Hassan about it. He's a man who likes to use others to do his own work. He likes to ride on other people's backs."

The Old Man of the Sea, thought Roskill. Of all the creepy fairy tales, that one had chilled him most in his childhood. And again there was method in it—Hassan's method. For he would only be using Aleppo's security system now as he had used Trans-Levant and the Ryle. And as he planned to use the Arab nations to destroy Israel for him.

"I think his plane will be the best-guarded of all, Major Butler," said Razzak simply.

"Then that only leaves you hijacking," said Butler. "And— by God!—if you've got one of his men in your pocket—" He stopped short as he saw the objection to what he had said. "But where does that bring the Israelis in? Are you going to hijack it to Israel?"

"If it were possible, it would be the most civilized way of solving the problem, that is true," the Egyptian said regretfully. "But I am assured that it is one thing the Israelis will not even contemplate. They are wise enough to leave such foolishness to the PFLP. And in any case, these are not innocent travellers to be threatened by one man—even if I could be sure of getting him aboard armed. No, Major— they would fight, as the Israelis fight."

He sighed. "If we could afford to fail I might have risked it. But we can't . . . We have to be sure."

Razzak paused, and his gaze settled on Roskill now.

So I know the answer, thought Roskill.

Take, burn and obliterate—nothing else would do. And for certainty he needed the Israelis . . .

The Israelis: orphans in a brutal world with time so much against them that Alexander's way with the Gordian Knot would always seem to them the simplest and the safest one. And however faulty their political wisdom might be, in the one field that Roskill himself understood their performance was unsurpassed.

And Razzak was still staring at him.

"Long-range interception?" As his eyes locked with Razzak's he felt the question mark fall away like a drop-tank. "They could shoot it down for you, couldn't they!"

If the Syrians and the Iraqis themselves were not to be trusted, nor the Russians either, the Israelis were the only airmen in the Middle East with the men and the planes to do the job. Roskill conjured up the dedicated professionalism of the pilots he had met and their mastery of the Vietnam-tested equipment the Americans had fed them. And of all people, the Egyptians would know just how good they were: *they* had been on the receiving end!

"Shoot down an airliner in broad daylight—they won't hijack it, but they'll shoot it down?" Butler barked incredulously.

"It will be at night and far out over the desert," said Razzak. "No one will see anything."

"And the Kurds will get the blame," observed Audley dryly.

"But—Aleppo to Baghdad," Butler persisted. "It must be six or seven hundred miles to the north, the air route. Can they do it at that range?"

"Five hundred miles, Major Butler. And they have American Phantoms. As to the technical problem of interception, no doubt Squadron Leader Roskill could answer for that."

Butler swung round. "Hugh—"

"Given the flight plan there'd be nothing to it, Jack. A piece of cake, as they used to say."

And that might very well be the crux of the thing: Hassan's mind, like Jack Butler's, would be earth-bound. If he had ever dreamed in his wildest nightmares of any sort of Israeli intervention he could not have imagined any threat from the airstrips so far to the south.

But with a competent crew and a late mark Phantom of the sort the Israelis now had, the 500-mile interception of a moving dot on a radar screen was no dream. It was a sentence of death.

"An aerial ambush?" Butler whispered.

"It's been done before." Roskill's memory suddenly came to his rescue. "It's like David said—there's nothing new under the sun, Jack. The Americans picked off Admiral Yamamoto that way in the South Pacific in '43—a beautiful precision job. And didn't the Germans try for Churchill when they thought he was on a Lisbon flight in '42 or '43?"

"I remember that. They killed Leslie Howard on that aeroplane," said Mary softly. "I remember that as though it was yesterday. He was such a marvellous actor, too."

They all turned towards her. She had sat there so quietly in the background, with the conversation flowing past her, that they had taken her for granted. Except that Roskill had marked the watchfulness in her eyes as they had settled on each speaker in turn. And now she seemed very sad.

"Of course, we didn't know at the time how his aeroplane had been lost," she continued irrelevantly. She looked thoughtfully at Audley, and then at Razzak. "If my niece and her friends were here, Colonel Razzak, they would say you were being very wicked—they would say that the policeman must never fire first, even to prevent a crime. Young people today aren't at all like the papers say. They are really very puritan—very sure they can distinguish good from bad."

Roskill felt a stirring of embarrassment. He couldn't see what she was driving at, and he wasn't sure that she could either. Yet vagueness had never been one of Mary's failings.

"But you don't hate them, do you—these people on the aeroplane?" said Mary.

"Madame—?" Razzak seemed disconcerted too.

"And I know how David feels," Mary went on. "Is your Colonel—Shapiro was it?—is he like you, David?"

There was a moment's silence, which lengthened into awkwardness before Audley broke it.

"Shapiro's a decent man, Miss Hunter. He doesn't always like what he has to do."

"I thought he might be," Mary said. "And if this . . . Alamut is allowed to take place, there might be war again in the Middle East?"

"Full-scale war—no, Miss Hunter," Razzak shook his head at her. "Hassan's great objective is nonsense. He will not achieve it even if we fail to destroy Alamut—I agree with Dr Audley absolutely there. He might wreck the cease-fire that is coming, perhaps, but that isn't what we are worried about."

The Egyptian sounded as though he set no great store by the cease-fire.

"What worries us, Miss Hunter, is how he plans to achieve this thing. We don't want to lose . . . anyone we can't afford to lose before he fails."

Mary considered him thoughtfully. "And if you and the Israelis worked together in secret this time, one day you may work together openly?"

Roskill looked at her sharply. That was more like the old Mary. It had never occurred to him that Razzak and Shapiro might also be playing another, much deeper game, and for even higher stakes.

Razzak said nothing. But then there was nothing he could say; the very idea was enough to make the Pyramids tremble.

Mary seemed to sense that quickly enough. She turned towards Audley.

"There are a lot of things that I still don't understand, Dr. Audley—David. But you asked me for my opinion before."

"I did," Audley didn't sound quite so confident now. It was almost as though she was speaking out of turn. "Go on, Miss Hunter."

"You said I had a stake in what was happening."

Audley blinked—that sure sign he was no longer quite in control of the situation.

"So you have, Mary," said Roskill tightly. To hell with Audley! "You and I have both got a stake of our own."

"That's just it, Hugh dear. We have to forget about Alan now, both of us. This is more important."

"But, Mary—"

"Shooting down that aeroplane is a terrible thing, even if they are all wicked men, which I'm sure they're not. I suppose I ought to agree with my niece—with what I know she'd say. She'd talk about means and ends."

She gazed at Audley. "But I would say that Colonel Razzak is right, and you must do what you can to help him. I don't know whether ends can ever justify means—but sometimes I think they absolve them. I suppose it's because Father made us all read de Vigny when we were young . . ."

"*Servitude et Grandeur Militaires?*" said Audley in surprise.

Mary smiled at him. "I know it doesn't sound like a girl's book. We had a Victorian translation of it called 'The Problem of Military Obligation' which made it sound even less like one. But when I read it I thought it was very sad and beautiful, I remember—we were what used to be called a 'service family', Colonel Razzak, you see. We did know something about obligations."

"'We are the firemen, free from passion, who must put out the fire. Later there will come the explanations, but that is not our concern'."

Trust Audley to dish up a bloody quotation.

And yet—damn it—there was something here that Roskill knew he had missed; something Mary was sharing with Audley and Razzak, and could not share with him.

"Madame," said Razzak gravely, "I give you my word that we shall put out this fire."

XV

"COLONEL SHAPIRO IS a very remarkable man," said Yaffe seriously. "A very remarkable man indeed."

Roskill glanced quickly at the Israeli agent, to make sure he wasn't taking the mickey. But of course he wasn't: he was a slender, schoolmasterish young man, old beyond his years and serious almost to the point of eccentricity, judging by his conversation so far.

"Then Razzak's equally remarkable," said Roskill tendentiously. Yaffe made him feel both irresponsible and argumentative.

Yaffe considered the proposition solemnly.

"Y-ess," he conceded at length. "Yes, I think you might bracket him with Colonel Shapiro. Just below, perhaps—but in the same general bracket. The men of the future!"

On the other hand, thought Roskill, in the present company of screwballs and mavericks the young man wasn't really remarkable: compared with Shapiro and Razzak—compared with David Audley, come to that—he was raving normal.

"Always supposing your people are willing to risk a Phantom far from home," he murmured. "I rather gathered yesterday that it still wasn't cut and dried. If it goes sour now they're going to be men of no future at all, I shouldn't wonder—or have you got some inside information?"

Yaffe grinned at him knowingly, taking years off himself as he did so. "I'm only an onlooker now—like you, Squadron Leader. But I don't think we'd be here if the plan had aborted."

It was true enough. According to Razzak, the very possibility of the British knowing what was afoot had nearly put the project off altogether—it was evident that neither the Israelis nor the Egyptians trusted them to hold on to a secret successfully. It was a tribute equally to Audley's reputation for good faith and to his ability to spin a likely tale to his own side that this second meeting was taking place at all. But now at last it looked as though Shapiro was ready to accept the flight plan details that Razzak had promised him at Firle.

And there, thought Roskill, was the rub: they now were as far as he could judge, on the very edge of the New Forest, a rendezvous even less desirable than Firle. And though both the Israeli and the Egyptian had official engagements in this general area at midday, one on Salisbury Plain and the other at Portland, these woodlands struck him as being even less suitable than the open downlands.

As if to echo his disquiet there was a distant and incongruous stutter of gunfire, which he had been hearing at intervals ever since they had left the car: somewhere not too far off, just over the rise to their right, there was a firing range.

"Well, I can think of a hell of a lot of better places than this to meet," he said grumpily. "After last time it's bloody well asking for trouble. Just because you happen to live here—"

"There'll be no trouble this time, that I can guarantee you absolutely," Yaffe interrupted him.

"Did you guarantee that last time?"

"That was—" Yaffe sounded irritated rather than defensive "—bad luck."

"It was somebody's carelessness."

Undeniably it was somebody's carelessness, whatever Yaffe said. But it obviously wasn't Yaffe's carelessness, because no one was allowed to make that sort of mistake twice—least of all, Roskill told himself thankfully, in the Israeli service. Which meant that if Yaffe said there was nothing to worry about, there was no percentage in getting flustered.

"I agree it's a poor place from the security angle." Yaffe was conciliatory now. "Not a place I would have chosen, even though I live here. But you'll just have to take my word for its security today."

Perhaps Shapiro's men were lurking behind every bush. If so they were skilled woodsmen; but then the Israelis did most things competently these days.

"Who did choose it then?"

"Razzak did, indirectly—it's rather unfortunate, but I believe he's been having quite a lot of trouble ducking his shadows. They've been sticking to him like leeches."

Majid, presumably. There was a strong suspicion in Roskill's mind now that the handsome captain might be one of Hassan's Watchers.

"I think the real trouble was that he couldn't shake them off without making them more suspicious," Yaffe continued thoughtfully. "And the more he shook them, the more suspicious they'd get of course. That was why he set up that meeting near Newhaven when he was already en route to Paris—"

"Which didn't work too well!"

Yaffe shrugged. "It might have been worse."

"So you think!" Roskill thought bitterly of Alan taking his early morning gallop. "And that was only because Hassan's man ran into one of our chaps. So what makes you so sure they can't do better this time?"

"This time?" Yaffe frowned. "Squadron Leader, this is *our* territory and *our* meeting."

Roskill stared sullenly at the leaf-strewn path at his feet. It was as full of holes as gruyere cheese, full of 'ifs' and 'buts'. Yet the Israeli was utterly confident—and so had been the Egyptian the day before when Audley had insisted in coming in on the final meeting.

And damn it—David Audley had been confident too. They were all so goddamn confident now.

"And you see—" said Yaffe, suddenly more cheerful again "—we rather think the heat's gone off Razzak now. With Majid on his way—"

"Majid gone?"

"Of course, you wouldn't know that. He flew out last night. A sudden urgent family crisis."

So that was it! And there'd be others like Majid across the Mediterranean and through the Middle East who'd be called away from duty by sick relatives and unforeseen family crises and every other excuse in the book to their final briefing in Alamut. It was no more than the expected pattern, after all. But it was a relief nevertheless to come up with one second reason for this relaxation of tension.

"Mind you," said Yaffe, "I do still agree with you about this place." He waved a hand at the woods around them. "But you can blame the Egyptians for that. They're rather sensitive about meeting us, and they insisted it had to be well out of London."

There was another distant rattle of machine-gun fire.

Yaffe grinned. "In the peace and quiet of the English countryside."

"What the devil is all that shooting?"

"That's the Territorial Army—or whatever you call it now—up on the Mereden Range," Yaffe's seriousness seemed to melt. "Every Sunday morning they have it for several hours. Then they give it to us."

Roskill looked at Yaffe in astonishment, whereupon the Israeli burst out laughing.

"I don't mean the Israeli army, Squadron Leader—the local Rifle Club, I mean." He patted the ancient golf bag over his shoulder. "I practice with the family heirloom every Sunday. It's the only way an honest man can keep a gun licence in your law-abiding country. Sport—yes, self-defence—no!"

"I still don't see why they had to meet at all."

"Razzak and the Colonel?" The boyish grin faded, and Yaffe nodded understandingly. "They insisted on that, too—it has to be face to face for the final agreement, just the two of them. I think when it comes to the final crunch they still don't trust us—the only man they trust is Colonel Shapiro."

In the end everything depended on Shapiro and Razzak. It was not really the logic of Israeli-Egyptian co-operation that was going to confound Hassan, because in real life the logical thing could usually be safely discounted; it was this million-to-one relationship between enemies.

"I don't know what he said to convince our people at home," Yaffe murmured, almost to himself. He looked at Roskill pensively. "It's very easy to be enlightened when you're not involved, Roskill. And when you don't have to make the decisions that involve your survival. We don't have that luxury—that's why so many of us have got a Masada complex."

"A what?"

Yaffe shook his head pityingly. "You British always think you're going to win the last battle, but we Jews expect to lose it—we've lost too many last battles. It takes a lot to trust an enemy when you feel like that."

"The Egyptians are trusting you as well."

"Not as much. We're the ones taking the big risk if they want to double-cross us." Yaffe sighed. "Oh, I know we've been after Hassan too—and what Razzak's given us fits in with our own information. And we can't afford to have Hassan loose any more than they can. But our security's a lot better than theirs. There's a pretty good chance we could protect our people."

Roskill felt in no mood to argue. But what Yaffe couldn't see—and what Shapiro had seen—was that if Israeli security succeeded in protecting its leaders from assassination when the Arabs failed to protect theirs, nothing would convince the

Middle Eastern countries that Israel wasn't at the bottom of it all. And maybe Hassan had calculated that too.

The trees ahead of them were thinning. If Yaffe's topography was right, the low ridge beyond the meadow just ahead was the vantage point from which they would be protecting the final rendezvous between Shapiro and Razzak, at which Audley was a self-invited observer. And there Alan would get the vengeance Roskill hadn't dared to hope for—an overflowing measure of vengeance.

It was strange that revenge no longer seemed to matter so much now that it was in someone else's hands. It was as though Alan had once more become no more than the victim of a tragic accident—or an innocent battle casualty among the thousands who had perished in a whole generation of Middle Eastern bloodshed. What made it futile was that it was not his quarrel: no one would carve the old 'dulce et decorum' tag on his grave.

Roskill was suddenly reminded of the Latin words scratched in the Bunnock Street telephone kiosk, which he had not had the chance to put to Audley . . .

"But we don't really have any choice," Yaffe said philosophically. "We've either got to trust them or go on killing them, and I'm fed up with killing. I don't ever want to—"

Yaffe's words strangled in his throat. He jerked forward convulsively, shouldering his way in front of Roskill and plucking frantically at his coat as he did so. The golf bag swung outwards striking Roskill a tremendous blow in the chest—

There was a chip of wood spinning in the air—

There was a noise—

The spinning chip and the noise and the golf bag hitting him had all happened in the same fragment of time, and in that millisecond—that same millisecond—Roskill's leg was swept from under him and Yaffe himself crashed back into him.

And someone cried out in agony and shock.

The trees whirled round him and the leaf-mould came up towards his face.

There was blackness and a terrible weight on his chest. Blackness and wetness and the weight on his chest that pressed him down, expelling all the air from his lungs.

Can't breathe—dead—dying—the chip of wood spinning in the sunlight—

"Are they dead?"

A voice a long way away.

A grunt. "At this range they are dead."

Roskill wanted to cry out that he was not dead—maybe dying, but not dead. And maybe not dying if only someone would take the weight from his chest.

But that hoarse grunt and that voice had been familiar—appallingly recognizable. He thought: 'If I cry out, if I move, then I *am* dead.'

"Are you sure?"

An English voice.

Grunt. The known grunt.

"Uzis make no mistakes. But we can make sure."

A third voice, not English, not known. Roskill felt the hope draining out of him and the lethargy of the inevitable *coup de grace* taking its place.

"My God!" The English voice again, closer and trembling. "You've cut them to pieces!"

"I told you—at this range—"

"But there was to be no killing here."

Hope flickered again. Roskill forced himself to take tiny, shallow breaths; it was difficult enough to breathe at all with the whole world crushing him down into the ground.

"No choice. They would have seen us, and they knew me—both of them." Contemptuous.

"They would probably have recognized all of us." The third voice was matter-of-fact. "And the Jew was reaching for his gun anyway. It is unfortunate, but he is right."

"So what do we do now?" The English voice still shook. "God! What a mess they're in!"

"We get them off the path. Then we go on."

"Go on? We leave them?"

"We leave them until we find out what Razzak is doing and who he's meeting. These two won't go away."

"Someone may find them, damn it!"

"Don't panic."

"Panic?" Anger overlaid the fear in the Englishman's voice now. "There was to be no killing in England—that was an order! You can't kill people here and walk away, can't you understand that?"

"We're not going to walk away. When we've got what we came for, we'll come back and deal with them. But Razzak comes first." The voice hardened. "How much time do we have, Jahein?"

"He left me five minutes ago—we have no time to spare."

"Oh, God!" There was a sob in the English voice: the man was crumbling.

"Look—" The third voice softened now, as though its owner recognised the danger that lay in the Englishman's collapse. Roskill strove to listen with a part of his mind, while the other part attempted to control his body—to make it lifeless. They already thought him dead, and half the possum's trick was in the mind of the hunter . . .

The third voice was wheedling, justifying, explaining: Majid had been wrong to have been so sure Razzak was a harmless fool—the dead Jew was proof of that . . . so he had missed something, maybe during the Paris trip when he'd been alone with Razzak . . . he had been over-confident and careless. It was even possible he was treacherous, and if so it had been a blessing that they'd set Jahein to watch too without telling him. But until they knew for certain they were all at risk now . . . and they needed him to operate the Shibasaki microphone—

"—We'll just carry them off the path—down there—in the groundsheet. Here, Jahein—help me with the Jew."

Roskill summoned up every last reserve of self-control: he mustn't brace himself as the crushing weight was lifted off him, mustn't breathe, mustn't twitch . . . he must be dead!

"Get his pistol, Jahein—"

The weight was gone.

"And get the other's gun while we hide the Jew."

There was a pause, and then a hand touched Roskill's shoulder, started tentatively to move him—and then stopped. There was a spasm of retching . . .

"Well?"

"He—he didn't have one."

"Huh! Well, it wouldn't have done him any good. Here—set the sheet beside him and we'll roll him on to it."

Unfeeling butcher's hands rolling dead meat—Roskill flopped awkwardly, heavily and loosely as he guessed dead meat would flop. The sheet enclosed him like a shroud.

"Hurry, now!"

There was a numbness in his leg and along his side—not pain, but numbness. That was the side on which he had fallen when Yaffe cannoned into him . . . As he was clumsily swung into the air, jumbled in the groundsheet, Roskill was suddenly fully aware at last that he had been hit, how badly he couldn't tell. But it couldn't be too badly, otherwise he wouldn't be conscious—or did one retain consciousness as clear as this while shock kept the pain at bay?

The swinging stopped and he was thumped down and half rolled out of the sheet, face down again . . . They were scattering something over him, leaves or dead bracken . . .

Someone—not Jahein—spoke urgently in Arabic.

Silence.
Merciful, life-giving silence.

He must not spoil it now: he must wait and let the silence flower into safety.

Roskill started to count slowly, first to one hundred—with

an extra ten because he had a feeling he'd jumped from seventy to ninety. Then another slow hundred . . .

His eyes wouldn't open: his eyelids seemed gummed together. Gently he eased his right hand towards his face and wiped them. He tried again: there was a small beetle, shiny black, exploring a twig six inches in front of him, and beyond that a wall of green. Somewhere close at hand a bird took flight, carrying its shattering alarm cry through the woods.

Roskill began to explore his body. The side was still numb, but he could twitch his toes inside his shoe. So far, so good.

With his right hand he began to feel gingerly down his back: it was soaked with blood—poor Yaffe's blood. As if the thought focused his vision he saw just to his right the Israeli's feet sticking out from under the edge of the groundsheet. He didn't want to look any further; Yaffe must have taken most of that burst of fire . . .

He felt the bitter anger swell up in his throat—after all the warnings he had had, to be chopped down—

The thought was cut off dead as his hand touched an enormous crater in the left cheek of his backside—Christ! He'd been shot in the arse!

He forced himself to touch the edge of the crater again. It couldn't be as big as his fingertips told him it was, but by the size of it, it had to be an exit wound. As he touched it he felt pain for the first time: his brain was telling him what his body wasn't yet ready to admit.

The question was—where was the entry wound?

Sudden fear drenched him again. It didn't matter where he was hit, but only that he get to hell out of here before they came back.

He wrenched the groundsheet back, scattering the bracken and sending arrows of pain up his side from the mangled buttock.

He raised himself stiffly on his hands and looked around. He was still close to the edge of the wood—he could see the light through the trees—but down an incline away from the path. He lifted his head higher and took his weight on his right knee.

Still not a movement anywhere. Away to his left he could now see the sunshine bright in the meadow, beyond a steep, sandy bank—there was a stream there at the meadow's edge.

He glanced down and caught his breath: he was covered in blood, saturated in it, his shirt and trousers sodden. God! No wonder they hadn't looked twice at him—he was like a slaughter house!

The thing now was to get away fast. He stood up—and cried out in pain and surprise as he pitched forward.

His leg wasn't there at all!

No, blast it—he rolled desperately to protect his back-side—of course it was there! But it felt as though it wasn't and whatever was wrong with it, he wasn't going anywhere on it.

Roskill pounded the soft earth in fear and anguish. He couldn't stay here, but he couldn't go far hopping or dragging himself. He felt thirsty and dizzy—two of the classic shock signs the squadron M.O. had dinned into his head. He was hurt worse than he'd thought.

Falling blood pressure, rapid irregular pulse; skin pale, cold, clammy and moist . . . he could remember Doc Farrell reciting the litany.

But there was something else Farrell was always preaching in his survival course—what was it?

"The sympathetic system overrides the central nervous system in emergency—the sympathetic reactions are directed towards the mobilisation of the resources of the body for the expenditure of energy in dealing with crises."

Man—when you're in danger the adrenalin pumps and you work at a tremendous peak of efficiency. If you went on living like that you'd burn yourself out in no time. But if you don't panic while you're there on top, you're a superman!

The superman wiped the blood-stained tears from his eyes and looked round him again.

The golf bag!

Trying not to look at Yaffe, Roskill slid the bag off the dead man's arm. The straps were stiff and slippery—like everything else the bag was blood-soaked.

The family heirloom: God, let it not be some ancient muzzle-loader!

He knew before he'd slid three inches of it out what it was: an old Lee-Enfield—the blunt terrier's muzzle, with the wooden stock and hand-guard, was unmistakable: the immortal SMLE.

Bullets? He jerked back the bolt feverishly.

There was nothing there. But of course there was nothing there: Yaffe would never carry a loaded rifle in his golf bag. Not to panic; there had to be rounds in the bag somewhere . . .

Unless he collected them at the Rifle Club!

Roskill fumbled with the strap on the ball pocket: small, stout cardboard boxes with metal edges. And nestling in the boxes lovely .303 cartridges, five in each of the little black chargers. Thank you, God!

Remember how it was in the old ATC days, when the Flight Sergeant forced them to learn the drill—and he had always found it easy to learn things by heart . . .

Draw back the rifle and hold it with the left hand at the point of balance . . .

It was easy still—*place the charger in the bridge charger guide. Place the ball of the thumb on the top round just in front of the charger . . .*

The rounds went down smoothly in a clean sweep. Roskill took another charger, pressed the rounds home and closed the breech with one round up the spout—no practice this time, with that last round safe in the magazine. He stuffed two of the little boxes into his coat pocket for good measure.

Superman was armed now, anyway—Lee Enfield against Uzi!

But not here. This was Uzi country; the old rifle liked the open spaces best, not the woodlands.

The meadow.

They would be coming back across the meadow.

Roskill set off, propelling himself up the incline on his right hip with his right foot, the rifle resting painfully on his collar bone, his useless left foot dragging behind him. But before he'd gone three yards he knew he'd never make the distance back up to the path and then along to the meadow—not in the time that must be left to him now. Not even that pumping adrenalin could disguise the weakness and the spreading pain down his leg.

He veered off to the left, towards the stream.

Downhill, even on the uneven surface of the wood, the going was easier—it was no more than agonizing. And the stream itself refreshed him: he lay in it, he dipped his face into it, and at the last he drank from it, watching the water redden as it washed some of the blood from him.

The cattle, or whatever used the meadow, had used this point in the high bank to get to the water—there was a mud wallow, but beyond it a broad track worn to the top.

Leaving a slimy trail of blood and water behind him, Roskill inched his way up the track. He knew the effort was squandering his energy reserve as he crawled, anchoring each advance with the rifle butt. But the line of meadow grass at the top was the Promised Land; to fail to reach it now would be to lose everything.

At last he could peer over the top, between the tufts. For a moment he couldn't focus: the landscape swam before his eyes.

Then it became an empty field—a much bigger field than he had imagined, at least from this worm's-eye view, with a barbed wire fence marking its frontier with a low ridge of heathland and forest scrubland. And there in the far corner to his left was the stile which he and Yaffe should have crossed just a few minutes ago.

Yaffe . . .

The hay-makers had taken the first growth from the field, and it was trimmed to an even stubble. But they had left an awkward patch providentially close to where he lay, beside

the stump of an old tree whose roots he had seen stretching
down out of the bank towards the water.

Roskill crawled the final yards to the protection of the
stump. For half a minute he rested his face against the rough
bark, breathing deeply.

Another sign that he was slipping.

But not yet, damn it, not yet!

Roskill carefully placed the rifle on its side in the grass
and took the spare cartridge boxes out of his pocket. He
opened them and placed the spare slips ready beside the
stump. He was appalled to see that his hand was white and
shaking like an old man's, the veins huge and blue.

He looked methodically around him again.

*A good fire position should permit free use of the weapon,
have a good field of fire, be inconspicuous and bulletproof.*

Wasn't there something else, though?

Be easy to move from . . .

Well, it was all those except perhaps the last. But that
didn't matter, because he wouldn't be moving from it, one
way or another!

He slid the rifle forward, checking the safety catch. It was
undoubtedly a very old one, with the open U-shaped backsight
which he'd heard of, but never seen. At least the aiming rule
was simple enough though: the top of the foresight must be
in the middle of the U, in line with the shoulders.

He could feel a roughness on the stock—there were Arabic
letters carved into it, and five little bright silver studs carefully
hammered in line below.

Trophies, by God! One stud for each life the Arab owner
had taken, until Yaffe—no, Yaffe's father more likely—had
missed becoming a stud and won it from its owner. The War
of '47, maybe . . .

And there was something else, too: further down were
there two holes—new holes which had flaked the polished
wood. Roskill looked in awe at the stock. No wonder the
golf bag had hit him so hard! Like its owner, it had taken
bullets which had his name on them . . .

He shook his head and looked up across the field again.

Jesus Christ! They were half-way across it! He'd been maundering over the Lee Enfield while they'd been marching almost straight towards him, and he hadn't even decided what to do!

Shoot first at long range and drive them off, warning everyone?

But it wouldn't warn anyone, because the T.A. men were still blazing away in the distance—and he'd likely miss at anything except point-blank range.

Which meant letting them get close, to see the whites of their eyes, when they could rush him if he missed . . .

Three of them. He saw them clearly for the first time now: Jahein, grizzled and watchful, with a raincoat slung over his arm to conceal the Uzi; the Englishman, spare, sandy-haired; and the third man, Middle Eastern, carrying a long, shallow black suitcase; that would be the Shibasaki telescopic microphone.

The Englishman would run. He hadn't wanted to kill and hadn't even the stomach to search a body. It wasn't likely now that he would try to be a hero. That left two—and two he could just possibly take. The two who mattered!

They were walking steadily, but not fast—three strangers out for a Sunday morning stroll in the country.

He lifted the rifle: *the sole object of a rifle is to kill the enemy.*

But the enemy heaved up and down in front of his foresight; it was like aiming at someone from a small boat in the ocean. He should have practised aiming—

Steadying now, though. First pressure on the trigger— *correct trigger pressing is essential.*

Damn it to hell! The safety catch was still on!

They were very close now. Roskill's bottom was a fiery crater too: he wouldn't be able to sit down for months—first pressure again—but if he missed now he'd never sit down again, ever.

He shot Jahein through the chest at five yards' range.

The bolt moved smoothly, ejecting the case, and slammed back. Jahein was on his back in the grass—

If the third man had charged him then—or fled—the barrel waved so wildly he couldn't have hit a house. But the man dropped his case and clawed in the grass for the Uzi which had fallen from Jahein's hands.

The Uzi was a death warrant. It gave Roskill a second to steady the barrel and then an easier shot than the last: the man was bending, almost stationary, with the little machine-pistol just coming up from the ground when his second shot knocked him down, sending the Uzi spinning.

Like the chip of wood spinning...

Roskill lowered the rifle. All the saliva seemed to have drained from his mouth: it was like a lime kiln. Thousands of rounds he'd fired, cannon shells smashing the targets, clay pigeons puffing into fragments, and never a shot in anger until now, when two dead men lay there—Jahein's heels were drumming convulsively a few yards from him...

The Englishman was running—not running, *scuttling*—like a rabbit across the field, twisting this way and that, towards the barbed wire fence.

Let him go then. The dead he had shot in self-defence and justice. The third time would be cold-blooded murder. And he was utterly exhausted.

Then it struck Roskill like a blow that they all mattered equally: if they had seen Razzak meet Shapiro, what each one of them knew might be—might be—

No more time to think, for this was a difficult shot. No wind to aim off into, but God only knew where the old Lee Enfield threw its bullet, high or low, left or right.

Except the instructor always said it wasn't the gun but the concentration behind it that hit the target.

Concentrate then. At this range aiming off didn't matter: the man had to reach the wire; it was too high to jump, so he'd have to stop and climb.

Wait and concentrate. It wasn't a man, but a piece of knowledge running towards the wire. If it crossed the wire into the thicket beyond it would be on its way to Alamut. And whatever happened, nothing must wake Hassan to the truth.

Squeeze with the whole hand until you feel the first pressure—he was almost at the wire . . . now he was climbing and it had snagged his coat sleeve—*restrain the breathing and continue that steady squeeze*!

God! Roskill winced as the kick seemed to travel down his body, exploding low down and spreading outwards, fogging his vision momentarily.

The man was crucified on the wire, half hanging over it. Then, as Roskill watched, he started to slide backwards the way he had come, jerkily as each strand of wire caught his clothing, took the strain and then ripped free. Roskill stared sickened as the body crumpled in slow motion to the bottom of the fence, one arm finally harpooned on the lowest strand. Inside the field.

He felt cold. A killer ought to feel cold, though. Jack the Giant-Killer. Wyatt Earp. Dead-Eyed Dick—no, not Dead-Eyed Dick. Dead-Eyed Someone, surely.

It would be nice to pass out now, warm and safe—cold and safe, anyway. But the damned adrenalin hadn't stopped pumping.

He frowned, trying to catch his thoughts: there was something else to do, that was why!

Something else to wait for with the family heirloom. Three more silver studs and room for a fourth now: two for safety, one for duty, but the fourth strictly personal—for Alan.

It was curious, he reflected, how it was possible to feel light-headed and clear-headed at the same time. He would have to discuss it in the squadron mess tonight with Doc Farrell—say to him he was dead right about the fear of God sharpening the wits!

Damn it all—he'd been so close—and then Audley had twisted it and forced the wrong answer on him!

The Firle meeting had been the key, not because Razzak had met Shapiro there—but because those dead men in the field hadn't been told about it by the Watcher who was dogging Razzak's footsteps.

Majid!

So Majid was the young man with the hot-headed little sister—Razzak's man inside Alamut.

That was why Razzak and Shapiro had been so scared, so bloody scared—yet so confident today that Hassan wasn't on to them . . . he'd never been on to them at all: so long as Majid had been 'watching', nothing of value ever reached Hassan . . .

So it didn't matter what Alan had seen, but only that Majid's lies about the Paris trip must never be exposed. For if they were blown, Majid was blown—and when Majid was blown there would be no Alamut flight, and Razzak's chance would be gone forever!

Oh, Razzak had been good, and never leaked Majid's true role to anyone! But he'd not been quite good enough all the same, because he'd fallen into the oldest pitfall of all: he'd despised his old dog, Jahein—his simple peasant soldier who was Hassan's extra insurance, unknown even to Majid. And in the end it had been the faithful old dog that had the rabid bite, not the sleek hound at his side!

And yet it had been the sleek hound that had made Alan's death a necessity.

Roskill patted the rifle. They wouldn't be long now. The meeting would be over, and they'd be waiting for him to trot up obediently. And then they'd begin to worry.

All he had to do was to wait, all alone with his thoughts and his handiwork; resolved now, all those contradictions and inconsistencies he'd pushed unresolved to the back of his mind. His desire for vengeance had blinded him then, but now everything but vengeance was stripped away.

Another wave of pain, above the steady throb of it, brought tears to his eyes. Much more of that and he'd pass out. Think of something nice then.

Isobel.

High time he resolved that, too. What he had was the
ashes of happiness, genteel planned adultery. But in a flash
of despairing self-knowledge he knew that he could never
give up Isobel, and no well-placed rifle bullet could cut that
knot satisfactorily...

Think about Harry. That debt would be paid, if only indirectly, through Alan. No *wergild* for them...

One Roskill seemed to float away, to look down on the
other one, the blood-stained, mud-caked wreck cradling the
rifle and shivering in the sunlight.

The detached Roskill could see clearly. He could see the
field. He could see the four of them at the stile. He could
see Butler clap his field-glasses to his eyes and could hear—
almost hear—his blasphemies.

A word to the others, and Butler was charging the
meadow—

"Over here, Jack!" the wreck croaked.

Butler swerved past the bodies without a second glance.
"Hugh—!"

"It's okay, Jack—I—look worse—than I am...Got all
three of 'em, Jack—pow, pow, pow!"

"Hugh, don't talk!" Butler's eyes compassionate, then
doubtful. "Three?"

Must get this bit right.

"One—over by the fence, Jack. But call the others, Jack—
got something important for them—get them now!"

Butler signaled urgently.

Now.

"In the woods, over the stream—Yaffe—help *him*..."

Never do for Jack to be around for the kill.

Butler stood up, glancing quickly from the men coming
across the field to the wood.

"They're coming, Hugh lad. They'll be here in a minute.
We'll have you out of here soon."

Then Butler was gone, splashing through the stream.

"You do that, Jack," Roskill murmured to himself, sliding the rifle forward, "you do that."

The barrel swept the field. A good field of fire, no doubt about that—all three in sight and in the sights if he could only hold the damn thing still!

Left—David Audley!

Bastard, bastard, clever bastard, David! Just how long have you known what really happened at Firle? Did you guess at the Queensway? But all the time you wanted to know *why*, and you couldn't have me running amok to spoil the game! So you headed me off and confused me with half-truths while you found out.

You clever bastard—even when you were bullying Razzak you were also telling him that he couldn't trust me, so he had to trust *you* . . . I was the threat, wasn't I?

Guilty, David. But no bullet for you—what else could I expect from you, David?

Center—Muhammed Razzak

You knew—and it would have been your order that killed Alan, Razzak—because you couldn't have your brave boy Majid blown before you let him take the Aleppo flight to Alamut. Is that what you've done, Razzak? Did you tell him where he's going? Just to make his cover perfect, did you forget to tell him about the Phantom?

Guilty, Razzak. But no bullet for you, Razzak—because you're quite a man—and you would have gone yourself if they'd have taken you!

They were very near now

Jake Shapiro

No style in killing, you said, Jake—but this is my style: an ex-British, ex-Arab, ex-Israeli rifle—just right for you if I can hold it still one second more . . .

You had the means and the motive and the opportunity, Jake, and everything said it was you from the start: *if he wanted you dead, you'd be dead*, they said.

Razzak wouldn't have had the men or the know-how. It had to be done, so it had to be your kill—just like that poor bugger on the wire had to be mine!

The man on the wire...

Oh, sweet Christ! thought Roskill: I killed that man for the same reason you killed Alan—the same reason, the same risk, the same necessity.

The same act.

The same guilt!

Roskill tried to concentrate and failed. But the effort took his last shred of energy: the rifle barrel wavered, then sank into the grass as he fainted.

EPILOGUE

BEIRUT, Wednesday.

Wreckage of the Trans-Levant air liner which has been missing since Sunday night has been sighted by an Iraqi Air Force plane near the Euphrates river.

An air force spokesman said that the wreckage appeared to be scattered over a wide area of the desert, and there was no sign of survivors.

Palestine guerrilla sources in Damascus have blamed the crash on Israeli agents, but there has so far been no official comment from Jerusalem. It is pointed out unofficially, however, that telephone threats had earlier been made against flights from Syria to Iraq by an extremist Kurdish organization, the FKL.

The aircraft, which was on a

scheduled flight from Aleppo to
Mosul, carried 37 passengers and
a crew of four. Among the passengers was Mr. Elliott Wilkinson, the well-known Arabist and
a vice-president of the Ryle Memorial Trust.